BLADES OF ARRIS
SITHE

USA TODAY BESTSELLING AUTHOR
STARLA NIGHT

Cover by Christian Bentulan
Editing by Linda Edits

For inquiries:

Starla Night
starla@starlanight.com
https://starlanight.com

to the
very last
star

ONE

CATARINE

The last thing I hear before I sneak out is my mom agreeing the planet Vanadis is terribly far away.

"But she hasn't been responding to the new drugs," my mother murmurs into the portable viewscreen while she sits alone on our single living room couch. "The Vanadisans have more medical knowledge than any other race. I'm sure this is what she wants."

I can't hear my dad's response on the viewscreen.

My mom glances over her shoulder at where I linger in the shadowed hallway. She tilts the screen away. "Don't cry right now, Mat. Did you ask about the advance?"

That's how I know she doesn't see me. They never talk about money in front of me. They don't want me to worry.

My throat tightens.

I'm sorry, Mom and Dad.

I time the movement of our all-female guards outside the brick building, disable the alarm, and slip out the side door into the tight alleyway.

When I'm seeking my fix, I am strangely clever. My

brain clears away the fog just long enough to get what I need.

And I must be clearheaded right now.

I take side streets through New Brussels to the club zone wearing my sheer white bodysuit, fur-lined heels, and neurolink cat ears. The color contrasts nicely against my golden-beige skin and dark brown hair. They know me at all the local places, bars repurposed from chunks of old buildings, so I can't actually go inside. But it's enough to be close by.

I make the recording while I walk.

Mom and Dad, you did your best to raise me and love me, and I'm sorry it wasn't enough.

Sending me away is the best choice right now. I promise it's going to be great.

So don't worry about me, okay?

Someday, I'll stand before you and show you the amazing things I've done. I'll be myself again. I'll be well.

I'll be the daughter who makes you proud.

Someday.

A man calls out in the local French, "*Hey, catgirl! You need a fix, babe?*"

I end the recording and turn in his direction. Soon enough, I have found myself in the arms of a man I don't know.

I don't want to need this.

I don't want to be like this.

My life, my future, my dreams have disintegrated around me, and all that's left is the craving. The craving to be whole. There's a missing piece deep within me, a hunger that no food can sate. I'm a bottomless stomach. And that's what I've been reduced to. A hole that cannot be filled.

My parents' guards break in as I'm riding the third

stranger. Or maybe it's the fourth. I've lost count. The men jump up, apologetic and embarrassed, which means I've been caught with these men before and I just don't remember.

But I grab on to the one that I am with and make him finish. It's the finishing that does it. Not semen, not dildos, not my climax—believe me, we've tested everything. Only after the pause, the heat, the spurt can I get the satisfaction that I need. The clarity.

And then it's over. That brief moment is gone. I'm already feeling soft edges on everything, as if my feet barely touch the pavement.

The guards wrap me in a blanket and take me home.

My mother stands on the front step with red-rimmed eyes, her white skin paler under the streetlight. She has passed the point of tears with me. All she does is sigh. "One more time?"

My eyes burn, but I try to keep it in like she does. I hold out the recording chip.

She slips it in her pocket and helps me into the shower, runs a full body scan, and calls the emergency medical service. Again. They try to send a male doctor, and of course that's not possible for me. I might try to seduce him. My mother stays for the health check from the female examiner, then wraps me in a fuzzy blanket and tenderly puts me into my bed.

All around me on the walls are the photos of things I once wanted to do. The friends I used to have. The dreams I carried like flames in my heart.

I used to have dreams.

I was going to be someone important. I was going to heal the sick like my mom. I was going to build bridges like my dad.

I was going to study the vast intergalactic empire we've unwillingly joined and become a great communicator. Reach out to the hundreds of other lesser worlds, conquered like us, and make allies. We all serve the same terrifying race. The Arrisans took over our planet in a day, and we're still scrambling to catch up.

But now my existence slips away from me like sand.

And my mom understands my frustration, but I can't even talk anymore to my dad.

We were so close. When I was a child, I used to crawl up in his lap and watch as he designed the great bridges that spanned uncrossable divides. There is so much rebuilding left to be done, and he was always busy, but he never minded taking me with him. He was big and protective.

Whatever got into me was something he couldn't protect me from.

And I know it kills him.

This sickness that drives me toward strange men also violently repels me from my male blood relatives. If I see a slide show of relatives, a memoriam of our Dutch and Malay ancestors that happens to include a man, I'll destroy the viewscreen. Why? I can't understand. My mind goes blank. I don't even feel angry when the guards wrestle away my makeshift weapons, pens, and scissors.

My dad lives in another country, another time zone. My mom gave up her career to take care of me, so my dad works twice as hard from afar. He was always the social one, and now he's all alone.

He'd do anything for me.

They both would.

And this voyage is my chance to do something for them.

My mom knows I'm grateful, but I swear that someday, I will look my dad in the eye and tell him the same thing.

Thank you for loving me as best you could.

Thank you for trying so hard to save me.

Thank you.

In the morning, my mom gets me up. I feel as rested as I ever do. We get dressed.

The cruiser is leaving from the North America space center, which is on a jagged mountaintop in Iowa. We breakfast in a cross-Atlantic chartered shuttle, then my mom signs the hundreds of contracts that promise I'm in my right mind, and my parents will not try to sue in the case of my unfortunate demise. I stare out the window and try not to make her signatures a lie.

I read that Iowa was once a flat farming region, but that's hard to believe. Fissures from the invasion's cataclysms break the ground in such a way that it's impossible to use the land for much of anything. The gangplank of the bulbous, alien-looking intergalactic cruiser rests on glassy rock that still smells like sulfur.

At the bottom of the gangplank, I give my mom a farewell hug. Her body is soft and comforting, just like the fuzzy blanket she wrapped me in last night. "Did you listen to the chip?"

"I will," she says. "After."

After I leave.

After it's too late to change her mind.

She pulls back. Her eyes are red-rimmed again.

It's okay that her tears are all gone. The tears I spill right now are enough for both of us. "Tell Dad I say goodbye."

She nods.

I don't want to hurt them anymore.

When I'm gone, my mother will finally be able to go join my dad again, and they can be together. That will be a good thing. I hope I remembered to say that in my recording.

Please be happy, Mom and Dad.

I wave goodbye at the top of the gangplank and then enter the spaceship.

The cruiser is just as my mom promised. There's a common area, a cafeteria with a fish tank, and I have my own room.

But the best thing of all? There are other women like me!

Not that I'm happy for them, but I'm so grateful I'm no longer alone.

They also know what it's like to go into a blind rage near their innocent male relatives. They've stalked dark alleys seeking a cure for a sickness that no one else can identify.

What's wrong with us?

Why did we get singled out?

For the first few weeks of our journey, we puzzle out the mystery.

We're from different continents, ethnic backgrounds, ages. One woman's sickness started a few months ago, and another has suffered for over a decade. Of course we're all humans. Nobody from the other conquered worlds ever visits our backwater planet. That's why I wanted to go out and make allies.

We give each other nicknames. I don't know who started it, but it's easier to be your nickname than who you really are.

I'm the diplomat because my face betrays little emotion, but the neurolink cat ears will constantly perk up or lie flat.

And I'm the only one who gets mental fog. The others all suffer different effects that worsen the longer we're in space, away from any men.

One woman faints. We call her the ingénue. Every time her heart rate goes up, she goes down. She has to wear a helmet to avoid head trauma. I carry her food trays in the cafeteria and stay with her until she wakes up. A sneeze knocks her out for two hours.

"Thanks for the nice cat nap." She stretches and tweaks my neurolink ears. "Get it? Because you have nice cat ears?"

I get it, and I want to compliment her, too. "Nice, um...nice..."

She waits patiently as I fumble through the brain fog to finish my thought, as pointless as it is. She says she doesn't mind my rambling, and that we have to stick together because we have the worst side effects.

"...head...thing," I finish.

She beams and taps her helmet. "It also doubles as a battering ram. I know my fainting makes me pretty useless, but if you ever had to break a pane of glass and I'm unconscious, just get another woman to grab my arms and heave-ho."

I want to tell her she's not useless, but it would take too long to construct the sentence—if I could even get it out—and so I just nod encouragingly. She gives me a bumpy hug.

The other women are just as kind.

For example, the housewife watches over us to make sure we eat our vegetables and brush our teeth. The king-maker stalks the halls with me, tall and proud and fabulous.

The ace is classically beautiful and loves to pamper herself, which somehow makes her self-loathing all the more tragic.

There are others who suffer, but I feel worst for the ace. The rest of us don't hate sex. For her? It's a terrible curse.

Please let the Vanadisans find a cure.

Our small group, from a defenseless, conquered planet,

travels alone with no weapons. We are a little raft in the black interstellar ocean.

But for the hope of a cure, we've all agreed to face any danger...

Right before dinner one night in the cafeteria, proximity sirens turn on.

Something—or someone—is about to hit us.

The emergency lights flash.

"Hull breach imminent," the computerized voice warns.

There's screaming. Chairs are overturned. Empty food trays clatter. A glass shatters.

"Evacuation sequence engaged," the computerized voice continues. "Enter the escape pods and await further instructions."

Evacuate? Us?

We're in the middle of space. The middle of nowhere.

I find myself in my cabin.

The captain drags one of us— the ingénue; she fainted— down the hall past me toward the escape pods. "Go!" she screams.

But...?

She comes back for me, grabs my elbow, and drags me down the hall. We pass empty portals where the other pods have all detached. She throws me into one of the last two pods. "Yours is broken. I can't seal it from inside the ship. Hit the red button to detach."

The captain closes me into the pod. She taps the glass. Through the tiny vacuum of space separating my pod from the main ship, I hear nothing. Her mouth moves. *Red button!*

My finger hovers over the red button.

She flinches and jerks her gaze behind her, then disappears.

Shadows darken the hallway.

Not human. Alien.

Wait.

Do I sense...?

Heat radiates from my center, pouring itchy lava into my veins. My sinews pull as taut as the strings of an instrument. My back arches, fingers flex, and the mental fog liquefies into primal need.

Uh-oh.

My brain is clever.

It remembers the safety pamphlets and complicated diagrams I read in the beginning. The captain locked me in the pod. But there is an override.

I stumble back into the cruiser.

The hall is empty.

But the burning ozone scent is familiar. I smelled it at the attack sites my father used to take me to as a child. Sites from the day the Arrisans discovered our planet and cracked it open like an egg.

There is also another scent.

Someone's coming.

A man.

No, men. Men are coming.

I turn and open my arms.

No normal person would do this.

I do not want to be like this.

This is a sickness.

It curls into my brain and drives me forward like a zombie.

I had dreams.

And now they are all gone.

All that's left is the craving.

Yes, come for me.

TWO

SITHE

I slide into nearspace like a held breath.

All comms are quiet. Battle armor sealed. Power to a whisper.

The Eruvisan pirates huddle over their kill: an outdated vassal-planet cruiser belonging to one of the many lesser races my warriors have conquered. Escape pods scatter like broken shards, and the slim pirate vessel, a modified missile carrier not capable of lengthy space travel, has attached to the cruiser like a parasite to a helpless bird, breaking the wings as it drains the fluttering vitality.

They have finally made a mistake.

I position my ship over their parasitic vessel, matching velocities, and crack my hatch.

Vacuum meets vacuum. Silent.

Descending to their ship like a shadow, I stretch my arms. Long, black blades emerge from the interior of my wrists. I pass over their vessel.

Comms first.

My left blade slices through the receiver relay.

I hook my fingertip beneath the bolt and thump my

right blade against the metal hull. Its subtle reverbera-
tion paints a picture on my hood, showing what's
inside.

Two males hunch over comms and rub their erect
sexual organs. They are so distracted, they do not notice my
pulse.

The Eruvisans are never distracted. That is how they've
escaped me so many times.

I walk forward using the tips of my blades to hook into
the metal and pulse a second time. Still hunched. Oh,
they've noticed the downed communications. One presses
the comm button furiously. The other looks up at me—
although I am invisible to him through the metal hull—with
a frown.

Kill.

My boots magnetize to adhere to the metal with a soft
clink which I hear inside my suit via suit-augmented bone
conduction. I draw back my left blade and plunge it through
three layers of alloy. The curving blade heats as it shears
electrons from atoms. I skewer both men through their
armored chests; their death shudders reverberate in my
blade-bones.

I lift my hand. The blade retracts. Atmosphere puffs
into the vacuum and then stops.

One of their bodies has probably plugged the hole.

Silence no longer matters, but the circumstances of
their distraction tingle my nerves with a vague foreboding. I
pulse my way across the pirate ship, taking more care than
usual. But nothing seems amiss.

Why did they not notice my arrival?

Eventually, I slice the hinge cables to breach their
airlock, flood and pressurize the small chamber, and then
stride into the atmosphere-filled pirate ship.

A dank film molds the surfaces. Bad moisture cleaners. They could not have operated this vessel much longer.

Their stolen cargo is stacked beside the grimy force chute.

I wave my palm over the origin mark. Symbols glow, reacting to my suit, and identify it as Arris cargo lusteal. Aphrodisiac powder. The sweet metal needed to bring on mating lust in Arrisan males and females is all that stands between our race and annihilation.

Anger flashes in my chest. After all the unimportant metal they've stole from us, this goes too far.

And yet, they successfully escaped to another system. I barely followed.

Why didn't they get away with it?

Why were they trapped here, on a lesser cruise ship, after evading a blade fleet?

The lessers on this cruiser could never have overpowered the Eruvisans.

So, how?

Their hull-cracker tube is still attached. I drop into the chute.

Their parasite ship gravity loses me, but momentum carries me until the cruiser picks me up. I land scale-light on the floor. Heat-proof, radiation-absorbing, sound-dampening, light-bending armor conceals my movements so that only the briefest stir of air marks my passage through the cruiser.

But something is odd. Unusual sensations like soft fingers slide up my back, somehow beneath my skin-fitted armor.

Something is different here.

The atmosphere is breathable, so I open the suit.

Strange scents assault my nostrils. The Eruvisan stench

chokes me with body malfeasance and waste-cycling problems consistent with their ship. Beneath that, the scent of the cruiser—no, of the lessers who once inhabited this cruiser—causes an odd tautness in my abdomen.

One escape pod door hangs open.

The scent intensifies.

I follow it to the bridge and stop. An incomprehensible sight greets me.

The Eruvisans are not dead as I expected. They are very much alive, and yet they have all ignored the most basic safety protocols. This mistake will end them.

They surround a small, multi-limbed creature lying on the floor making the strangest squeaking noises. One male thrusts his pelvis to its pelvis. Not it, her. Her pelvis. This seems to be a group mating ceremony, but the Eruvisans are not noted for mating outside their race, much less in the middle of a heist, so this whole scenario is senseless.

Strange.

My implant projects ship status and species information in the same impersonal way it attempts to translate the guttural grunts and cries.

"Oh, yes! Yes! More!" *Male grunting noise.* "Almost there!"

This vessel originates from our colony Humana, and this unfamiliar female is one of the humans. She seems to have five limbs, four of which grapple the cold-blooded Eruvisan, and two sets of ears. The extra nonfunctional limb and one of the sets of ears belong to another species of animal on the Humana home planet, wherever that is. Galacticus? Somewhere outside the eighty-nine asteroids? It is so difficult to keep our conquered worlds straight.

She encourages the Eruvisans to mate with her, and they have clearly been in space too long—or perhaps they have gotten addled by their poor environment—and so they oblige.

I have a duty to announce my intentions. I deglass my suit to become visible and drop my hood. "Eruvisans."

My words disappear into the noise of their wrestling. The thrusting male slows and stands, his leathery green sex organ erect and dripping.

I clear my throat and try again. "Eruvi—"

"Oh, please, no. Just a little more," the female begs. "I was so close. I almost remembered. I almost...please."

Her words are strangely effective. My midsection tingles.

Another Eruvisan unfastens his trousers and kneels between the female's legs.

Honorable or not, I will not wait. My blades emerge from the bones of my wrists.

The Eruvisan nearest me catches the shimmer out of the corner of his slitted eye. He turns slowly and then hisses. "Blade!"

They all freeze.

Finally.

I give the proper warning. "You have stolen from noble Arris. All who wish to face judgment in the pits of Ranna, remain still. All who wish an immediate death, move."

The silence stretches.

Will this truly be the day I take prisoners back to Ranna? I flex my wrists, extending the blades in promise.

Everyone moves at once.

I don my hood, not bothering with stealth, and unleash my blades. Scything the room, I paint the bridge in blood. The work of death is effortless and it is my greatest skill. I kill so that the empire of Arris lives.

When it is done and the last disease-ridden thief drops, I cross the spongy blood-soaked floor and pull in my blades to touch the console. This is Arrisan technology. I would understand it even if my implant didn't automatically translate the colonial scribble into honorable text. Opening a comm channel to our military, I transmit my coordinates to the nearest fleet ship, a new dreadnought christened *Spiderwasp*.

Now, to wait.

I rest in the captain's seat. It is covered in strange pink fabric, taut at the top and loosely wavy beneath. The implant whispers that the lesser humans call this design "frills."

I lean back in the seat and close my eyes. It has been a very long time since I have rested.

A wobbly voice reaches my ears. "Can I move?"

The lesser is the only one who remained still and thus she is the only one who remains alive. I do not care. She is a problem for someone else now. "Yes."

She rises. A mess of flesh, torn fabric too delicate to withstand wear, and dripping with bodily fluids.

And yet something about her disturbs me.

I ignore it. The *Spiderwasp* can possibly reply in 27-695, 27-694, 27-693...

"You're a blade?" She steps over a severed torso and wobbles when her bare foot lands on a hand. "You took over Humana in like a day." Then she stops as though she's just noticed. "They're all dead."

I do not answer because it is obviously true.

"But I never got my clarity." She turns to me with new intention in her eyes. Her back flexes, sinuous, and her movements become slinky. She grabs the long, bedraggled appendage and curls it around her wrist in a way that she seems to think is enticing. She lowers her chin and looks up through her lashes. "You're a man."

"I cannot help you."

"Oh, sure you can." She slinks toward me and leans forward to emphasize the valley between her breasts and curves of her shoulder, her waist, and the roundness of her ass. When that elicits no response, she releases the tail and wraps her fingers around my forearm on the armrest. "Please?"

It is a unique experience to be approached by a lesser who has no fear. Rarely do I allow anyone to touch.

But her dream is a delusion. Lust only hardens my jack in the mating arena sparked by heated females who have ingested lusteal, the aphrodisiac powder.

I have entered the arena and mated five females. Each time, I held absolutely still as the female climbed my nude body and impaled herself on my erection, then took her pleasure until she demanded my seed. The arena is stressful, mating is uncomfortable, but being selected five times is a rare honor. I always perform.

So this female lesser looks at me with clouded eyes and runs her tongue across her orange-smeared, bloodied lips. "I'll make it worth your time."

Explanations take too long and anyway are beneath me. I hook my index finger in one of the sealing seams and crack the skinsuit to display my flaccid jack.

She looks down, and her lips curve. Her eyes form happy crescents. She lifts my jack as though it is a precious gift. Then drops her mouth on me. Wet heat caresses my male member. Her head bobs up and down.

Strange heat pulls into my loins.

My blades pierce the skin at my wrists. This lesser is

doing something to me. And that should be impossible. "What are you doing?"

She lifts her head and beams. "Getting you ready."

Ready?

She leans back and tucks her bedraggled hair behind her true ears. Splaying her knees settles her weight. She dips her head to create more stimulation.

I grasp her hair to stop her.

My jack has firmed and is partially erect.

Strength leaches from my fingers. How...?

She pulls free from my lax fingers. Her mouth closes over me another time, and her tongue caresses my heating length. Her breath tickles my crotch, clever fingers encircle my shaft, and her other hand cups my sac. Little moans send shocks in the backs of my heels and twitch my tendons. I curl my fingers over the armrests.

How is she doing this? What is she doing? How am I reacting?

Shock and disbelief prevent me from protesting. I expect this moment to end. And also, I do not want it to. Hot blood-rush thuds in my ears like the first time I ejected my blades and entered a ring for combat.

She releases my jack from her mouth and stands, one hand between her legs stroking her feminine crevice, her gaze lit on my jack in anticipation. Using a confidence I can't understand, she pulls my waist forward and rests her scuffed, stained knees on either side, straddling my legs. Her weight barely burdens my thighs.

Tilting her head, she teases the collar where the skinsuit meets my hood. "Don't say much, do you?"

There is nothing to say.

The unnatural female licks her sticky fingers, smiles knowingly as my jack jerks in response, and positions the throbbing, hard tip of my long shaft against her bare, wet crevice. She sinks onto me, nesting our pubic bones—hers dusted with rich brown curls, mine dark as silent sky—with a satisfied moan. Her innards clasp me in a humbling embrace as though I am enveloped by the warm ocean of my youth, and then she begins to move, drawing away and surging close. Thought, memory, sensation is sucked away, leaving me floating on the crest of a deep oceanic peace.

"Oh yeah, that's good." She rolls her hips to take me to the hilt, thrusts and writhes, and elicits more electric shocks in my body. Her rhythm drives me deeper into the comforts of the chair, and I stiffen my abdomen to control her wildness.

Controlling her is an illusion.

Her body bounces against this new resistance, sucking and popping, slamming me with half thoughts and rolling me over with a chaos of sensations. Her thighs, small and yet powerful, clench my waist. Her ass, round and juicy, slaps my lap. Her breasts rise and fall with the artificial gravity.

Her fingers creep across and squeeze her own breasts, then one hand entangles in her hair, stroking her extra set of ears. "This...yes...you...*Blade*...mmm." Her body suddenly convulses. She collapses against my chest, a satisfied groan wrenched from her throat. We both breathe heavy, hot gusts of air, and I have never felt more like a male.

My muscles ping. Unfinished impulses meeting caution. Is it over?

"Oh yes. It's been a long time since I've been able to feel that." She pats my pectoral, takes a deep breath, and rights herself with new energy. "I've got to do that again."

No. This strange addictive sensation is not over.

She undulates her hips across my abs, driving my jack

in deep and long, and then thrusts, hard, fast, and undeniable. All the muscles of her body tense, including the tiniest in her face, and she gasps in release. Then she clenches my shoulders, locking her forehead to mine, and impales herself over and over onto my jack with enough force to loosen the floor weld of the chair. She is an animal. In that moment, so too am I.

Her eyes, foggy and feral, fix on me. "Do you feel it?"

The question unlocks something deep inside. My balls draw up and tighten. Eye to eye with the creature who should be a lesser, who should be as unimportant to me as the cushion, who should be unable to incite my lust, my body snaps. Hot seed shoots from my jack and buries deep in her hot, wet center. A second shot, a third spatters her insides.

Her body crests against mine, and she shatters. Gasping, crying, shaking, she arches hard enough to roll off backward.

I catch her around the waist, locking her in place, jack to socket, until the last shot of seed spurts into her shuddering body. She hangs motionless off my lap. I ease her off and settle her at my feet.

Gone is the confident female who commanded me to sate her lust.

One hand slowly brushes the disarrayed locks from her face. The eyes that only moments ago were fogged now sharpen with clarity. Her arms tremble.

She takes several deep breaths.

Gags.

Then cinches an arm across her chest, hugging her biceps, hunching in on herself. Wide, frightened eyes scan the blood-spattered, weapon-burned bridge. She looks away.

My blood diffuses into my body and empties my engorged jack. I return it to the safety of the skinsuit. The suit seals up, evacuating the foreign molecules, so I am returned to a normal state.

But I will never be in a normal state again.

A ping on the center screen informs me the *Spiderwasp* has sent a response. It takes some time to connect with this lesser technology.

"What...?" she asks quiet, confused, and also awed. "What did you do to me?"

I have no answer, because my question is a mirror.

What has she done to me?

THREE

CATARINE

O h no.
I've gone too far this time.
Way, way too far.

The man stands and twitches his gray suit, resettling it over his broad, all-too-human back, tapered waist, muscular quads and calves. The cowl has fallen back, revealing black hair and pallid skin, and he pads silently across the blood-soaked carpet on gray boots. The black lining his fingernails could just be polish, the spikes on the backs of his ears a quirk of biology.

But the molecule-thin blades nested like a chevron tattoo at his wrists prove he is the deadliest member of the conquering race. A foot soldier, known as a blade, from the conquerors of Arris.

Why, if the Arrisans had superior ranged lasers that devastated hundreds of planets like they'd devastated Humana, were their foot soldiers trained and armed to win a war single-handedly? Old joke. Because every part of Arris is terrifying.

And I have just sexually assaulted him.

I have assaulted him in the ship's theater where we used to spread blankets and eat popcorn and pretend we were still on Humana, in a big science experiment together, one that would be over soon.

He presses the communication button.

The movie screen activates, and another brutal, pallid Arrisan fills the half dome. He leers over me.

Terror jolts into my bones. I scramble around the back of the captain's chair.

"*Spiderwasp* in," he barks. "We acknowledge your priority call. Intercept in two clegs. Prepare for the majesty of the High Command's newest flagship, blade. *Spiderwasp* out."

The screens go blank, and the orange blood sprays become more visible.

As do the ribbons of flesh beneath my bare feet.

I am crouched in someone's entrails.

Silence cuts my ears with its sharpness. The stench of burnt oxygen and sour waste pierces my nostrils. The world fractures around me like peering through broken glass. Too sharp, too real.

The foot soldier replaces his hood and turns.

His face is barely profiled in the cloaking shadow of the assassin's cowl. The suit moves like a normal cloak, but a sheen of black underneath deflects light like spilled oil. He flexes his fingers. The curved blades emerge a fraction from his wrists. He fixes on me.

No.

I scoot around the captain's chair, trying to make myself small.

Please, no.

Oh, please—

"What did the Eruvisans do to you?"

His voice is toneless and quiet.

Like a serial killer.

I want to look away, but I can't in case that's how I miss when I die. "Nothing. Everything. I don't remember."

The shadows where his eyes should be widen slightly. He thinks I'm tricking him. Like I would even know how.

I can't feel my hands anymore, and my ears ring, but somehow, I still sound calm. "They came down the hall from the cafeteria and surrounded me. I begged them to... ah...have sex with me."

Even at the point of death, this is still shameful and embarrassing. Worse because the fog hasn't rolled back in. It seems blasted away, gone forever, leaving me with ugly slivers of panic and regret.

"One of them screamed that they didn't have time, but the other one with filed teeth and a really big, uh, bazooka? Already had his pants-thing open, and he said they had time because they had to collect the cargo. He carried me back to this room, and I had sex with them."

He doesn't react. No movement. Just partially extended blades and silence.

"Then you arrived."

He turns away, the cowl hiding his whole face, and stares over the miasma. "And?"

"You killed them all."

He toes one of them, then crouches and holds his hands at an odd angle. The suit extends beyond his wrists to cover his fingers. He paws at a victim. Gore travels up his gloved fingers. He stands and strides to another. Searching. "And then?"

"Ah... You were there..."

What does he want me to say?

I remember he was not eager. When I came on to him,

he showed me his flaccid cock, not in invitation, but in dismissal. And I hadn't cared. Other people's feelings never bother me when I need my fix.

Pins poke my toes. Blood flow. I need to move.

I ease onto my knees.

He glances back at me.

I freeze.

Please don't kill me.

He slowly stands. Hands at his sides, his suit retracts to reveal his gray fingers again and the blades at his wrists. "You were never in their ship."

The tone is flat, a statement, but I don't want to miss a question. I shake my head.

His fingers flex again. The blades extend past his fingertips and retract. "Where did they encounter you?"

"The hall by the escape pods."

He moves his arm.

Wait. He wants me to show him?

I use the captain's chair to pull myself to my feet. My muscles have locked up. I totter across the theater and into the hallway on stilts. Sodden fabric sticks to my damp legs. My heart thuds as if a stranger is pounding my chest with his fist.

He moves behind me like a shadow.

This is how the Arrisans murder people.

My neck prickles.

He's close, his arm lifting, his blade sliding out, and while I'm turned away, it slices—

I whirl.

He's standing on my other side, several feet back, giving me plenty of space.

My arms tremble.

I saw the reach on his blades. They swept the room.

They cut through a wall. There's no safe distance on this ship.

But his shadowed face orients on me, so I gesture at the obvious. "That's my escape pod."

"Where were you before?"

Before the emergency? "In the cafeteria. I was... No, my bedroom."

He tilts his head as if to ask which is it?

"I was in the cafeteria with everybody when the emergency lights flashed. Then, instead of going to the pods like everyone else, I went back to my bedroom and grabbed my ears."

His cowl lifts fractionally.

"I have to take my ears whenever I leave the house. There's a tracker inside, and if that malfunctions, the ears are memorable, so people can say if I've gone past."

One of my parents' compromises. It's also good at attracting the kind of man who'll try anything once. I become other, exotic. And the neural link is the only thing that can convey my real feelings sometimes. While I stand stupidly, the ears flatten and convey my inexpressible regret, shame, and sadness.

That's how it used to work.

I take off the ears.

They are spattered with blood.

And now I can see with terrible clarity.

Terrible, injuring clarity.

I always wanted to be cured, but not this way.

It's probably fleeting anyway.

I know where he wants to see next.

My bedroom.

"Show me."

All right.

I lead him down the hall. The carpet is trampled and blackened. Was it always like this? Surely the invaders didn't leave the grime in the corners. The black circles on the walls, though, are new. Weapon marks.

There's a circle next to where the captain's pod was.

Someone shot at her?

I hope she got away. I hope that my being stupid didn't doom her.

I pass around the grand cafeteria to my chamber.

This is a big fancy ship. We had to pay a lot to be on it. And everyone has their own bedroom, like a real old-fashioned human cruise, back when we had those in the oceans and everyone had cabins.

Here's mine.

It's compact but nice, like my old grad school dorm, and I even got to outfit it with the things we put in storage: teak dresser, matching night table, overstuffed reading chair. On the dresser is a framed picture of my family. Me and my mom anyway. Because that's safe.

He pokes in the closet, under the night table, and then peers into the inch-wide gap between the floor and the bed. He rises again and hovers his hand over the fuzzy white comforter. "What is this?"

"My bed? It's for sleeping."

He looks into the stall behind the dresser. "And this?"

"The shower. For washing off."

"Why?"

"It's normal. We don't have space suits like yours on Humana."

He continues his search.

I hold the cat ears and unclip the tail. My breasts hang out of my torn nightclothes. The ears need a delicate wash, and I don't want to set everything, still bloodstained, on the white bed.

He passes me and lifts the picture, looks behind it.

"What are you looking for?" I ask.

He presses a button on the frame.

The picture flips to my college graduation, my mom on one side of me, my father on the other. On my father's other side is the prime minister of Malaysia.

I brace to...

Oh.

I have no urge to attack.

My father beams, one arm around my shoulders, an impossible grin splitting his tan-olive face. My mom must have hidden it inside the frame, knowing that after my brain cleared, I was going to be able to look at us and feel happy.

And I can actually look. For the first time in four years. I don't go blank. I feel...

Oh, sad. I really hope someday I can see him again.

The hooded assassin studies the picture like he's trying to figure out what it means.

My legs start shaking again. I'm so tired, exhausted, like my tendons are unknitting and I'm a puppet about to collapse. Everything stings.

I never feel like this after my fix. The fog, the numbness, the insatiable craving rolls in before the liquids have dried.

But now they're sticky and gross all down my legs.

I feel beaten inside.

And still I have this wonderful, horrifying clarity.

Maybe it's because I'm just so scared. I know that I'm about to die.

But maybe something else has changed. "That's my family."

"Lesser families..." He looks at my rattling knees. "You're sick."

Again, it's not a question, but I feel compelled to answer. "It's shock. After a shower, I'll be fine."

"You're blooded."

I'm really sure the blood—which is orange—isn't mine. "I have a medical kit in the bottom drawer."

The concept of drawers seems strange to him, which opens up all sorts of other questions, but he finds the kit and takes it back to the bed. He sorts the contents, studying their labels, opening tubes, sniffing the contents. They're all basically new. This is my after-sex kit. My mom packed a new one.

He holds up the only ointment that's half emptied. "It's Arrisan."

"Yeah, it's the best stuff we have."

He looks back at the tube in, what, surprise?

But he doesn't know much about us if he doesn't know about families or beds or anything like that.

I'm about to collapse, and if I hit the floor, I'm not getting up again. "Do you mind if I take a shower?"

His cowl twitches.

He doesn't mind...probably.

I end up dropping everything on the carpet and stagger into the narrow stall. We're supposed to close the stateroom door before we shower to make sure the moisture-collectors funnel all the liquid back into the system, but I can't summon the will to risk walking past him again. I just can't.

I flip on the water, which automatically starts the roaring suction fans. They dry my skin almost before the tepid drops hits me. The biggest planet-side luxury we lack is a bath. The ace and the kingmaker complained about it a lot.

This drizzle feels rapturous.

I lather on dry soap, shampoo, and conditioner, and massage my scalp between rinses. The hose extends to access every part of my body. As it cascades a few inches across my skin, it doesn't just wash away the last half hour. It washes away the last four years of my life. Everything I saw, everything I did, everything that happened. It's all rolling off and disappearing up to the ceiling drain.

The stinging gets a lot worse.

Cuts appear all over, but something sizzles with waves of discomfort *down there*, which is so weird. I haven't felt anything in my body, especially *in* my body, in a really long time. The water makes it worse, but I feel like I have to rinse it clear. What exactly happened? I can't get a good look. Contorting to the front, to the back...no. I need a mirror. There's one in my—

He stands right outside the shower.

Watching me.

I flinch, nearly dropping the hose, and it sprays my inner cut again. Ouch, ouch, ouch.

His hood has fallen back very slightly. I can see the outline of his chin. His lips part.

I flip off the shower and retract the hose, wait for the fans to dry me, then limp cautiously past him to the bed and the open medical kit. On the small cuts, I can use regular pain cream, but inside...well, there's a reason I have this half tube of Arrisan ointment. I put it up where I think are the edges of the wound. It turns warm and then numb, but there's still a lot of pain. I didn't get it quite right, but it's going to have to do. The ointment is really too precious to use.

He holds out his hand.

But I need it.

The words never leave my mouth. He can have whatever he wants. His face has receded into the cowl again, nothing but shadow. I drop the tube in his palm.

He motions for me to turn around.

The tip of the blade flashes against his wrist.

He's going to kill me now.

Oh.

No.

Please.

I had dreams.

My heart thumps like a drum.

Please.

I face the bed.

"Bend down."

Like the guillotine.

I rest on shaking palms.

Why did he let me have a shower if he was only going to bloody my bedroom?

The air coasts over my bare backside as he approaches.

If he wants sex, that's fine, I can do sex, that's not a problem, but he isn't giving me any vibes for sex, his hood means instant death, and I really want to live, I want to see my parents, I want to—

Is that hiss the sound of his blade sliding out?

I clench the fuzzy blanket and squeeze my eyes shut.

Something very softly brushes me down there.

Huh?

Another delicate brush, and then my folds are gently parted and his finger dips into me. A sensation of tiny brush strokes paint my bruised canal. The area warms and then numbs.

He isn't killing me.

He's...healing me?

Down there?

I don't know how to feel about this.

I mean, I have a vivid memory of writhing on his nude body. I know the weight of his balls, how his cock feels in my mouth. I know his taste and the fullness of taking him while arching my back.

But this is different.

That was then. I didn't know what I was doing then.

This is now. When both of us clearly have our senses.

Although I guess he had his senses then too. I'm the only strange one.

He retreats.

I straighten awkwardly. The cut does feel better.

He gives me back the tube, capped. "It's deep. You'll need another application. And start treatment for Eruvisans parasites. They take a few goras to mature, but bloodworms will eat your skin off."

That's good to know.

My mind is reeling. I pull on a clean dress. It has a loose drape similar to his, but the closest color I have to oil-slick gray is eggshell blue. My feet slide into my flats.

He waits at the doorway. "Come."

I grab the medical kit and carry it like a clutch. I wish it was ten times bigger and made of steel, but I've heard their blades can slice through literally anything, including plasma.

We stand abreast. I dare to look up.

He must have pulled back his cowl to peer into my nether regions, because his face is exposed again.

It is not what I expect. Smooth cheeks. Blunt, almost too-large nose, flat eyebrows tapered to a point at his temples, and a well-proportioned mouth. He's not handsome, but ordinary. With his black hair, he's almost Desi, maybe mixed. If it weren't for the gray of his skin, I wouldn't be surprised to pass him on the street.

But his eyes are too light. Pashtun.

"Show me the other rooms."

"Of course," I murmur, hardly knowing what I'm saying. "I'll show you anything you want."

He holds my gaze for a second too long. His eyes are silver-gray. Like his cowl, like the rest of him.

Then he turns away.

And I get this weird feeling. Yes, I assaulted the deadliest alien ruling the universe. But maybe, just maybe, I'm going to survive.

FOUR

SITHE

She unnerves me.

We walk through the hall of the cruiser. I keep her on my right within easy scything distance. Dividing my attention this way is a product of long training, but I do not remember such heightened awareness since my trials.

I still feel her fingers on my skin.

A shudder crawls up my spine.

This cruiser has the bilateral symmetry of a pollinating insect, which is why this type is called a harvester. The oblong open cavity in the center is surrounded by a colonnaded hall. Smaller storerooms, which these lessers have unwisely transformed into sleeping quarters, are the pollen seeds. They are supposed to be filled with raw materials to support space travel. A ship modified like this has nowhere to store supplies. It must make frequent stops.

Whoever sleeps in a storeroom that is breeched will not survive.

I enter the next storeroom. Again, it is not filled with

supplies but with a puffy shelf, an odd moisture box that she called a shower, and assorted smaller objects.

She pauses in the doorway. "This is the bed of the housewife..." A delicate frown crinkles her forehead and makes my fingers twitch. Her brow clears. "Lia."

Then she looks at the blades showing in my wrists and steps back.

Yes. Keep your distance.

You will not catch me unawares again.

She swallows.

I prowl through the room. Like the rest of the cruiser, it smells vaguely of lusteal, but there is no clear source. This room is largely identical to hers, down to the small square image of people baring teeth in some frozen rictus.

"That's Lia's husband and daughter." The lesser's voice remains even. "Her family."

Such a strange concept. Family.

She backs away from the doorway, and I pass her, continuing around the colonnaded hall. Retracing my steps, I realize I am a different person from when I entered this cruiser.

In an emergency, the ship should lock down along the colonnades, sealing off each storeroom from the hallway and sealing the hallway from the central cavity.

Foul liquid drips from the pirates' hull cracker; it was inserted at the rear where the hallway is narrowest, preventing the host ship from cutting off access to the inner cavities.

She wrinkles her nose.

I will keep my hood closed.

Slight vibrations under my feet indicate the engine room. I kneel and rest my hand on the square door, and the picture of what's beneath appears on my tactical display.

The combustion engines will have had to work harder to combat the moisture and environmental effluvia flowing from the Eruvisan ship, and also vacuum from my entry, because their breached airlock is likely not perfectly sealed.

Is it worth opening the engine room? I glance at her for the answer.

She titters awkwardly. "You want to see? I don't know anything about the engines, but I can do my best."

I do not know anything about engines either. "Is there anything strange about your fuel?"

"Fuel? I don't think so. I could read about the engine, or we could pull in the captain's pod. She can answer any questions so you can go away happy."

I complete the circuit of the cruiser.

There is only one entrance to the bridge.

It smells worse now that the bodies have settled. Are there no cleaning robots on this cruiser? This mess will foul their ship as badly as the Eruvisans'.

She stays in the doorway while I operate the magnet that will pull in the escape pods. "Which is the captain's?"

"Hm? Oh, it was the last one to leave the ship."

The one floating closest, then.

The magnet controls do not respond.

They've been modified, like the cleaning routines.

And like the cleaning routines, that decision will kill them.

The decision to use the pods was bad anyway. They're designed for limited use in atmosphere. No one should ever leave a ship in space. Better that salvagers find your charred body and mark your name on the list of the fallen than you drift, a deserter, to become a new asteroid among the stars.

As lessers, perhaps they do not share my fatalism. All

life seeks to prolong itself just a little bit longer. Just on the off chance that they thwart fate and survive.

I expected to feel the compulsion of lust again inside this room.

However the Eruvisans passed the metal aphrodisiac from their stolen cargo to this lesser, it should have left residues in this room. On their bodies.

But I feel nothing.

Somehow, they deposited the lusteal within her without leaving a trace.

What does it mean?

More questions pile up.

There is a strange ache in the base of my spine just above my hips.

Questions like *why* don't bother me very often.

But I am also never trapped with a creature I can't trust or assaulted by impulses I can't understand.

I am a blade. I am control. I fear nothing. Others fear me.

There is no more to be gleaned from this room.

"Did you call the captain's pod back?" she asks as I pass, giving her a wide berth as always.

"No."

"No?" Her pitch rises, and she lurches. "Why—"

I whirl. Bracers up, hood down, fingers spread so my blades are obvious and crossed.

She stops abruptly.

A long beat passes.

"S-sorry." She flashes a shaky grin and fists the shimmery blue fabric, drawing it tight against her thighs. "I just tripped. I didn't mean to startle you."

I am not startled.

But I did not reach my position by being easily misled.

"I was just hoping we could call the pods back before they get too far away."

I rise slowly. "No."

"Did the attackers do something to the controls?"

She means the Eruvisans, and it's doubtful. "Control of the pods has been routed away from the bridge."

She blinks slowly. Her eyes are large and an odd color. Black rims a sultry brown that deepens as it approaches her pupils. They contain peaks and valleys like a secret desert. "Routed away...to the captain's pod? The captain is the only one who can control the magnet?"

"Yes."

"Can we communicate with her?"

"No."

The delicate frown returns. Thinking through the problem.

And then her stomach makes a cavernous noise. She covers her belly. "Do you mind if we visit the cafeteria? It's where I was when the emergency lights went off. Where we all were."

Perhaps it is dangerous to keep her behind me.

I gesture for her to go first.

She moves quickly to obey.

For the moment, I still have the edge.

Two edges.

She walks, breathes, bleeds like any other lesser.

I confirmed it when I applied the sealing ointment to her inner passage.

But something in her is different.

Even now, it is calling out to me.

Again.

Her scent curls around me.

She walks before me, weaponless, and yet she will chain my mind.

Compel my body to act.

Not again.

This time, I am prepared.

Even though she is giving all the signals of a defeated lessor—fear, submissive posture, overtures of friendship—she also fearlessly handled me, touched me beneath my suit, put me in her mouth. Thinking about it causes unnatural heat to flood the region again. I have to adjust my suit.

Two clegs cannot pass fast enough.

The food units are standard issue and filled with raw materials from Humana. She offers me a tray, but the programmed contents are barely identifiable, and I will not enter a rest state—during which I clean, meditate, and refuel—until the assignment is complete.

"Are you sure? These are pretty great. They can make latkes or empanadas or mee goreng."

There is a small but non-zero chance that she was exposed to the lusteal through the food processors. "Give me one of each."

She programs in another meal and carries the plates to a table. Such a strange, wasteful use of this space. She folds herself into the cage of the chair. Then she uses her utensil to eat something called carbohydrate noodles.

I rotate the chair ninety degrees so there is an obvious exit and balance on the edge.

Humana's food has a mineral aftertaste and the texture of paste. I need no more than one bite of each substance dissolving to an unsatisfying mush to confirm this is not palatable nor the source of the lusteal. A science officer would have to make the final determination, but I also doubt these substances are healthy.

"Not hungry," she notes around a big mouthful. "I'll eat fast."

It does not matter.

Quiet tones echo, and odd sprays of light flicker on and off, highlighting different parts of the room. Like the frills on the captain's chair, the fuzz on the floors, and the unsecured bed shelves, these decisions make no sense.

The inner colonnades have embedded viewscreens showing fake space scenes. On the walls separating the cafeteria from the bridge, flat creatures swim inside a bubbling liquid tank. Although not a bad idea to store potable water behind transparent aluminum, this is also fake.

She presses a button in the center of the table. A glass cylinder rises filled with potable water—which is real—and she consumes it with a tiny sigh.

But I am not fooled.

Her eyes rove my body.

She is still on edge.

Waiting for me to let down my guard.

"So the Eruvisans stole something from you, huh?" she asks, tension ringing her strange, compelling eyes. "Is that what you're looking for?"

In a sense, yes. "They put metal on you."

"Metal?"

"Aphrodisiac. The reason I could react."

"React?" She chews slowly, and her oddly-colored eyes descend my body to my groin, obscured by the table. She swallows. "Oh, yeah. I think I've heard of that. Your race used to, um, reproduce in cycles, or what we would call heat —if you don't mind me calling it that."

Heat is very accurate for the sensations once more filling my lap.

"But after the...um, the destruction of your home world, you changed your biology to remove the mating urges."

"We learned to control them."

"Because you removed the parts of your body that cause it to go into heat and refined those parts into a biological 'metal' called lusteal. Isn't that right?"

It is odd that she should know so much about my people but I should know nothing of hers. "You study us?"

"As intently as you probably studied the, um, cause of your home world's destruction."

"Why?"

"Because we weren't sure if you were going to destroy us." She pokes the tines of the utensil—fork—into the noodles. "Or if you still might."

We do not destroy lesser planets. We protect them.

Unless they threaten the empire.

She suddenly lets out a puff of air. A small laugh.

I notice nothing amusing. "What?"

"Oh, just..." She sets down her fork and leans back. "I was supposed to eject with the rest of the pods. How did the Eruvisans dust me without me knowing? Well, I was in the middle of getting my fix, so I guess they could have done anything."

Her fix. Implying that she was broken and needed repair. "Human biology requires fixes."

"I have a disorder. That's why I'm on this ship. I've undergone so many tests trying to figure out why, for the past four years, the need for sex has been constant. Before then, it was more normal."

"Once or twice a decade?"

She lets out a huff of air again. "More like once or twice a week. I mean, a gora."

How horrifying.

Her brows lift. "It's not so bad. When it's with someone you care about who you've chosen to be your partner."

"One partner?"

"Well, for a lot of people..." She seems to be measuring her words carefully. "You're allowed to be with as many people as you want, but it's equally common to choose just one."

"You choose?"

"And they should agree to be chosen. There's consent. There's supposed to be consent." She worries her plump lower lip between her teeth. The bunching of skin mirrors the gathering of fabric beneath her swollen mammary glands. *Breasts*, the implant informs me. Much larger in these lessers from Humana. "I'm sorry. I knew you didn't consent."

True. So she'd understood that?

And she *touched me* anyway?

"It must be like your lusteal," she says. "Getting in your mind, forcing you to mate without any choice."

"Lusteal doesn't force us to do anything. It prepares us to act. It does not require us to act."

She tilts her head. "Then why did you?"

That question has been bothering me this whole time. There is no satisfying answer, and so I settle on an unsatisfying one. "Surprise."

"Oh. Because I...right. Whatever's gotten into me is way worse than your lusteal, then, because I can't control it at all. I'm sorry."

No wonder she continues to eye me. "You suffer still?"

"Usually I get a few moments' relief during the refractory period."

Refractory period?

"Oh, don't worry," she assures me. "Right now, I feel very in control."

She mated with a crew of Eruvisans.

Then she mated with me.

And the mating act is not unusual for her species. It's not rare. Twice a gora? Meaning every few shifts?

The Arrisans have purified reproduction into the most efficient method. The best warriors in the empire are chosen for rigorous genetic combinations in the arena, but most new Arrisans are grown from stored embryos.

The intensity of the real act, the driving primal need that demands satisfaction... Lessers must endure this broken sensation constantly.

What an impossible way to live.

And somehow she is forcing me to experience it. Outside the confines of the arena. The need is building again, heat pooling, engorging me, concentrating my thoughts.

When she touched me, I should have scythed her.

I should still.

Her apology means nothing. She knew the rules.

And yet I didn't scythe her.

My shock was total. I was confused. But I was not paralyzed. Somewhere inside, I made a decision not to enforce the rules. And I think I'm still trying to reconcile that unprincipled decision with the hyper-moral blade I think I am.

"What happens when the *Spiderwasp* arrives?" She rests her wrists on the table, showing surrender. "You're going to turn over the stolen cargo?"

"Yes."

"And the dead Eruvisans and their ship?"

"No." The *Spiderwasp* would have no use for them.

"You're just leaving?" She studies me intently. Those odd irises are hypnotizing. She is doing something to me again. "Leaving me behind too?"

Of course. She is nothing to my mission. How is it not obvious? "Yes."

"Alive?"

That is up to her.

"Assuming that we part friends," she adds.

Allies... We will never be allies. I am Arrisan and she is not.

But assuming she does not interfere with my orders, I will leave her and her damaged ship behind. "Yes."

"Do you think we can actually get to our destination with the other ship attached?"

I would not fly in this modified cruiser even before the Eruvisans cracked it. "Close the chute and detach it."

"And me? Do you think I can reach Vanadis before the bloodworms eat off my skin?"

I am no science officer.

But I have a sudden driving need to see her interior again.

A need that I should resist.

A need I have been resisting, but now I'm all too aware of it. "It is time to apply the ointment again."

She opens the medical kit, holds the Arrisan ointment in her hand for a long moment, and then rests it on the table. Her movements become less coordinated. Her fingers fumble with her blue fabric. "Did you want me to apply...?"

"I will." I pick up the ointment and rise, adjusting my hood for optimum vision.

She bends over the table and bunches her fabric like clouds above her plump cheeks.

The split where her body parts and allows her partner—

her chosen one—to tunnel his jack into her socket is tan-pink and looks like the softest substance in the universe. What is the function of these small dark hairs?

Hot blood pumps into my lower body. My abdomen hardens, and my heartbeat localizes in my spongeflesh, engorging it.

The only sound is our breathing. Hers increases to a ragged edge.

Why did I say I would do this? I already checked her interior when I applied the ointment the first time. And yet I am here, before her, the tube of ointment in my hands.

I squeeze the ointment onto my fingertip and touch her—

She jumps.

I freeze.

Tremors escape down her legs. She sucks in a deep breath and releases it. "Okay."

Using my other fingertips, I part her flesh.

As a lesser, her biology will not be as compatible with ointments created for Arrisans. The deep scratch will require multiple applications to fully seal.

But it has disappeared.

What is this?

There is barely a shadow to indicate where the scratch was before. I slide my finger across the inner skin. It is moist, soft, and whole.

The ointment has healed her *faster* than it would heal the same scratch on an Arrisan.

"What...?" I close my mouth. What does this mean?

She rises onto one elbow and tries to peer over the fabric. "Is it bad?"

"No. It has healed."

"Oh. Good. And the bloodworms?"

"You will need to visit a medical center."

"Right."

But we are still arrested in these positions.

Maybe she did not heal faster. Maybe I mistook the size of the injury before. Maybe she has a strange ability to seal over injuries while they are still healing.

Or maybe she is affected by the substances used on Arrisans even more than we are.

So many questions I should never try to answer. My role is to execute and report, not to wonder.

And all while my fingertips are still touching the softest substance in the entire universe.

It is one thing that feels exactly how it looks.

Heat floods my jack.

"Are you done?" She rises up on her other palm and cranes her neck to see into my face.

If I couple with her, the heat will leave me. It will flow out into her where it belongs. If I take her on my terms, instead of having my fluids torn from me, I will be able to control this.

And she has already chosen me as her partner.

But before I make a single movement, she pulls away and straightens, the fabric piling onto my wrists. "You have to ask every time. They have to agree. Every time."

As if she can dictate to me. This lesser who took my body without my agreement, who wrenched feelings from it, who compelled me.

Her very gaze is hypnotizing.

I ask. "Will you?"

Those long lashes flutter. She focuses on my flat cloak. "You want me?"

I separate my suit to expose the critical part.

My jack, hot and throbbing.

She reaches her hand out to touch it.

I angle away. There is no need to experience the mouth, the fingertips. I am ready to couple and lose my release in her. Get my own fix so that I can repair this fissure in my brain.

Her fingers curl around empty air.

She meets my eyes. "What's your name?"

I have so many. Blade, Arrisan, destroyer. "Sithe."

"Sai...th." She sounds it out, her tongue curling around the unfamiliar syllables. Perhaps I was mistaken about needing her mouth on me. One taste of that sensation was not enough. "You have to know my name to ask me."

"What is your name?"

"And you have to call it when you come."

"Come?"

"Release." She fixes me with those impossible eyes again. The desert irises of untold mountains. "Say my name. Catarine."

Also an odd name. So many syllables, and they tumble across one another.

"Say it," she demands.

And, as I've decided to yield to the compulsion jetting through my taut body in order to control it, I accept her rules. "Will you agree to be my partner, Catarine?"

FIVE

CATARINE

The assassin—the blade—Sithe—looks like a nightmare cloaked in gray, and yet he asks so politely.

The same way that he informed the green-skinned Eruvisans of their fate. Calm, patient, and fully intending to cut them down without a second warning.

He let me live.

And here we are.

I obeyed his rules. Now he is obeying mine.

You have to know my name. How many people have I had sex with in my life? I barely remember the names of my shipmates. In the four years since I lost myself, I have never demanded anyone's name.

But in those four years, I have never had sex with all my senses.

I will not forget this.

And if his story is right—if he's a typical Arrisan who goes to a mass orgy once or twice in his life—then he will never forget this either.

I do not want to die.

And I'm pretty sure now that he has no intention of killing me.

But just in case.

Just in case...

Sex with him gave me back my clarity, at least for a little while. It's not so much that I owe him. It's that I want to know exactly what it was that did it.

How long will it last?

How much longer until I become sick and stupid again?

But I am making a choice right now with this blade. Sithe.

For the first time in four years, I am making a choice to have sex.

That, in its own way, is kind of amazing.

His hands still cup my buttocks. He stands too close. Coiled power unsheathed. His cock is full, taut, and straight as an arrow. How funny that his blades curve but his cock doesn't. I've seen hundreds of cocks in the past years. They go every which way, and every which way has gotten me off.

Still...

I take a single breath. Another.

His scent is vanilla with a hint of male.

Entirely different from the homey foods—mee goreng fried noodles and comforting coconut rice—that I've just eaten.

His scent curls in my nostrils. Tingling fills my breasts, pinches my nipples. I know what he feels like inside me, and I'm about to know again.

I choose this.

"Don't cut me." I turn and bend over the table again, as if I can really make demands, and then spit in my hand. I have to push his away to rub the liquid on my parts.

His eyes glitter with interest. "Do lessers of Humana always put their mouths on their sex organs?"

A stark reminder of what I am to him.

Not that I once forgot. "No, but without foreplay, I need lubrication."

"You can self-lubricate." He seems to be making a note. "What is foreplay?"

"Like I did with you. Touching, licking, sucking. But it can be other things."

For some reason, thinking about *other things* gets things moving for me. A localized slipperiness wets my fingers as much as I wet my skin. I'm not worried about it hurting—I've endured a lot of rough sex over the years or even demanded it—but it would be nice if my first sexual experience after coming out of the fog was actually, you know, nice.

As impossible as our circumstances are.

His warmth approaches. A breath of air. His hands slide down my thighs and then up again to part my cheeks. He was staring at me when he was supposed to be applying the medicine. Now he is staring again. Searching for something within me like he searched within the ship.

An interminable sensation of waiting forces my heartbeat faster and faster.

Before he even touches me, my breath hitches. "Go slow."

His cock grazes my entrance. Probes. And pushes through.

Centimeter by centimeter, he enters me, slow as dark sweet soy sauce, taking me at my word. And on he comes, stretching my pussy wider as he tunnels deep until his thighs snug against mine and his abdomen curves over my buttocks. Seated against each other, we connect as deeply as two separate beings can.

And then he does something with his hips to grind himself even deeper.

Pleasure lights me up.

My womb shudders.

This is the A-spot, the G-spot. Every letter spot, even letters in alien languages I haven't yet learned, is this spot.

He slides back, releasing the pressure, and then surges into me again. Slow, steady, with a little kink at the end that drives a shudder of release through my spine. Again, and again, as unbreakable as an avalanche, as unstoppable as the tide. I taste sex in my throat, I want to arch my back and cry. He is wrenching four years of forgettable encounters into one that will break me into pieces and pulverize the shards. I bite my lip to hide that I'm coming again and again.

He pauses—while I am shaking from so many minor but unmistakable orgasms—and a hand touches my hair. "You were louder last time."

"D-did you want me to be loud?"

"Maybe." He winds my hair into his fist. "I want to bite your shoulder."

That could be amazing, but I don't know where he'll stop. We're not at breaking-the-skin levels of trust yet. Even though his cock is buried in me. "Please don't."

He pulls me up by my hair. His breath ghosts over my bare skin. His other hand cups my neck, my swollen breasts, the curve of my waist. His scent makes me swoon. I can't stay upright. He smells like intoxication. He lowers me back down to the table and releases my hair. My elbows shake and then fold, and I melt into a pool. He pushes my dress up over my back, baring me, and kneads my hips. "Unleash your voice."

So I do.

He surges into me again, and that unstoppable orgasm escapes my mouth with a moan. A sigh. A sob. It is every pornographic soundtrack, but it's real. And him? He's touching me, gripping me, studying me. He could go for days. This doesn't even excite him.

"You can..." I sob another climax. "...go faster..."

He does.

Faster and faster, his cock rams into me, shaking the table and shoving it across the cafeteria, creating a wave within my body where one orgasm doesn't cease before the next one hits, and they synchronize faster and faster, lifting me higher and higher. I will never forget this. I have no words for this sensation. A great pleasure wells within me, leaving all previous sexual experiences behind, remaking me in the fire that is his cock thrusting into my center.

He groans as he comes.

So, even he can make a noise.

And the flash bang of the orgasm blinds me. Deafens me. I have never experienced anything like this. Climax washes through me like a great whirlpool sloshing my life's juices with sparkles of well-being.

This is what I was created for.

The meaning of life...it is this.

I am a human, and I have a body for the sole purpose of feeling this depth of centeredness right now.

He waits a long, long time. His warmth covers me like a blanket. He compresses me against the table, but it is not a burden. More protective, really.

And then he slowly uncouples.

My life force drains out.

At least that's what it feels like.

I could sleep for a week right now.

Since I just had about a hundred and fifty orgasms topped by...I don't even know what to call it.

I have no desire to die.

But if I did, at least I had that.

He moves behind me, and then I feel the feather-light touch of his fingers brushing ointment on me. In me.

"The scratch came back?" I manage against the hard plastic table.

"No, new ones." There's a frown in his voice. "You advised me to go slow. Humans bruise easily."

"Yeah, I guess so." Worth it, though.

Such an odd series of coincidences have brought us together here now. A coincidence that I should have this unique disorder that compels me to have sex. A coincidence that, in the vast infinity of space, thieves carrying Sithe's stolen metal should stumble upon our teensy little ship.

I wonder if my exposure to lusteal will complicate the Vanadisans' ability to develop a cure. We lost contact with them shortly after embarking from Humana. Our ship doesn't have the capability for intergalactic communications —we have to deviate from our route to match velocities with Vanadisan satellites, and we unanimously begged the captain not to do it because it would prolong the already-unbearable, celibate journey—so they might be anxiously wondering where we are.

And I have so much delicious clarity right now.

My refractory period feels infinite.

Maybe it's the lusteal that's prolonging my period of clarity. I didn't feel any different after getting dusted—somehow—by the Eruvisans. I didn't even notice it happening, which means there are no immediate side effects aside from being able to turn on Arrisans, and Sithe says that's not a big deal. Lusteal causes nothing more than a normal erection in him. Nothing like the compulsion I feel.

If lusteal was even a partial cure, I would beg, borrow, or...well, not steal, obviously. I'd ask Sithe for a little lusteal for the other women.

Maybe the cause of my clarity is Arrisan sex.

That's the moment everything really changed.

Well then, lusteal could come in handy again. We'd just have to also find Arrisans who aren't busy and won't execute us for daring to talk to them.

Lusteal doesn't exist on Humana. It doesn't exist naturally anywhere in the universe since the Arrisans created it from their own bodies and have total control over it. I've seen a picture in a digital textbook. It was black and glittery, like mica.

If I only knew the cause of my illness... I had so many tests. So many. We all have. They tested for everything.

Everything.

They tested for space viruses from dead galaxies in case we happened to be exposed to a chip of an ancient asteroid. I'm sure they must have tested for lusteal.

All the Humana doctors can say is that there's no mechanism for head injury, no obvious brain damage, no foreign substances, no chemical imbalance, no hormone disorder... All the noes. No yeses. That's why we've put all our hope in the Vanadisans. They've studied alien biologies forever. If anyone can figure it out, they can.

Arrisan ointment is effective, and it's made from components not found on Humana. If their lusteal is the cause of my clarity now—if it could give me and my shipmates even a temporary cure—it would be worth whatever price the Arrisans demanded.

Yes. We would all pay any price.

He finishes applying the ointment, and I roll onto my back. My dress is a mess. My hair is a mess. I'm a mess. His movements are controlled, his suit sealed up again except his hood, which is down around his shoulders.

He looks ordinary, but neat. Everything in its place. I will always be drawn to a man who moves with purpose, who keeps himself tidy.

Ding.

He stiffens and pulls up the hood, disappearing into the depths. His silver eyes are the last thing to go, like a spooky Cheshire cat, and then the shadow swallows even that.

I clamber off the table.

He strides to the saltwater aquarium wall and hits a button.

The fish disappear to reveal the blunt-featured Arrisan from before. "*Spiderwasp* in. We are ready to accept the stolen cargo, and your next assignment is waiting. We will match velocities in ten clicks."

"There is an environmental factor."

"Which is?"

"A lesser was exposed to the lusteal. She metabolized it and caused a reaction."

The blunt-featured male squints.

Uh-oh.

I want very much to hide behind the table, but in case he's actually squinting at a screen near ours, I don't want to draw any more attention to myself.

"Convey the lesser to the science officer. *Spiderwasp* out." The viewscreen returns to festive fish.

But everything else takes on a dangerous shade of gray.

Sithe stares at the tank.

Then he swings to me.

The hood is up.

He is a shadowed monster. Not a man balls-deep who ghosted his lips across my shoulders and told me he wanted to bite me. He is an elite soldier, the special forces of the deadliest aliens to conquer the universe, who executes assignments and enemies without question.

Dread seeps into my veins. Ice pumps through my heart.

I thought I was going to get to stay.

The words die on my lips.

He lifts his chin so his eyes appear in outline from the hood's shadow. "Ten clicks."

Ten clicks.

Until I have to go to a ship filled with Arrisans.

In this crumpled-up dress.

My legs are all sticky. "May I take a shower?"

He was staring behind me, but now he fixes on me. "Seal your door."

Ominous.

His hood darkens to black, and he strides aggressively past me, almost at a fast glide that makes him both smaller and more nimble. He crouches beneath the pirates' ship and then leaps inhumanly high like a grasshopper. His forearms cross, and his black blades flash out. A beetle's deadly pincers. He disappears.

I do not know this person.

Nothing but a name.

The floor shudders. My fork clatters off its plate.

He's doing something to the pirate ship.

Something that threatens the stability of my ship.

Run.

I move on legs I cannot feel into my bedroom and slam the button to close my door.

The light remains red. It never was good at closing. The

captain was always working on it with a tool set, cranking on panels, and swearing.

"Nothing like the smell of ozone in the morning," she'd say with a funny-shaped screwdriver clenched in her teeth. A wire would spark with a loud pop and she'd swear.

"You'd be a knockout if you didn't swear," the king-maker would tell her, polished hand on her generous hip, stylish head cocked.

"The swearing is what fixes it."

"Then you should swear a lot more. You're straddling this line, holding yourself back, and 'suppressed frustration' isn't a good look. If you went all-in on class or you fully embraced your rough edges, you'd be gorgeous."

"My great uncle told me all the pretty girls died off in the Second Flood," the captain had muttered. "So there's no hope."

"My dad's side died in the Second Flood," the ingénue had piped up. "An Arrisan ship by my mom's house blew up so big that the clouds gathered and it rained glitter for twenty-seven days."

"My kin died in the Great Quake." The kingmaker had crossed her arms and leaned against the wall. "I'm just saying that some people are naturally pretty, but you have to work on it."

"Mm." The captain's tone had turned dry. "Thanks for clarifying."

But I have none of the captain's tools. And even if I did, I don't know how to use them.

I do know how to swear. I slam the button again and again, chanting it like a prayer. "H. H. H."

H stands for the worst thing that can happen in space. Hull crack. What I'm afraid is about to happen again.

And it also stands for—

The door closes. The red light turns green. Sealed.

Huh. The captain was right. Swearing did fix it.

The wall jolts beneath my shoulder.

No time to celebrate.

I run into the shower and rinse off the mess, tensing for the drizzle to hit any cuts, but the Arrisan ointment is miraculous and it never stings.

Ah, I left my medical kit in the cafeteria.

But I am going to an Arrisan ship. The ointment is only precious because we have so little of it on Humana. They have plenty of it in their ship.

Please don't let me die.

I finish my shower and send my dress through the cleaning cycle. The shower seals and my ears pop. The shower windows tint and then return to normal, and it unseals with a hiss. I put the now-cleaned, slightly ozone-scented garment back on.

It's still my best chance to connect with Sithe. I am a lesser to him, but I must try to make myself as similar to him as possible. It's a psychological principle that people like and are more drawn to others who look or act like them. Sithe isn't human, and this principle barely works on Humana anyway, but alone in space surrounded by threats, it's all I have.

Outside shoes. I definitely need outside shoes.

A knock echoes from the wrong side of my room.

Unsettling.

I finish dressing and scoop a few things into a day pack.

What about my cat ears?

I sit on the bed, holding the clean pair.

November first, I awoke with a massive headache that morphed into cramps and then a throbbing bone ache in my hips. It lasted weeks and scans couldn't find anything, but it marked the first symptom of my descent into madness. That year for Halloween, I'd been silly and dressed up like a black cat for my workplace party. The ears were simple fabric. They have neurolink ears for all sorts of animals, including unicorns. I think I focused on cats because it was the last time I was normal.

Sithe's voice comes from the intercom. "Open the door."

I leave the ears behind.

The button works a lot better at opening than at closing.

His silver eyes take me in, and then he recedes into shadow. Turning his shoulder, he strides silently down the hall to the escape pods, away from the pirate ship.

The cafeteria looks undisturbed. I must have been wrong about him cracking the hull.

Until I reach the escape pods.

A mouth like an anglerfish bites into our ship. Long jagged black teeth pierce the metal frame. A shadowed interior gusts cold air.

A gaping hole has been carved out of the hull and rests in the middle of the hallway.

That's not going to be okay. "Wasn't there any way to connect our ships without damaging ours?"

"Not in ten clicks."

No apology. No reasoning. He has irrevocably damaged our cruiser, at least as badly as the pirate ship did. Probably a lot worse.

When the captain comes back, how can she connect to the cruiser? She isn't wearing an evac suit in her pod.

My stomach churns.

What will happen to everyone?

What will happen to me?

He strides over the jagged barrier and into the gray interior, a shadow moving deeper into shadow. "Come."

I cannot remain here.

I hug my day pack.

There's only forward now. No backward.

I walk into the mouth of the beast.

My footsteps echo, boots clattering loudly.

As I move, the tunnel shrinks in, closing up behind me the way his clothes seal over his body. I hurry to catch up to him. The tunnel terminates in a small hollow just a few strides across, like hitting the back of the throat. The way I've come seals and smooths like skin or fabric.

I've been swallowed.

He turns around to face me and leans against the far wall, wrists down, hood back, eyes staring straight ahead.

The ship walls fold around him. His fingers twitch. The air between us tints. He's facing me, but I don't think he sees me at all.

Are we moving? There's no sensation of movement.

Everything is still and silent.

Should I be still and silent too?

But I can't forge a connection in silence. "What's happening?"

"We are matching velocities with the *Spiderwasp*."

We're flying, then. It's not cold, but my fingers are like ice. "Can I see?"

The walls around us change to show the outside, and it's not like the viewscreens in our cruiser which have an unreal patina. It's like looking through glass, which is insane because I know how deep we are in his ship...although it's nothing like the ships I've been on. Humana has received the dregs of technology, and this is the pinnacle of the empire, so I guess I don't know anything about it at all.

Behind me floats our cruiser. It was such a pretty clam-shaped spaceship with a pearl glued onto the widest part—

the communications array for the movie theater, which was actually the bridge.

The pirate ship hangs off its back like an ugly tick.

There's a sad puff of debris by the gaping hole from which we've just detached. The other women's memorabilia have been sucked into space. I wish I would have figured out how to close all the doors at once, but it's also a stark reminder that none of us can ever go back.

Which bits of dust glittering among the stars are the escape pods?

Hopefully, the captain can see we've left and everyone is still close enough to be pulled back.

It's a lot more likely someone will find our cruiser than a pod.

But it's also really unlikely anyone will ever find our cruiser.

It's still moving at hundreds of actungs per cleg, but looks like it's standing still against the background of stars. Since we must be increasing velocities to match the other ship, we're leaving it behind.

On the other side of Sithe lies our destination.

I walk around him—because it was a trick of the optics and he's actually leaning against a column in the center of the room, not a dead end—and rest my fingers against the false glass.

There is the *Spiderwasp.*

A giant evil haystack. Haystack? The top is blunt and rounded like a fist while the bottom tapers to straw-like strings. I think of a spider wasp as a flying insect that preys upon tarantulas. A number survived the cataclysms, and we keep both—wasps and tarantulas—at a healthy distance. This is something different.

"What is a spiderwasp to an Arrisan?"

"A sea creature."

Yes. The tentacles hang down as some sort of jellyfish that stings. We maneuver to rendezvous with the underbelly. These tentacles, in fact, do sting. All the ends are guns.

He leaves whatever he's doing and stands behind me.

What's going through his mind? The person who communicated with him on the first transmission had told him to appreciate the majesty. "Is it majestic?"

"It is new, and so it is the most powerful."

Power equals majesty.

His hand brushes my forehead.

A lock of hair was hanging in my face. He tucks the stray lock behind my shoulder and smooths the others.

...What?

The silver in his irises glimmers as his gaze snags against mine.

Then he recedes beneath the hood until only the curve of his temple, jutting chin, and jawline on one side are visible.

Nerves squiggle in my belly.

Is this curiosity?

Or a hint of caring?

Can I prompt him to take care of me?

To protect me?

He casually, thoughtlessly, doomed my shipmates because he couldn't wait the extra clicks to non-destructively connect our ships.

It would be so very easy for him to do the same to me.

We're flying into a nest of killers just like him.

I really don't know what's going to happen next.

SIX

SITHE

The *Spiderwasp* is a top-class dreadnought.

As Catarine turns her odd eyes away from me to it, her expression is the correct one.

Fear.

Its planet-ending array makes even me a little uncomfortable. It was built for one purpose.

To establish dominance.

No one will ever best the Arrisan empire. We will strike first. We will strike hard. We will force all others to cower before us, and no race in this universe will ever threaten us again.

Her hair is long and textured, finer than mine, and a darker brown than her eyes.

I can still feel the threads against my fingertips.

"What kind of ship is this?" she asks quietly.

"A dreadnought."

"And what do you do on it?"

"Conquer." Is there any other thing that you do on a ship?

She taps her fingertips against the screen. "What about your ship? Is it as big as the dreadnought?"

I flick a finger at the screen she's touching. The schematics of my ship appear in ghostly outline against the *Spiderwasp*. It is a smaller version, but all Arrisan ships are all built on the same principles.

She must note the similarities. "Is it a sea creature too?"

"It's a sinusoid."

Her head tilts and that little frown reappears. "A wave or a blood vessel?"

"A type of seed. Mine is optimized for space travel and speed."

Originally, the sinusoids were all our race had that could escape the Harsi. When their deadly maws crushed our great ships, our stations, our planet, the smallest seeds slipped through their teeth. And though we have modeled the dreadnoughts on some of their technology, we are still most comfortable in sinusoids, I think.

"Does yours have a name?"

"A number."

"Oh."

In the worst case, my ship contains genetic materials as well as tools to implant a host. There is enough food to last several generations so long as everything is properly recycled. And it has, of course, weapons.

We can restart our race anywhere so long as one of us survives.

Arris will live so long as one ship survives.

We pass into the massive array.

Long threads dangle, nearly invisible, electrified, capable of cutting us into pieces. The ship navigates them, although the gravity inside is at odds with the movement, and she sways.

These long wires are necessary. Dreadnoughts have instant communication abilities with Arris Central and the other ships of the empire. In the worst case, it could become the new command center around which all fragments of our race would rally.

We pass through the communications array to the weapons.

Each barrel fixes on us—autotargeting—and then deactivates.

"Those guns..." She watches the biggest one power down. "They look powerful."

"They can push planets out of orbit."

"Like what happened with Humana. You pushed us a little bit so that we would have more perfect growing conditions for your food."

Did we? "Every planet must contribute to the empire."

She offers a small smile but it does not seem to indicate happiness.

No one feels happiness when they're being swallowed by a dreadnought. I dislike yielding control, but their loaders can pilot my ship through this nasty course and into the cargo bay better than I can.

Perhaps I will research Humana during my next rest.

I can imagine her standing within the waving fields of nutrient vines, her hair flying in the desert winds, the lessers she calls family crossing to help her harvest cubes as the evening turns a comforting shade of twilight maroon.

Probably this is an image of Arris I have superimposed over her world, but she looks at peace.

The screens flicker as we approach the open bay. It is nearly time to dock. The ships communicate their codes, and the passageway unfurls to my cargo bay.

I lead her to the airlock. She stands beside me, sober and brave.

And then suddenly, she opens her small bag and brings out the square of her family. "If I don't have the chance, could you send this back to Humana? I didn't get to see my dad for a long time because of my illness, and I'd really like it if he could know that my last thoughts were of us together as a family."

It is highly unlikely I will be able to do this. How many ships fly from Humana? I have never encountered them before, and my assignments have sent me over a large region of the empire. "You should hold on to it. Or cast it into space. It will arrive faster."

Her chin wrinkles. She nods abruptly and jams the square into her bag. "Sorry. I understand."

Good, then.

The lock light turns off.

They are opening my airlock?

Because of the environmental factor, right. They will open in near space to suck out any potential foreign objects in vacuum. It's a reasonable precaution, but a problem, obviously.

With no warning, I crack my suit and swing my arm around her. The suit flaps against her. I pull her hard against me.

She squeaks against my chest.

My airlock pops.

The suit suctions tight around us. It is designed for my size and compresses her uncomfortably hard.

The puff of air exiting my pressurized ship pulls us out into space.

Only us, because everything else in my cargo bay is secured.

Gravity is less here, and we rotate gently. My stomach dives for my throat.

She trembles against my bare skin like a small animal. Her palms splay across my pectorals. Her head rests against my shoulder.

This is a strange feeling.

She must be at the right angle to see out through the hood, because she gasps. "Stars."

Yes, they rotate above us.

I time the rotation as we and my ship coast the rest of the way into the dreadnought's cargo bay and step back onto the lip of my ship just as the *Spiderwasp*'s gravity takes over and sets us down inside. Atmosphere floods my ship. I release her.

She stumbles back, resting her palms on my ship's wall for balance, disheveled, mouth open, and nostrils flared. Her eyes silently communicate her total fear.

It is appropriate.

And yet, there is a strange urge in me to pull her back beneath my suit. Walk with her to my room, complete my rest, and accept my next assignment with her hidden against me, as if she is not there.

Such a strange fantasy.

Like the questions that drove me to investigate the cruiser when I should have simply waited with my prize until the *Spiderwasp* arrived. Like the urge to mate her, bite her. I should not want these things. I should not ask these questions. I should not feel these urges.

My ship glides to the elevated dock. Engineers slouch on box chests, tools ready to inspect and repair. Because this is my ship, but it does not belong to me. Nothing belongs to me.

I'm a weapon of the Arrisan empire. I'm a blade, but I

do not own myself. I am wielded by the hand of the empire, and if I break in that hand, then I weaken the empire. That is why I strive not to break.

The engineers do not share my philosophy.

Portable tools, scanners, and straps to clip on thicker protective gear dangle from their high-visibility green overalls. It makes them look oddly puffy unlike the slim profile of an ordinary Arrisan.

I wear the highest grade of armor, nearly impervious to my own blades, and my blades can cut into anything.

But their tools can slice a ship in half.

The walkway extends. I cross onto the *Spiderwasp*'s metal pan. Catarine smartly shadows me.

The crew stands and turns to their boss.

The head engineer, Atana, swaggers up to us like he's larger than the standard build, but physically, he's very ordinary. He has the normal short black hair, gray skin, and four-pointed ears of any other Arrisan, and yet his silver eyes hold mine aggressively. He has the temerity to clench a long igniter punk between his teeth. It smolders.

His lips curl back so far that he exposes his canines. "You got some metal for us?"

I do not like engineers, but in hundreds of missions, I've never had a problem with them. "In my cargo bay."

He ambles past me. His gaze flicks to Catarine. He stops.

She cautiously returns his gaze. Not overly friendly. Not entirely submissive either.

It is smart. She draws as little attention as she can.

But it does not work.

His nostrils flare. He scents her. And then his pupils dilate.

I ease onto my heels, gliding without hardly moving because I will not turn my back on him or on his crew.

He looms over her. His tone darkens, menacing. "You brought a lesser?"

I take one sharp step and cut off his gaze. "She's infected with lusteal."

His chin lifts. He can see her over my shoulder. "I didn't know lessers could get infected with the metal."

I don't like the feral interest in his eyes. And I don't like the way his crew forms up behind him. I don't like the way that everyone in all corners of the giant bay is suddenly looking at us.

Atana curves his lips, causing the dangerous lit punk to rise. "Looks like cargo."

"She's not."

"We'll take charge of it."

"She's my charge."

"Down here, blade..." He takes a meaningful step toward me. "Everything's mine."

I bare my left wrist.

My blade shoots out and curves toward his temple.

It is meant to be a reminder. A warning.

But he whips up his right forearm in the same fast flicker.

A hard silver dagger clashes mine.

He's a blade?

His are straight. Silver. Steel.

And his grin mocks me. "You want to try me? Class of 2-8? I'm class of 3-2, and I'm happy to shatter you. We have upgrades."

This is why I hate engineers.

Arrogant braggarts, the lot of them. They hold the fate

of the ship in their hands. As goes the ship, so go the occupants. They are the only caste in the empire trained to subvert the rules.

And this department is led by a blade?

I had heard that the blades were being removed from classes and distributed throughout the empire. We must remain mission-ready to face the Harsi and no longer have enough assignments for new blades. Arrisans are nothing if not efficient users of resources. Why not have an engineer who's also a blade?

But this is a mistake.

Engineers have one mission: keep the ship alive. If a captain wants to pull some maneuver that will jeopardize the ship, engineers are trained to disobey. Who gives a blade to a man trained to disobey?

Blades do not have a fraternity. We do not have a brotherhood. All we have are orders. And one mission. To keep the Arrisan empire alive.

Class of 3-2 might actually be faster than me. Atana definitely has more support.

"She's bound for the science officer." My voice goes so low, it almost growls, in case he does have some sense of orders.

He glances at the engineers behind him and releases his blade. It retracts, and so I do the same to mine.

He smiles and steps back. "Well then, why didn't you say so? Can't keep the science officer waiting."

A low rumble of laughter accompanies this statement.

They know something I don't.

I have an unsettled feeling.

It increases as we stride through the ship.

Catarine scurries behind me. She said nothing during

the exchange with Atana, neither shrinking in on herself nor expanding to challenge him to a fight. All she did was watch. That was wise. There is nothing she can do as a lesser, and now she is careful not to make our journey more difficult than it has to be.

Every hall we walk, every juncture we pass through in the winding veins and arteries of the dreadnought, gains us more interest. Arrisans who are supposed to have tasks slow and stop. Arrisans who are supposed to focus turn and look.

I have walked through dreadnoughts a thousand times. No one ever looked at me. I have transported lessers before. Criminals, ones who screamed or fought for freedom. Ones who should have drawn attention and did not.

The lingering aphrodisiac taints her.

A curling sensation twists the muscles around my spine.

I scent her everywhere within me. In my blood. I feel her still pressed against my collar. Against my thigh.

My blades rub against my bones.

If anyone approaches like the engineer did, I will cut them.

It's my mission to convey her, so it's natural to feel this intense sense of purpose.

We spiral deep into the lower recesses. This sector is filled with engines, weapons, metal, and of course a few stores. Just in case.

It is also the realm of the science officer. He needs to be close to where they might take in specimens.

I have never been to this one, but I have been to science offices before. The entire wall is blocked off, and the doors here are double insulated. Unlike the rest of the ship, which, of course, seals perfectly in every junction, these walls are blast-proof, shockproof, mostly weapon-proof. Few areas of the ship are more reinforced. Even my blades would have a little trouble cutting through.

A little.

I stop before the scanner and pull back my hood. It reads my implants. The doors slide open silently despite their bulkhead size, and we enter the office.

This one is strewn with remnants of scientific study. Samples from different planets pose in lifelike displays, most in successful hunts. Victors grasp prey, shake it in a death snap.

Catarine stops short.

Her muscles tense. She doesn't breathe.

I can see how these scenes might upset a lesser.

But my assignment is not complete until she enters the examination room. "He will inspect you. Ask him about the bloodworms."

Her odd, sere irises meet mine. She takes a big breath and straightens. The dress gathers attractively beneath her distinctive breasts. "Thank you."

"Yes."

On an overhead speaker, the science officer speaks in a dry tone. "And you have delivered your cargo. Very good, blade. You may go."

And so I will.

Catarine lifts her shoulders and her chin. She looks regal, almost Arrisan in this moment. "Goodbye, Sithe."

I nod.

She strides into the barren examination room. Its tinted doors close.

She is gone.

My assignment is complete.

I turn and walk out.

The science office doors close behind me. Silently. I feel

the air movement on the back of my neck and replace my hood.

My implants direct me to the crew's quarters.

I am to rest there before I receive my next assignment.

Turn. Walk away.

I obey.

The science office hallway disappears behind a corner. Another one. There is a juncture full of Arrisans who pay me no attention. Another.

I can no longer smell her.

Her scent fades and so does the feeling in my fingers. My lower body. I feel nothing from the knees down.

But my implant pings.

Turn here.

The crew quarters are this way.

Sharing a dorm with other Arrisans is not restful, but I can usually shut them out, ignore them as I await instructions from my superior at the Arsenal. That is fine. I've done what I need to do. All the questions are gone.

An engineer blocks the walkway to the grav tube. He's repairing the slide. I deliberately avoided the grav tubes with Catarine because she wouldn't understand how to ride them, and we drew enough attention simply walking.

I must reach the bunks as quickly as possible. It feels like small insects are gnawing at my ligaments. If I must go around, I will surely lose my pride.

"How long?"

"As long as it takes," the engineer replies, flippant.

That means I should wait. If they know a repair will take clegs, they tell me.

"So you brought in a lesser that was infected with the metal, huh?" He leers. "Did you enjoy it?"

Anger flashes through me, hotter and more acidic than I have ever felt.

This male must be young or has especially bad genetics, and I want to hurt him, really drive home how ugly his question is and how much it is beneath me. "I've been to the arena five times."

He drops his fingers, limp-wristed to show surrender, and licks his chapped lips. "Some of us have all the luck."

"It was not luck." But that is too harsh, perhaps. "And it was not what I expected."

"The boss enjoyed it when he went." The engineer curls his lip and mimes putting an igniter punk in his teeth. "He said it was intense."

Atana would say that.

The arena is intense, but in a totally different way from mating with Catarine. Feeling her on my own terms was like getting something back. Something taken from me in a way that I hadn't even realized I had lost it.

And all her small noises, her ways of sighing and twisting and lifting her hips to take me in only incited me to want more. Instead of counting every thrust to gauge if I could release faster, I didn't think of numbers at all. I explored her like a new planet, charting her solar cycles by listen and feel. Taste. Scent.

And now...

She is with the science officer.

Where she belongs.

"You think he's going to figure out how the metal got in?" the engineer asks.

Yes, the science officer will. Maybe he'll even extract it. And then she'd be released. Free to return to her strange planet and her lesser family, a fragile existence but unburdened by the Arrisan responsibility to defend all races.

"You think he's going to mount her like the others?"

That draws my attention back to the squat engineer.

Science officers don't commingle with lessers. They never interact with their specimens. Usually, they aren't even in the same room. Just as the science officer directed me from the intercom, he would perform any examination remotely.

But the engineer is salivating for my reaction, and so I give him disaffected confusion. "Mount her?"

"Yeah, you know. Like the other specimens on the walls."

On the walls...?

"Do you think he'll do it so she's getting attacked? Maybe her hand up, begging for her life? He better not leave the metal in her body, or else he'll have some night visitors, if you know what I mean."

Wait, *mount her* on the wall?

But those specimens had their blood drained and organs removed. Their eyes are coated with a film to retain liquidity. Their brains are sliced into thin sheets and scanned into an archive. The sheets are then thrown into the recycler. Maybe one is saved in a cabinet.

If she is mounted on the wall, then she won't go back to her family. She'll never stand in the middle of a field of vines while the desert wind whips back her hair. Her family, the humans on the square image in her little day pack, will never surround her.

"It's a point of interest now. A lesser who took in the metal." He scratches his cheek. "You think it's been enough time he probably already got started?"

I turn on my heels and walk toward the science office.

My implant pings.

This is the wrong direction.

My next assignment is behind me.

I am not supposed to be here. I am not supposed to do this.

My heart beats faster and faster.

Blood roars in my ears.

No one looks at me.

I break into a run.

What am I doing? What am I doing?

SEVEN

CATARINE

This is creepy.

Everywhere I walked on the ship, I saw *them* looking back at me. Gray skinsuit robes, naked stares tracking my movement like hungry ghosts. I have entered the land of grim reapers, and I am the only one who is alive.

They're all silent. No one breathes. When their hoods are up, that's terrifying, but when their hoods are down, then you can know that their silver eyes are following you.

And they all look so similar. Short black hair, gray skin and eyes, almost no difference in height or weight or musculature. That's what happens when your entire planet dies and the scant survivors throw everything into creating supersoldiers. Their creepy sameness adds to the unsettling sense that something is wrong.

I thought the engineer was going to kill Sithe and take me. Would that be better than where I am now?

The walls of the science office are a canvas painted in death. Friezes of monsters killing monsters in three dimensions. Slides that click over labeled parts, including human bits and pieces. I really hope those were willing donations.

There's a difference between science officers and doctors.

The Arrisans do not have doctors. Doctors pledge to do no harm. This concept is foreign throughout much of the universe, but especially among the Arrisans. We lessers are weak and need mending, but if Arrisans are damaged in such a way that they cannot be healed, the honorable act is to commit suicide. At least it was in their early history. Now, I think, they no longer recycle bodies into emergency food cubes, but they still have historic rations that were once people. And not all of them were dead when they were processed.

But then Sithe said to ask about the bloodworms, implying that I could actually still survive. Like the science officer's just going to examine me and then I could get treatment, because what's the point of treating someone who's not going to stay alive?

It seems crazy, but this is his world, not mine. His confidence gives me a little bit of strength. I know I'll never see him again, but at least I could say goodbye with my head held high. I wanted to give him a smile, something nice to remember me by, but that was impossible. It was all I could do not to cry.

And now I'm inside the smaller room. It's an operating theater, maybe. There's no place to sit, just barren, empty walls.

But I thought the same thing about Sithe's ship, and it transformed like crazy. He could sculpt the walls like clay. I don't have any idea how. Technologies that fall to Humana are the knockoff brands. We've stuck wagon wheels on snow plows, while the Arrisans are driving showroom models.

And I stand in the middle of this box and wait.

The ceiling is glass. Maybe. It's dark like a hood, and you can't really see what's up there. Since the door has closed and the interior walls look the same, I feel like I'm inside an oubliette. Because I haven't moved, I know for sure that the exit is behind me, but if I had walked around even a little bit, I think I would already be disoriented.

A face appears overhead. The science officer. Pallid, older, with sharp cheekbones and brow ridges lit from beneath. He looks terrifying.

"So you were infected with our metal. How?"

His tone is dry and impersonal. He doesn't look at me. He's looking at something else, distracted.

"I don't know. I—" My voice cuts out. Nerves. I take a slow breath to center—still breathing, something is right—and try again. "Sithe can't figure it out."

"Sithe? Is that the name of your medical scanner?"

"No." Wow, it never occurred to me that they didn't know each other's names. "It was the Arrisan who brought me here."

"I see. And how did you get infected?"

I just told him. "I don't know."

"I see."

He's seeing something that's definitely not me. Or at least not my answers. "What are you doing?"

"Analyzing you." He seems amused that I asked him the question, so that's good I think. "You, in fact, are embedded with the metal. I had serious doubts. No lesser has been affected by lusteal before, no matter how much they were exposed. Not from Humana or anywhere."

"You've exposed people from Humana?"

"Well, not me, but someone has. In the interest of science."

And there was no other person affected in the whole universe. Just me. By touching those pirates, by begging them to put things into me without a care, I exposed myself in a way no one ever has before.

I really, really regret that right now. My body droops. My lips, my lids. I have no strength in my jaw to even talk.

"Why don't you lie down in the middle of the examination room?" the doctor—no, science officer—very reasonably suggests.

I really am so very tired. But if I move, I'll forget how to escape. I lean against the door. "I'm okay."

"Interesting. So, tell me. You interacted with the blade."

"Yes, I did." My head is swimming, but honestly, it's nothing like what I experienced on the cruiser. I can still string together thoughts. "I'm supposed to ask you about bloodworms."

"What about them?"

"If I have any in me because I had the contact with the Eruvisans."

"Oh. Well. They won't trouble you. I promise you that."

My shoulders slump. "That's a relief."

One last thing to worry about.

I mean, one *less* thing.

Hmm.

"Yes, indeed. Because..."

Abruptly the room shifts, and the floor tilts.

I fall to my knees.

It's just like I thought. Just like on the other ship. The wall cups me, but in a way that makes it feel like I'm falling through the floor. My fingers claw at the smooth sides as I fall farther and farther from the room, which is now an actung away. I can't scramble up the sides to get out.

If only I can lean forward...

Wait, no. The dark ceiling is still above my crown, which means the door to escape is still behind me. Somehow. I need to lean back.

A bright light sears my eyes. "Do not fight the machine."

"It...what are you doing?"

"Examining you."

"Still?"

"Oh, I tested your surface information. But now I must go deeper."

The light turns yellow. My heartbeat sounds loudly in my ears. The machine is doing something. I'm about to be sick. I have to lean forward, get away from it.

A high-pitched noise, a terrible mosquito whine, drills into my ear canals. My bones shudder. I feel it in my teeth.

I clench them. "Is it going to hurt?"

"You will not care about pain."

And he's right. An array of terrible implements descend from the ceiling. It's horrifying. And yet I barely care. The yellow light centers above my eyes, guiding lasers. My mom does surgery with those sometimes. The yellow light traces the path and then the circular saw cuts.

"Very nice," he murmurs. "Note: Heart rate is steady. Compliance-gas levels are supersaturated. Any increase risks epoxy, and yet the specimen remains upright. Is the presence of lusteal strengthening her weak lesser biology? She resists as if she has blade-levels of mind-control training. Quite intriguing."

In regards to fighting to control myself, he's right. I've had years of training.

But there's no need for a shock test. "You don't have to frighten me. My heart rate might not show it, but I'm already terrified."

"Oh, I know. This test is a bonus." The smile permeates

his tone in dark anticipation. "Very soon, you'll not care about this at all."

I'm about to become one of the slides.

"Note continued: It's impossible to conduct the examination without damaging the entry doors to theater two. Contact engineering to schedule a repair and blame the lesser for noncompliance."

The whine sharpens, and the yellow light changes to magenta.

I'm going to scream. The saw is going to touch my skin, and I'm going to scream.

"Wha—?" The science officer's surprise is louder than the saw. "Why are you here? This is my domain. Exit."

A longer pause. The light flickers to yellow and the active pitch lowers, but I can feel the heat of the saw clawing away at the air just before my forehead. I ease away, even though it means descending to where he wanted me on the floor. The saw whines above me. My stomach lurches. I'm going to throw up, and it still looks like I'm an actung through the floor.

"This is not your assignment, blade."

Wait.

Could it...?

"The specimen is mine," the science officer snaps, and the light abruptly changes back to magenta.

It sears my eyes. I've gone right into its path. My vision tunnels on the blurred saw.

It's coming it's coming it's coming—

A black shadow flashes in front of my eyes.

Kak-zhing!

The saw makes an injured sound and bites me at the hairline with a resounding *thunk*. Heat and pain splits open my brain.

It's got me. It's done it. My skull is split.

Oh no. Oh, wow. Oh, H.

The floor snaps to the right place. I'm resting on it, my knees splayed, dress puffy.

The machine coughs and splutters over me. It's even worse than my nightmares. Wires spark and scalpels scrape.

A wheel spins, then stops. It's empty. The toothed saw is missing.

The sudden silence is too loud.

Sithe's gray arm snakes around my waist and hauls me back. My daypack is still looped around my shoulder, incredibly. It slides off as he sits me upright.

Hot liquid cascades down from my forehead. It spatters my dress with red spots. I wipe it away from my eyes.

Blood.

It hurts.

My head hurts.

Really throbbing bad.

Another man—the science officer—jogs out of the middle office. He wears a gray robe in a lighter shade with a blue stripe up the back, and his dark hair has streaks of gray. Black lenses hover before his eyes. But his expression isn't ordinary.

Of course, at this moment, neither is Sithe's.

His blade arcs out so fast, it's a blur. The sharp edge rests against the science officer's jugular.

"You broke her." Sithe kneels and holds me against his chest. His rage is cold. "After I said to freeze."

"Heh." The science officer eases onto his heels. He does not make the gesture of surrender, but his caution is unmistakable. He swallows, and his skin brushes Sithe's black blade. "You invaded my domain."

"I ordered you."

"Your orders have no dominion here." But the science officer sucks in a breath as though he realizes arguing is not a good idea. "It's not broken. The skin is torn, but the skull is intact."

"I don't believe you."

"Lessers bleed." He flicks his gaze to a case etched with their long-life symbol, a six and a nine superimposed. "Clean it up. You'll see."

"Pass the medical kit to me."

The science officer slides the case across the floor to us. Despite the movement, Sithe's blade never wavers from his throat.

"Open it," Sithe orders me.

I fumble with the closure. On top is a cleaning cloth and sanitizing solution. I break the packet, and solution dribbles on the floor. My hands are shaking the worst of my life. Sithe retracts his blade and helps me apply it to the cloth, then presses it to my forehead. It stings, but not as badly as I think it should. He folds the cloth, pressing different sides to soak up the mess.

There's no mirror. Whatever he sees makes him grim and also seems to reassure him. The science officer must be right. I won't die.

The science officer turns his back on us and studies the wall above the super-thick prison doorway.

A circular saw is embedded above the main door. It sparks.

That's dangerous.

Oh. Wait.

When the saw blade was descending toward me, I saw a black shadow that must have been Sithe's blade. The saw must have hit it and ricocheted into the bulkhead.

I was moments from no longer being me anymore.

The muscles tighten around Sithe's mouth. He studies me.

If I don't say something, I'm going to start shaking again. "I asked about the bloodworms."

A slight divot shows his frown.

"Infested." The science officer turns. One side of his mouth curves into a nasty smile. "Completely. It's already too late for her. She'll be paste in a few clegs."

Even I know that's a lie.

Sithe rises, pulling me up with him, and loops the day pack strap over my shoulder. "Give me the treatment."

The curve deepens. "For the good of Arris, I'll irradiate the remains."

His blade ejects from his wrist just a little in warning. "There will be no remains."

"On the contrary, blade." The science officer is downright giddy. "You are looking at the first lesser to be embedded with lusteal. My name will be inscribed in the ledger of unique finds. Perhaps my inferior status will even be reversed and my father's genetic code may be reauthorized for continuing our bloodline. Now, release my prize specimen and trot off to your next assignment. Remember, you already transferred ownership."

"I changed my mind."

"You're a blade. You can't change your mind."

Sithe pulls me past the science officer toward the door.

The science officer throws out his arms as if he intends to hug us.

A long dirty-metal blade, flat and kinked in the middle like a boomerang, slices into our path.

Sithe drops me and flicks up his forearms to block the strike. His blades are much thinner and more curved. I thought of him as a scythe, but this science officer is like a praying mantis with his kinked blades, bug-like and deadly.

"You're one of them too?" Sithe's voice is low and tense, as if it's taking a lot of strength to hold back the wider, blunter metal emerging from the science officer's wrists.

"Class 2-6. Ukuri." The science officer smirks as he pushes. "As an older class, I never thought I would cross with the deadliest blade in the Arsenal, but here we are."

It's funny that Sithe says *one of them* and not *one of us*. He's a blade too. It must be strange finding out that everyone is special forces when you expected ordinary soldiers. But it doesn't make much difference to someone like me either way.

"You cannot take Catarine," Sithe says.

"Your lesser belongs to the empire. Don't be confused by the metal."

"You cannot take her."

"You're affected by it."

"So are you."

Sweat beads up on the brow of the science officer, Ukuri. "I'm affected by nothing."

"No?" Sithe shoves Ukuri's blades back. "Then how can you obstruct a blade executing an order?"

Ukuri's blades lower. His gaze darts from Sithe to me and back again. He licks his lips, seems surprised by the sweat. "You execute no order."

"How do you know?"

"You told me."

"And? Since when has the word of a blade meant anything but compliance to a science officer?"

Ukuri's nostrils flare.

Then he slowly straightens. His flat blades retract. The

smirk returns. "You win for now, blade. There is a proper order. The lesser will be back."

Sithe also retracts his blades and takes my elbow again, this time keeping himself between me and the science officer.

But it doesn't matter.

The doors open.

We pass through.

The science officer stares me dead in the eye. "I'll see you again."

The doors close, shutting him inside.

EIGHT

SITHE

I am striding down the halls, my gaze darting in every direction. My body is shaking. Blood is squeezing through my veins like it's being pumped under pressure.

This whole ship is full of blades. Anyone whose wrists I can't see could be one of them.

Catarine stumbles against me.

My hold on her elbow tightens. She can barely walk, but I want to run. And I don't know in which direction.

Arrisan gazes follow me as I pass. Every juncture, every hall. Every open doorway and room falls silent.

I'm at the highest threat level since finishing my training. At no other time in my life have I felt this hunted.

They're all looking at her.

They're all looking at me.

I avoid that hall—there's the engineer, still working on the grav tube—and wind through the levels until I reach my original destination: the crew quarters for the lower quartile.

On any large ship, the crew is spread out, but the

majority sleep in shifts in a central dorm. The walls of the hex-comb always have open tubes, and Catarine is small; I can probably fold her around me and we can slide in together. No one will know.

But to get to my assigned tube, which is near the top of the wall and easy to climb into by myself unencumbered, I must pass the food units.

A group finishing a shift is taking their nutrients, chatting, subdued. They stop talking. Even their crunching falls silent as we enter.

I pivot away from them to an abandoned bench and rest her against the wall.

Her eyes are closed. Blood mats her hairline. The scar looks shiny.

Every time I see it, I get this swelling of...I don't know what it is. Seething. A terrible buzzing starts behind my ears, and if I open my mouth, it will come out into a roar. As if something has been taken from me.

In training, I never really cared about the exercises that drilled us into alignment with the empire. Nothing is as important as Arris. I already agreed, so the exercises were easy. I've never cared about the assignments they give me. If it's hard, it will take longer, but I've never turned one aside.

And now...

The other crew members glance at us from the corners of their eyes.

What did I tell the science officer?

You cannot take Catarine.

I don't know what to do about this.

My words bind Ukuri.

Because blades aren't supposed to lie.

Her day pack slips down her shoulders. She jolts and grabs it, clutches it to her chest.

One crew member elbows another. Low mutters fill me with dread.

They know that I don't know what I'm doing.

No, that's not true. This is where I'm supposed to be. I'm on my mission.

But there's the problem of what to do with her.

I'm supposed to rest, but how can I? How can I when the moment I turn my eyes away, someone will take her? My blades jerk and slide into the sheaths in my wrists.

I need to think.

The wall viewscreen displays open tubes. I click through to find one lower to the floor where I could slide in with her, do a better job at cleaning her, and let her rest.

One crewmember stands and dumps her empty bowl in the recycler, but instead of going to the recycler near her, she crosses too close to Catarine to use the one closest to me. "What's that? A pet?"

"She's my..." What do I say? "Yes."

"Looks contaminated."

Another two crew members form up behind her. We are all the same model—short black hair, gray skin, silver eyes—and the leader's chest is flat and hard like any male's. About half the ship's crew is usually female. The extra point on her ears is what gives her away.

We Arrisans have engineered ourselves to have little dimorphism. A woman's body will change at the arena, swelling and softening to prepare for conception, but after she completes her duties, it will melt away just as a man's jack softens and tucks up against his body. She will have nothing so heavy and unbalancing as the permanent soft parts of a lesser like Catarine.

I have never once considered my crewmates' body forms outside of the arena, and I only do so now as I evaluate whether these ones will be a problem. None have chevrons on their wrists.

But that doesn't mean I can start a fight.

The first one sniffs. Her pupils enlarge. "It's got a strange smell. Something...itchy."

Staying here will not work.

I pivot to face them, forearms lightly crossed. "Don't you have somewhere to be?"

They shuffle back respectfully.

I pull Catarine up by her elbow. Such a thin, pointy bone. She staggers against me.

"If it's damaged, you have to take it to the science officer," the first one says.

They all shift uncomfortably.

So, Ukuri is some sort of ruler over the lower quadrant.

I drag Catarine to the viewscreen and widen my search, specifically looking at other sectors for sleeping arrangements. The ship's computer interfaces with my implant, supplying the rooms I'm qualified for, and I choose the one farthest away from the science office.

The viewscreen shows me room schematics. Fine, confirm that one. I select it.

Blades are allowed to commandeer any room commensurate with our rank. I never bother because who cares? Others say they cannot start an assignment unless their body is fully rested, but I feel it's a weakness. Everything is training for the unexpected.

This is training.

Actually, that feels a little better. Calming. I'm back in alignment with my core requirements. It calms the strange and terrible buzzing.

Catarine drops her head to my shoulder.

I collect her sliding day pack, wedge my arm around her

waist, and exit the dorm. We stride directly to the nearest grav tube. It's in good repair. I clamp her to me and enter, and we spiral up the tube.

Floor by floor, so many eyes turn and meet mine.

I want to stop and envelop her in my suit, but watchers will know. They will know.

And I must act as though I'm simply obeying a directive.

The problem is that it's my own.

And I do not issue directives.

I only obey them.

What is going to happen next?

The question pulls my spinal cord erect like a string.

A noose.

We reach the commander's hall and my new private room, so very recently vacated.

This room is a safe hollow. I'm not afraid anymore. It is private and quiet. The previous occupant still has a stimulant pack boiling on the hot sands.

I cross the small space and rest Catarine on the fully supported wall bench. She melts against the gray architecture.

Her food was such a soft texture.

I really must read about Humana. "Can you eat our nutrients?"

"Kibble? Yes."

I do not know her word for it, but I dispense some from the private stores into a bowl and pour the boiling stimulant over it. Normally, we eat these separately, but maybe the nutrient cubes will soak up a little moisture and get closer to the mash she's used to. I fold her hands around the bowl.

She cracks her eyelids and takes a deep breath, then coughs. "Raw stims?"

"I think it will help." Is there any way to drink it other than raw?

She tips the liquid into her mouth, wincing and shivering, and swallows. "Nothing like the smell of ozone in the morning."

"It smells nothing like ozone."

"My captain drinks it raw. Drank it. Raw." Her lips, slightly curved, return to a flat line. "Is it too late to help her?"

We must already be a thousand macrotungs from her disabled cruiser. "Yes."

"Maybe the Vanadisans showed up and saved the pods."

They are closest to Vanadis space, but still not close. And why should the Vanadisans care about a bunch of humans?

The Vanadisans are one of our ally races. Their planet consistently provides useful compounds and biological modifications, and respectful trade has been more productive than domination.

But there are easier ways to acquire lessers than coming upon a wreck of them in the middle of nowhere, even if the Vanadisans do frequently sell their salvages and castoffs to lessers like the Eruvisans.

I say nothing. Catarine has endured enough pain today.

She crunches the nutrients slowly, wincing again, but swallows what is probably an acceptable amount for her body weight. She sets it aside with a sigh, rests her head against the wall again, and closes her eyes.

This is so different from before.

Before, in her cruiser, she was many things. Obedient, aggressive, cautious, mysterious. But overall, she was vividly alive. And the difference makes me feel twinges I don't understand. Twinges that burn within my chest, and I want to tear them away. Tear something. But tearing away at my own flesh won't heal her injury or return her strength.

I finish off her nutrients and wash the bowl in the hot sands—it is real stone shell, after all—and cover the entire brazier with cold ceramic. A brazier is a luxury better suited for planetside, but there is something indefinably comforting about hot sand.

And then I once more bring out a medical kit. There is one in the stores in every room in every quadrant because every segment that can be sectioned off, in case of hull breach, must be self-sufficient for as long as possible. Just in case.

I kneel before her.

The cleaning cloth absorbs and sanitizes. It verges on her cut. She sucks in her breath with a hiss.

Should I carry on?

She grits her teeth. "Just finish."

Understood.

I'm not used to caring for others. Occasionally, the people I transport die in my care, and for the first time ever, I wonder if any of those deaths could have been prevented. Normally, I'd just make a calculation that their lives were not worth the resources. And my calculations have never been questioned because I log them for confirmation. But she is worth all the resources.

I finish cleaning and spread the ointment across her forehead. The cut is deep. And this skin here is thin. Is it the same as mine? We look similar, I think, but we are really very different inside.

I check her for other injuries, a brief once-over, but the only injury is where the saw bit into my blade and detached. It flew past my shoulder. I reached her at the last possible moment, and when I close my eyes, I relive it.

So while I prepare for my rest, I do not close my eyes.

She opens hers. They're brighter and more liquid, and those odd irises fix on me, watching me remove my skinsuit and enter the cleansing bath—another luxury—and chant my mantras. Deep satisfaction flows into my bones. Everything is in alignment. My implant tells me I am doing what is right. An assignment will be forthcoming.

And that will be another problem.

There will be many times I'll need to go places where she cannot possibly follow. I have sacrificed more ships to accomplish my goals than many blades have ever piloted. It is a contentious item in my record, and if I were less scrupulous about executing my assignments, I might not have been selected for the arena so many times.

I cannot risk leaving her alone on a ship.

The unsettled buzzing returns.

I've done something that cannot be undone. This resting state is false. I am treading on stolen time.

Her eyes close again.

I pick her up and set her in the resting pod. The walls encase her, sealing up tight, and a hood covers her head. The air before her eyes tints as the protective particles thicken.

Her voice sounds tiny. "Is it really okay to sleep now?"

"It is. No one will come."

If I cannot fall into my normal rest state, I will do the next best thing: silently chant the thousand sacred lines, over and over, as I sharpen my blades.

NINE

CATARINE

I feel like crap.

There's no equivalent in Arrisan Standard. The language we learn in school, the one we use to communicate because it's the language of the empire, is a formal and controlled language. They don't have expletives or negatively charged words. You have to construct "crap" by using the building blocks to describe "unsanitized waste products that belong in a recycler," which doesn't have the same ring.

Crap is a word I learned in elementary school while following my father across the devastation of America and siting new bridges and great works. English is a delightfully flexible language, and so it has survived in crevices across the world.

I don't think mainland America will ever flower into a land of a hundred languages like old Malaysia. But it's hard to say. There were once eight million of us and over a hundred living languages, and now there are less than two million, and we can barely cling to our official Malay. My father used to sing me lullabies in my grandparents' disappearing languages with great sadness. We weren't even hit the hardest by the great floods.

I most often talk and dream in a pastiche of argot. But on Humana, we still have a lot of words that have no translation, and one of them is crap.

Why don't the Arrisans have a specific word for unsanitized waste products that belong in a recycler? In school, teachers would say it's because of their superior diet. And considering that Arrisan kibble tastes like pebbles and has the same crunch, I almost believe them.

Chewing hard food causes straight teeth and broad jaws, so maybe they know some secrets after all.

Regardless, I feel like I've been punched in the face. In the mouth, at least. I want to roll over until I feel better, but I can't move.

Huh.

It's because I'm snug beneath a...a tree? I'm wrapped completely up in some sort of bark-like gray shell. My face is shadowed by overhanging roots. I've been eaten by the earth.

This bed has a strange, immobilizing warmth. It's really hard, but also kind of comfortable, like a body-sculpted chair. The room, visible in a narrow view, is tinted. This must be like their hood technology. In a sudden hull crack, this little bed would survive as an escape pod all by itself.

Because the Arrisans are super careful about space travel.

I bet the honeycomb bunks in the dorm I vaguely remember from yesterday...yesterday?...could seal with the same technology.

Yesterday is a planetside word, like today and tomorrow.

In space, ships set their chronometers to Arrisan Standard time, which counts out sets of ten. Ten instants equals one click. Ten clicks, one cleg. Ten clegs? One shift.

Two shifts equal a day, but days are not twenty-four hours like on Humana. Oh no. And clicks aren't exactly minutes, and clegs aren't exactly hours. But after ten clegs, you're ready for a rest, that's for sure.

So, yesterday-ish, a lot happened.

Things are really different now.

I wriggle to get my hands free.

Moving loosens the shell. The gap widens as the hood recedes. My shoulders, thighs, calves, and every muscle twinges with acid buildup. The boots pinch my ankles.

Maybe I've been in here longer than I think.

Tugging my dress free, I clamber out.

Sithe perches on a bar overhead. This is a vertical room, increasing the illusion that I was resting beneath the roots of a tree. He drops down and lands on the balls of his feet. The barest whisper of air flutters across my skin. He is soundless.

He rises and faces me. His hood falls back, revealing his strange silver eyes. They focus on my forehead, and his lips part.

I'm beginning to see more things in his expression that I couldn't tell before. This parting of his lips is him focusing. And then his lips close and his brows slightly lift. He's upset about my injury, but also accepts it. "You respond well to the ointment."

"Yeah, I don't even have a headache. You returned in the nick of time."

He looks away, brow lowering, and his jaw flexes.

He's upset.

Oh no.

I touch his arm. "Thank you."

He looks down at my hand on his forearm, then flicks his gaze to my profile and turns away.

On the cruiser, I would have thought he was angry, but I don't think he is. Or if he is, he isn't angry at me.

Saving a lesser must be nothing to him. Like putting a crane fly outside instead of crushing it with an idle swat. My thanks makes him uncomfortable. Perhaps he feels awkward and doesn't know what to say.

I sit in the same wall seat as last night.

He opens the hot sand brazier and pours a stimulant pack into a copper cup. It has a handle about as long as his forearm and rests on the cool ceramic cover. He dispenses kibble into a bowl that looks like a neatly sliced eggshell with a mottled outside and a pleasant blue interior. This is what he served the stimulant in last night.

It's interesting watching him use traditional utensils I've only read about. It's peaceful, these relics from the Arrisan home world that has ceased to be.

And totally different from the honeycomb dorms where the crew—and apparently he—usually sleeps.

Here is definitely better than the examination room in the science office.

But it opens up a whole new realm of questions. "What happens now?"

"I await my next assignment." He hands me the stim-kibble soup, closes the brazier, and sits in the wall hollow across from me.

Raw stim grates on the palate with an almost choking bitter taste, and it barely softens the grist. Humans used to separate the chaff from the wheat, and I don't care what the resource scientists say, kibble is the chaff.

I choke down a too-big mouthful. "And me?"

"You come." The taut skin around his eyes very slightly softens. "Unless you prefer to stay."

"Stay? Won't I be taken back to the science office?"

He tips his head in confirmation.

"No, I'd prefer to go with you, thank you."

His expression returns to neutral.

Oh. Was he making a joke?

I eat what I can, and again he finishes the extra food for me, drops hot sand over the bowl so it hisses to sanitize and cleanse it, and then seals up the brazier. My stomach isn't completely sure I've eaten food, but resource officers at school assured us we would be healthier if we switched from noodles and curry over to nutrient cubes, so it must be fine.

Humana has a very small intergalactic export business with a few cool storage-stable fruits and spices. Our food isn't very palatable to the rest of the empire.

Sithe resumes his seat and folds his hands.

We wait.

I'm okay with waiting. Especially considering the alternative.

My forehead itches.

The expression on that science officer's face as we left— slightly maniacal grin, entirely confident in himself—plucks chilly fingers on my spine.

I'll see you again.

The sooner we leave this dreadnought, the less opportunity he has to fulfill his dark promise. "When will you get your assignment?"

Sithe fixes on me. His breathes deeply for one full cycle. I saw him do this last night before I fell asleep. This and rub his blades against each other as if he's training to murder the entire ship. "I don't know."

"They don't have work for you?"

"After we changed rooms, my new assignment was deactivated."

After he rescued me. "Is that normal?"

The muscle in his jaw flexes again.

Uh-oh. "Did you get in trouble?"

"Not yet."

Not...yet?

So he's going to get in trouble? "Are you going to have to give me back to the science officer?"

His blades twitch at his wrists. "He will never touch you."

"What happens if they order you? Can you say no?"

He compresses his lips.

Does he have no answer? He's so certain that Ukuri won't take me, but if he can't say no...

Maybe this is a much bigger deal than I realized.

I know how everyone looked at me on the way to the science office. I heard the crewman who approached us in the dorms for the short time we stayed there. Lurid curiosity colored his tone.

As a single blade, Sithe walks among alien races all the time, but maybe the average Arrisan doesn't. And now I've come to them stinking of their aphrodisiac metal.

Sithe has gone to the group orgies before, but most of them probably haven't, or they're like the science officer, stricken from ever reproducing. The Arrisans are poster children for eugenics. They worship rules.

Sithe broke one to save me.

This room is very nice.

Maybe he broke more than one.

"Are you going to be okay?"

He flips his wrists upright and examines the chevron pattern where his blades emerge. "I will be fine."

He can't fight everyone on the ship. Does he really intend to try?

He honed his blades for a long, long time last night.

I can't imagine going against the empire. Sithe has impossible weapons, but he's still just one man. I walked the halls with him yesterday. He got on the hands-free elevator and flew up an air tube, and I saw just how big it is on the inside and how many Arrisans are in here. This dread-nought's not even a small city. It's a big one.

And the science officer has blades, too.

So does the engineer, Atana.

How many have Sithe's same capabilities?

He's stuck his neck out for me in the most literal sense. The Arrisan empire is terrible to its lessers and vassal planets, but it's not a whole lot nicer to its own people.

I am less than nothing to him. A few clegs ago, we didn't even know each other existed, and he's just potentially doomed himself for me. "Why?"

One brow lifts. A question.

"Why did you stop Ukuri?"

His gaze unfocuses, and he nods as if he's been asking himself this very question for some time. "Lessers invest in families, an inefficient distribution of genes, and so when a lesser family loses its child, they weaken their empire. You are the only child?"

I nod.

"Your father and mother gathered all their resources to train and perfect you?"

My throat tightens. "Yes."

"Then your small empire must endure. There is no risk to the Arrisan empire. If you're a singular case reacting to the lusteal, then there's no reason to hurt you, and if you're not a singular case, the empire can study another. Go back to Humana where you belong."

He saved me because he saw the picture of my family?

Sithe looks convinced of his principles, but there's no denying that he's uncertain how it will play out. I don't know how to honor the choice he's made or express the gratitude I feel for what he's done.

I stand and cross to him.

He turns his wrists down and rests his fists on his thighs. A gesture of surrender, of peaceful intentions. But the skin around his silver eyes tenses. Wondering if I'm going to berate him. Tell him he's an idiot. I'm guessing that's the source of his tension, because I can imagine those types of thoughts.

And so instead I loop my arms over his shoulders and press forward, between his parted knees, and rest my chin on his head.

He very gently leans against me. We are just two creatures in this vast universe. All I can give him is comfort. And I have to rely on him for literally everything else.

He arms settle around my waist. "Is this foreplay?"

"No, this is comfort."

"Comfort?"

"To convey feelings that have no words. Like, 'I thank you. I honor you. I gift you the softness of my arms and the steadiness of my heartbeat, and I promise to share my emotional strength. If you need someone to show you kindness, I will show it to you for a little while.'"

He takes a deep breath and lets it out. "Like a mantra for rest."

The Arrisans don't pray, but his actions last night did look like prayers. "It can be like that. We share this comfort with our families and others we want to help feel better."

We stay another long moment. His breath tickles my bare collarbone. The earthy vanilla of his suit mixes with the bitter raw stim and the hot sands into a unique yet almost addictive scent. I inhale deeply. My breast brushes his cheek.

"I am not unwell," he says.

"Sure." I pull back. "I didn't mean to imply you needed to feel better because you're ill. It was the first one. To convey feelings without words."

He catches my left wrist in his hand. His thumb strokes the soft inner skin.

Though I haven't mindlessly craved sex since he cleared my head, I could just enjoy it with him. I could enjoy it very much.

"Is this foreplay?" he murmurs.

"Anything can be foreplay—any glance, any touch—between partners who have consented."

"There is always an order."

"We can follow any order that comes naturally." But I'm describing nature to a man who takes a snifter of a mineral—I think—and then enters some crazed group orgy. What would he consider a natural order for sex? "Um, naturally, you become aware of shared feelings. A desire to explore and learn about your partner, find out what they enjoy, and then give them pleasure."

He studies my face.

I'm not lying. I lift my free hand in initiation. "May I?"

"You may."

I cup his jaw and, with my thumb, stroke his cheek. His skin feels smooth like mine, but rougher, more masculine. I have no plan right now. I just want to know this man who might have sacrificed everything for me. We are together in this beast, perhaps the jaws have already snapped shut, and all we know together is the darkness.

Who is this Arrisan Sithe?

He feels as human as me. I trace my fingertips along his even brows, down his ordinary nose, across his malleable mouth, over his firm chin, and back toward his hairline. All such normal features.

Except his ears. They look like mine up to the curve, and then he has four small spikes pointing behind him. I expect them to be hard, but like his nose or ear, they are warm cartilage.

When I reach his earlobe, he catches my wrist. Now he has both of my wrists trapped. "It feels strange."

"Strange like..." There's no proper word for what I'm asking. "Ticklish? You want to laugh?"

"Not laugh. Something..." His gaze drifts lower. To the hollow between my breasts. And back up. "And then?"

"You can continue exploring with your fingers, your hands..."

"Your mouth." He remembers my description of foreplay from the cruiser, clearly.

"Yes, an early step of trust and intimacy is a kiss."

He inclines his head.

Since he still holds both my wrists, I lean forward, rest one knee on the bench beside his hip, and lower my face to his.

His lashes flutter. He doesn't understand what I'm about to do.

"A kiss means you touch lips."

His gaze flicks down to my mouth and then back up. He pulls my wrists very gently, drawing me forward into him.

Our lips brush.

He doesn't move at all. The press of my mouth to his is the same as my thumb to his cheek. Curiosity from him, but no reaction. And so I press again, more firmly, and a third time, with intent.

He no longer pulls my wrists. He's gone slack.

I draw back.

His gaze centers on me. He parts his lips, rubs the lower one with his tongue and teeth. "I feel something."

I do too. A shift in my center, the flooding of heat into my core, awakening, preparing, inviting. "There are more nerve endings in our lips than in our palms or our sex organs."

"Kissing engorges the spongeflesh."

I'm really not familiar with this terminology, but it's hard *not* to make something into a euphemism for sex when that's all that's on your mind. "Yeah."

"And then?"

"And then...you do what feels right."

"Which is?"

"More kissing or touching or exploring. Whatever you want." Oh, and in case it's not obvious, "And your partner agrees too."

The little divot appears between his brows. This concept—that there are no rules, that he's allowed freedom—seems foreign to him, I guess. He releases my wrists and sits back. "Show me."

I hold on to his shoulders and straddle him, pulling up my puffy dress so my knees rest on either side of his slim hips on the bench, my butt on his thighs. He is like rock, like iron. Like sitting backward on a chair. It's easy to find my balance and settle in with several inches separating my breasts from his chest, more space between our bellies.

He makes no move, so I pick up his hands and curve

them gently around my waist. Securing me. Then I cup his cheek again and find my way to his mouth. His lips are damp now, and he meets me more firmly. I will lead this dance, and he will follow.

It's funny, but I don't have a fraction of the experience with kissing that I have with penetration. Before my illness, I had boyfriends. One I even planned to marry someday. But that was over four years ago, and my feelings about intimacy are still jumbled up. This is a bit of trial and error for me too.

A simple push, pull, a little nibble with my lips followed by tugging with my teeth, and he parts for me, meshing and splitting, languorous and sweet. I must taste like bitter stim and kibble, but he tastes indescribably male. Heat pinches my breasts, and the hard rods of his legs stimulate my pussy.

I tease his lips with my tongue and meet his, testing him. He mirrors my actions, and when I sup from him, he steals the same penetrating taste from me.

His strokes feed my hunger. And he tilts his head the opposite direction, driving me back and then luring me forward. He makes me crave something within him that I can't identify but also can't live without.

And his breath gusts out. His arms slide around my waist. He pulls me forward so that I straddle his waist, a clinch that drags my taut nipples and heated pussy across his hard planes.

His suit is impenetrable, but I can feel what's beneath. I hook my fingers at his collar. He leans back and rests his fingers beside mine, allows me to peel the suit apart to bare his chest.

This upper torso I have felt but never seen. He has some markings that I don't understand on his right shoulder. Thin, black lines like scars, but not accidental.

His large hands knead my waist.

And I peel his suit down to expose his abdomen. No body hair, just smooth planes that ripple when he subtly shifts me, adjusts. The suit parts below his waist, revealing the points of his hips. His cock springs out, hard and ready.

I've seen this before. His cock is hard as a coil, thick and warm with his blood, and it pulses in my hands. His testes are smaller, flatter disks, tucked up against his skin despite his heat and arousal.

He stills. I suppose that's normal when you cup a man by the balls, no matter how many blades he can impale you with.

And I'm finding this exploration fascinating myself. He's not inhuman. If we met under a different circumstance, I would probably not think we were that different at all.

And yet there are some differences.

He pushes at my dress. "Do I bare you?"

"If you like." I feel enough wetness between my throbbing lips that I could put him in me now and ride him hard. "There are no rules."

He curls his fists in the fabric and tugs. The seams complain. "There are always rules."

I move his hand to the fastener hidden beneath my arm and close his deft fingers around the tiny bit of metal. "The rule is that you both have to enjoy it. And ask for it and agree to it and want it."

He parts my dress and explores my body just as I have explored him. His gaze flicks between what part he's stimulating—my nipples, my clit, my whole pussy—and my face. Waiting for me to shout at him to stop, that he's done something wrong, that he can't just do as he wishes so long as I agree.

This is such a strange thing for him. This man who has always lived under strict rules.

And when I'm a limp, heaving mess of needs and hungers, he draws me against him and seats his cock deep inside me. We face each other, totally bared, but seeing each other for perhaps the first time.

His grip on my hips tightens. This part, he feels confident about.

Rocking in our own rhythm, he torques his cock into me, wringing another mess of little climaxes that well up into an unstoppable fountain of mind-altering, soul-shattering release.

And because we're facing each other, I know when he comes. He goes totally still, except his elbows tremble. His expression doesn't even change. In comparison, with all my arching and crying out and moaning, I must be like the wave crashing against the shoreline.

But given enough time, even the shoreline will completely change.

And sometimes the collapse happens in one single wave.

TEN

SITHE

Holding Catarine's relaxed, satisfied body against me works better than all my mantras.

I'm calm again. So very calm.

What is it about her small but precious weight that makes everything okay? Even though, where the other Arrisans are concerned, I have leapt off a very great precipice, I feel there is ground somewhere beneath me. And when I am moving my hard jack within her soft socket, the ground doesn't matter. I feel as if I can fly.

And my release... It is not the tormented explosion that I demanded of my body in the arena, but an asking, an invitation. She's always saying, "You can do what you want if everyone agrees." As if there is a choice.

Now, she lets out a long sigh that ends on a groan and pushes herself upright, then wriggles to clamber off my softening jack.

I check her for injuries.

"What are you...oh." She stills for my examination. "I don't feel hurt. You were gentle."

I'm getting better at understanding the ways we fit

together and how to move to reduce her bruising. I allow her to sit upright and flip my suit closed, sealing myself up again so that the moisture is cycled away and I'm tucked, snug and dry, ready.

She wobbles onto her feet and stumbles.

I catch her, my arm stiff for a handhold.

She leans on me.

I am now a person that others can lean on, it seems.

Her knees shake.

"You didn't consume enough nutrients," I chide her, rising.

"It's not from that." She continues to lean on my forearm as I move to fix her deficiency. "Impossible as it seems, my muscles are sore. I'm out of practice. And I think my senses were numbed before, so I never noticed when I overexerted. But now, with you, I'm back to how things are supposed to be, and I feel everything." She wrinkles her nose and rubs her bare legs together. Her sweat shines. "Ick. Everything. Do you have a shower?"

She makes no move for her clothes—because why would she? I forget how nonfunctional her attire is, little more than cloth wrappings.

I retract the hot sands to expose the cleansing bath, efficiently situated together, but I don't trust the data the unit might have on humans, so I set the temperature to her current body heat. The light changes to red, and I open the lid.

She squints. "Is that gel?"

"It will cleanse you." She must not have been paying attention last night. I remove my suit, grip the sides, and stand on the substance, remaining still as it slowly submerges my body to the neck. The oily peach-orange viscoplastic slides into every crease, adheres to every pore.

Her body temperature is a little cooler than mine, but I still feel suspended, weightless, and totally enclosed. This is how I imagine we are before we are born.

And then I push my hands out and grip the sides again, rising as slowly as I sank. The viscoplastic peels off, removing any dirt and sweat my suit might have left behind.

She pokes the substance. "What about my hair?"

I sprinkle the powder on her hair. It clumps. She shakes her head, and her fluffy brown hair swings across her shoulders. The clumps fly off like snow.

She scratches her scalp, and the flakes beneath her nails turn her lips down. "Agh! What is that? Itch powder?"

"Small eggs. They will hatch into a microscopic animal that will—"

"Lice? You gave me lice?" She digs in her nails, scraping like crazy.

That is so funny. I mean, I'm sorry she's upset, but what a silly thing to be upset about.

My short laugh makes her slow and stop. She stares at me through the wild nest of what used to be her hair. "You smiled."

Hm. I suppose that is a rare expression. Not much amuses me.

I don't think about the things I lack very often.

Until now.

I pull out a wide-tooth comb that draws the oils through her long hair and tames the unruly halo. The hair bugs on Humana aren't beneficial, it seems, but this microscopic creature is more like the mite that lives in eyelashes and prevents crusts from falling into eyes. We are not natural hosts for the hair bugs, though. They have to be refreshed every few kortans. And her hair is long, so perhaps it will require more tending.

Arrisan hair grows short naturally. It is an advantage not to provide our enemies with an extra grip.

Why does the hair of other races grow so long? This would be the kind of question that I would put to the science officer, but thinking of Ukuri even by accident makes my blades twitch. He will never touch Catarine again. Never.

She twists her hair up against her head—the viscoplastic would take forever to peel off her long strands—and climbs into the cleansing bath.

Again, the wildness of her expressions draws forth my amusement. She wants to appreciate it, but her lips pull down in horror, then her expression lightens as she reconsiders, and then she settles on a wobbly place in between. "It's like ooze. Or slime. Kind of comfy, but kind of like it's going to swallow me."

"It is much better than a drizzle shower."

She pokes her tongue out the corner of her mouth. "Environmentally? I could see that."

Indeed, the viscoplastic will never overwhelm the moisture collectors. It is neutral in every sense of the term. And, in an emergency, the viscoplastic can be used to lubricate certain engines.

Of course, anything that leaks into where it doesn't belong is a hazard. Especially in space, which is so unforgiving.

Her face is funny again as she gets out, shivering, and pats down her belly and legs. "It wasn't bad. I can get used to it. It's just different."

Her true feelings are obvious.

Adorable.

She lifts her dress. The stains are rust-colored now, and she scrapes at the hard patches. "Is there a way to clean my dress?"

My suit repels most materials, and her weak fibers wouldn't survive our cleaning methods. "No."

"Well, I guess I won't be going anywhere." She fastens it, cloaking her form, and for some reason, that process is just as interesting to me as when she showed me how to remove it. The dress conceals and also hints at what I know lies beneath. Perhaps this fabric is not so useless after all.

The communication panel in the wall chimes.

Her eyes lock with mine.

It is time.

Time to find out the consequences of making a choice.

I close the bath and shoo her away from the view, into the corner. She perches on top of the resting pod, her feet drawn up, her dress trailing.

I sit in the wall seat and activate the communication panel. It slides across, encasing my body with controls and a screen that shows far too much of the room on its sensors, but not Catarine.

The captain's face appears. "You are not in your assigned quarters."

My formerly assigned quarters, yes. That is obviously true and requires no response.

Yet he wants one. His lips press together.

My heart thumps hard in my chest.

"Do you have my assignment?" I push, making it clear that I do not answer to him.

"No. A complaint has been raised against you by the science officer for damaging his equipment and taking his specimen."

"She is mine."

He blinks once. "Yours?"

"Yes."

"You were supposed to send the lesser to the science office for examination."

"He did not examine her. He damaged her."

"It's only a lesser."

"She is not to be damaged."

The captain's eyes narrow. "Report to my private conference room. We'll review your orders." The viewscreen goes dark.

I push free of the communications enclosure, leaving it out in the room.

Catarine stands to meet me. "They're going to force you to give me back, huh?" She's not stupid. "You didn't answer me when I asked. Can you just say no?"

Can I? "I have received no countermanding orders."

"Can you countermand yourself?"

Essentially, I have already done so. To take Catarine and change rooms, I have acted on orders that do not exist by *believing* them into existence. Because I must have orders. I must follow the rules.

Acting without orders? Like an undirected lesser?

The buzzing starts in my brain. All my muscles tense. I do not know in which direction to attack.

No, no. I have an order. I am following it. Even though it is one I have given to myself.

And we are back to calm.

But it will not hold under examination. "I need a reason. One the captain will accept."

"Okay." She rubs her temples. "We're going to figure this out. Has anyone else ever done anything like this?"

"Countermanded orders?"

"I was thinking something more intimate, but I guess if I'm the only one who's ever been affected by your metal, the answer would be no. Are you allowed any privileges because of your rank?"

"This room."

"Right, this private room. And you have your own ship."

"The ship belongs to the empire."

"But you have the privilege to pilot it. I see what you mean, though. Are you allowed a companion? A friend? Someone in your environment to provide support?"

"Not from Humana."

"From anywhere, really. Just to establish a precedent."

"Blades do not have companions."

"Or, um, any living creature?"

"Science officers collect specimens. Some have called them pets."

She taps her index fingers against her lips. "Seems a little precarious, but depending on how the empire feels about pets..."

"They have no significance outside the science offices."

"That's what I was afraid of." She paces the small space, her dress swishing. "Are there any great legends from the past or historical figures that take companions? Or women? Your royalty? King or general or...?"

"The leaders have no restrictions on using lusteal, so most build houses."

She stops. "I thought Arrisans didn't have families."

"Not houses like lessers. Stables. They indulge in their own genetics programs, always striving for the greatest efficiency."

Her shoulders lower from the tense hunch. She rests her hands on mine. "That's so sad."

"Is it?"

"It seems devoid of comfort." Her soft smile takes in the

cleansing bath, benches, and sleeping shell. "Although perhaps that's not a priority for Arrisans."

Comfort is necessary to a creature like her. She's easily bruised, and I have a great need to protect her.

"Can you skip the meeting, get in your ship, and pilot it away?" she asks, releasing me and hugging one elbow.

"The captain must authorize any departure."

"Maybe..." Her gaze lingers on the communication panel. She bites her lip. "Maybe you can say that you got new orders to go..."

"He'll confirm our orders with my superior at the Arsenal."

"Can he? Don't we have to drop into nearspace to communicate?"

"Not on a dreadnought." I take her to the communication panel and show her. "All dreadnoughts have immediate access to anywhere in the empire."

"Even Humana?"

"Yes, if your communication nodes are set up properly to accept transmissions, then even Humana."

"If I could figure out how to put that to use..." She shifts her weight from foot to foot.

I love this alive version of her. As on the cruiser, she is thoughtful, inquisitive, and speaks with such resonant clarity. Her words hold weight, more than most Arrisans I have heard.

Which is why my blades are sharp.

Ukuri will never take her.

Orders or not.

"I wish there was some way to sway the captain to our side." She shakes her head. "If there were some legend or something in your cultural past, some epic about alien companions that he might respond to..."

"As a pilot class, his education differs from mine." I seat her in the communication panel and show her how to operate the controls. "You can read?"

"Arrisan Standard, yes."

No other language matters. "Fictions are not taught to the blades. Perhaps there are points in our history that answer your question. The *Spiderwasp* is new, so it carries the most complete copy of the Arris Central archives."

She focuses on the screen, scanning through thousands of headings leading to billions of entries. All knowledge of the empire is contained here. Her jaw goes slack as she scrolls on and on and on. "Is there, um, anyone I can ask about the organization?"

"Domain experts exist in the noncombatant class."

"And you know them?"

I shake my head.

It is past time to leave. The captain would have already expected me.

But I no longer feel the heart-thudding fear.

"Try to delay the captain until I can find something that will sway him to our side." She exits the communication panel and follows me to the door, watching as I prepare to leave. "Can anyone come in here while you're gone?"

"No."

She lets out a sigh of relief.

But that's not strictly true. Anyone with a higher rank than mine can enter. And anyone with orders from someone higher can also enter.

So if Ukuri came here while I was gone...

"Here." I dig out the small tracker from inside my hood. "This is keyed to me alone. When you press it..."

The communication panel dings, and my implant whispers the coordinates for the tracker.

She takes the small button and peeks inside her dress.

"Not in your clothes. Here." I spread the fine hairs at the back of her neck and stick the tiny dot just inside the hairline.

"I might press it in my sleep."

"Pressure doesn't activate it. It needs your finger." I step back. "Try it."

She brushes it with her fingers, and of course nothing happens.

"Press hard."

She tries again, then jabs it with increasing frustration. "Are you sure? Maybe it doesn't work on—"

The communication panel dings, and my implant tells me that my skinsuit is in front of me.

"Oh." She lowers her hand and rubs her fingertip. "Yeah, I won't do that by accident, I promise you."

"It works anywhere in nearspace. So, even if you're outside this ship, so long as we have similar velocities, I'll know."

"So long as I still have my hands." Her smile wobbles.

I arrange her hair to cover the button. "If they cut off both your hands, that will be a problem."

"Are you...are you making a joke?"

Affirming the obvious is a pointless waste of time, and yet when I do it for her, I find it amusing.

So many sensations I have felt today.

And I feel another sense of reassurance. Her question led to a solution. It's clever and something I didn't consider. She sees things I don't.

In the empire, no one has choices.

With her, I do.

I slide up my hood, open the door, and enter the hall.

"I'll wait for you," she says. "Try not to kill anyone you

don't have to. Unless you have to. I mean, I guess that's what I mean."

I lift my chin for her to see my face. She needs the reassurance too. And what she sees there causes the tentative smile to return. She gives me a gesture—a wave of friendship, the implant tells me—and then the door slides closed between us, sealing her in and me out.

I whirl.

Try not to kill anyone you don't have to.

Ukuri's blades surprised me. As did Atana's.

This dreadnought is not as it seems.

But me? I am exactly what I seem.

This calmness, this certainty is what I need to feel. I am a blade, and my word is law. My blades are all that I need. I would not attack other blades or other ships as a matter of courtesy. We stay in our own orbits. But if I need to? The planet of me will fight.

Catarine does not give orders.

She gives permission.

And right now, I will take it.

ELEVEN

CATARINE

After Sithe leaves, the first thing I do is return to the archives.

The molded seat cups me in an odd way, and my eyes center on the screen. My back is to the wall, and the rest of the room, including the door, is visible through and beside the screen. I finally appreciate something about Arrisan architecture.

You know, I feel a little bad for the Arrisans. How awful it must have been to lose their home world, and how much they must have changed as a result. Look at how this nice room is more vertical than horizontal, how the bed is like a hollow beneath a tree, and how their walls are stuffed with stored food. They must have been some sort of peaceful squirrel species who got shaken out of their trees, and now, they're right angry little chipmunks.

Chipmunks with blades for incisors who bite planets with their little teeth.

Anyway.

I scroll again through the archive. It's sort of like the time I helped transport books into the rebuilt national archives. So many manuscripts all jumbled together in boxes had an organization scheme that was known only to the librarians.

Where to start?

I spend way too much time reviewing indexes before it hits me. The most obvious thing is to look up Humana. If any of us lessers actually did something important enough to register in the Arrisans' eyes, it will be there.

...

The entry is short.

There's a mysterious string of numbers, then how far Humana is from Arris Central, which is the main administrative center of their empire. Next is Humana's rank in food production, which is our designated purpose to them. After that, there're very few descriptions of the people, the climate, and the nonhuman species. There's a whole heading for biodiversity, and it's blank.

Then, a list of incidents.

Our history starts when we were discovered, then immediately "integrated" into the empire for our own protection. The planet was moved twice into a better production orbit; however, the second move was probably overshot because our production output declined.

No word about the floods, the quakes, the volcanoes blotting out the sun for years, or the apocalyptic destruction that might have affected food production.

I'm not even sure Humana knew about the second move, to be honest. Maybe someone did, but all the cataclysms sort of blur together when you're reading that chapter in school.

And the aftershocks, we still feel those. My dad has to plan around them when he rebuilds our greatest works.

At the bottom of the entry is a small note on current

events: *Due to the overcorrection of the second move, an orbital readjustment will be authorized during the next resource governance session.*

What?

There's a link, and it takes me to a long list of items awaiting an authorization. The other lines read like "increase quotas for Munderian logs by .02% for Sector 28 usage" and "decrease Quaderi flume output by .009% due to new accords."

We don't even merit our own ruling.

Whether or not to plunge Humana into another cataclysm that will definitely affect food production targets is going to be rubber-stamped by some committee in...oh, I can't even do the conversion from Arrisan historic chronology to Arrisan standard dates right now. I'm too upset.

Or the fog is rolling back in...

That jolts me upright.

I jump out of the communications enclosure and pace.

No. I'm mentally clear. And I have no sexual cravings. The fog is gone.

Those weird marks translate to twenty-eight standard goras, anyway.

See? Clear as a bell.

Twenty-eight standard goras... So soon. Less than half a year planetside. We couldn't get up food production no matter how hard we tried. And honestly, we probably already tried. It's amazing how hard you try when an Arrisan gunship is on the other side of the request.

To say nothing of a dreadnought like this.

I rest on my heels.

What was Ukuri saying about how they've never found a lesser who reacts to the metal? They have zero lines about our biology. It's like nobody's gotten around to studying us because they can't be bothered.

It just...it's so upsetting. I know that I'm nothing in the scope of the empire and they don't care about Humana. But this little line could cost millions, even billions of lives.

My day pack has rolled behind the brazier. Good thing the metal encasing it is so cool and nonconductive. Look at that college picture my mom slipped in. All of us smiling at the recorder. I was so excited because I'd gotten accepted to my top grad school. We'd just visited and looked at houses together. My parents were going to rebuild one for me so they could have a place to stay and visit in between their global projects. It's still my future, even though now it feels more like a dream.

And it's one I fiercely want to protect.

My dad acted like it was no big deal that the prime minister stopped by at that moment for a photo op. He said it was easier to be famous because our world has grown so small.

How much smaller can it become?

I swipe across the digital frame. The metadata includes a note. *Call anytime. Would love to hear from you. Mom and Dad.*

All right, then.

I jog back to the communication panel and exit the archive. The calling interface is weirdly similar to what I'm used to, so even though the moving wall is crazy advanced in a way that I can't even understand, the communications technology for crossing galaxies hasn't changed a lot from calling down in orbit, which every kid has done at least once on a field trip.

So, I input the call routing...

Error. Nearspace coordinates invalid.

Uh...

Oh, wait. I flip back to the archive, record the string of numbers that suddenly looks a lot like nearspace coordinates—and I'm not even a navigator—and click back into the calling interface. Take two.

There's a long silence.

Oh, H.

My heart begins thumping. I can't feel my fingertips.

Is it actually going to work? Really?

I feel clear. Not angry. Here's hoping...

Beep. Beep.

The screen resolves into darkness. No, a crescent of blue light outlines the lower part of the screen. A man's sleepy face weaves in front of the night light.

It's been four years, but some profiles I will never forget, even as he cracks open his dark brown eyes at the viewscreen. "Hello?"

"Dad?"

His mouth drops open and he blinks, much more awake. "Catarine?"

"It's me." I'm going to start crying. Tears just well up in me. My eyes flood and my voice shakes. "Hi, Dad."

"Catarine." His voice sounds rough. He coughs into his fist and shakes the lump resting on the bed behind him. "It's Catarine."

My mom rolls over with a moan and then drags herself upright. "Where now?" She's still asleep and thinks my minders are calling because I've escaped again.

I try to joke. "I bet you thought you were done with the midnight calls, huh?"

She flops back in the bed.

My dad laughs and rises. "Let me put on tea." He putters into the kitchenette—they must be staying at a hotel

—and flips on an electric kettle. "I thought you wouldn't call for a few months. Are you already cured?"

"Not yet. But at the moment, I'm fine."

"Yeah, I guess so." He pours a packet of herbal wellness tea, which I know from experience looks like twigs and dried berries, and tastes like it too. "I'm so glad to see you and hear your voice. Live, you know, instead of those recordings where you look half asleep."

"Me too." I have to swallow the lump in my throat. "I need you to do something important."

"You look really good, Catarine. Really *good* good. I'm so glad."

"I know, but...I don't have much time. Please listen, Dad."

He sinks onto the bed.

"I need you to contact a professor at Harvard. He's friends with..." What was the kingmaker's real name? "Allie. He gained notoriety for his paper on the economic role of vassal planets in Arrisan empire building. He's an honored chair now, I think."

"Yes, a quick moment." And my dad just takes charge of the problem, posture straight, profile focused, his hands typing out of view of the screen.

Him working in profile is such a familiar, nostalgic sight. The tears well up again, and I'm just so grateful to be able to see him and talk to him normally one more time. Even if I don't survive the *Spiderwasp* or Sithe's conference, at least I got to see my dad once more. I hope that someday I can give him another big hug.

My dad reads his screen. "Dr. Ramin Ghaberi, Centennial Professor of Economics at the Second Harvard University, H2U."

Did Allie ever give me the name? It must be him. "It's

critical that I talk to him right now, please. Use any method you can to get a hold of him."

He picks up his pocket-network phone, stands, and walks across the room. He's wearing his white pajamas with the black stripe around the hems that could almost pass for day clothes and, in times of crisis when he had to rush to a building site after an incident, certainly have.

My mom crawls to the edge of the bed and squints into the screen. Her dark chestnut hair falls across her face, and she tucks it behind her pale ears. "You sound clear."

"I'm having a moment of clarity. Don't ask how."

So of course she immediately does. "What happened?"

"You're not going to like knowing." But I give her the broad strokes. We were stopped by Eruvisan pirates, I got dusted with Arrisan lusteal, and then I met a blade. "I don't know how long the clarity will last, but my response to the lusteal generated some scientific interest."

She studies me with her unflinching warzone face. She's walked through enough of them on missions funded by *Medécins Intergalactiques*, a nonprofit Humana-wide medical organization that will someday expand to cover our galaxy once we figure out how to thrive off planet. We now know her work will always be necessary. Sharing cataclysms and a common alien enemy didn't bring humanity peace, it turns out. We still have the same old problems. There are just more of them now.

"You know what would be great?" I say, trying to distract her. "If you could send me all my medical records and tests. Everything."

"We sent copies on the cruiser."

"You did! That's...kind of too bad I didn't remember it sooner."

She raises one brow, the only indication that she understands I'm no longer on said cruiser. "I'll gather them again."

My dad sits beside my mother on the bed, causing her to sit up and scoot over to make room. They make such a comforting, familiar picture, her pale hand interlocked with my father's darker olive grip. "I have Dr. Ghaberi on, and he's going to accept your call now. Do you want the number, or should I just transfer you?"

"I'll take the number, thank you, and transfer."

He reads out the number, which I record on the metadata tag beneath my parents' information. Then my father smiles again. His eyes form the familiar happy crescents. "I'm so glad to see you again."

"Me too."

"We're going to see each other again really soon." He puts his arm around my mother, the realist in our family, and squeezes her. "I just know it."

My mom rolls her lips inward, which is what she does when she wants to believe in the best too.

My dad just beams, and I can see the tears in his eyes, and that makes me have to sniff because I'm going to start crying again. "I love you, Catarine."

"I love you too."

He reaches forward and clicks the transfer.

The viewscreen switches to a slender Iranian man with distinguished gray highlights. The dawn peeks through his closed blinds, and he looks really, really angry to talk to me. "You're the daughter of this bridge builder? You think it's okay to contact a stranger like this?"

"Yes, Dr. Ghaberi, I do. The Arrisans are planning to move the orbit of Humana again. I'm calling from their newest dreadnought, *Spiderwasp*, and I would like to send the entire archive, everything I have right now, to the Harvard servers. Can you accept it?"

He gapes at me.

But we don't have time for this. Someone could come through that door at any moment and take me away, cut me off, anything. "Can you accept it?"

"Yes." He runs a hand through his hair. "Yes, it depends on how large it is, but yes."

"All right, I'm going to begin transmission."

"Who are you again?"

As the archive is copying to their data servers, I give more details. My parents don't need to know how precarious my position is. My mom probably guesses, and they both know how dangerous space travel is. This man is a professor, and he knows other scholars. If there's something I can do here, I want him to have the background.

"You forged a relationship with a blade?" He sits in a large chair and crosses his ankle on his knee. "How? Their people are robots. They bred out emotions."

"I've seen many emotions on this ship." Mostly territorial, from the engineer to the science officer, but they are definitely not robots. "They're all focused on serving the empire, but their eugenics program is so strict that any deviations risk their genes. The science officer apparently lost his chance to reproduce due to some action of his father. He wants to dissect me to earn it back. The leadership, of course, exploits their privilege."

"You think that's why your blade saved you? Is it even possible for your genes to combine?"

"He's already visited the arena and his genes have been passed on, unless his actions doom his offspring like the science officer. But they're all raised centrally, so I doubt he knows his parents or his children. He said he saved me because a lesser family is like a miniature empire, and he didn't want to weaken mine."

His brows rose. "That's surprising sympathy. If only there was a way to make the rest of the empire to share it."

"That's why I sent you the archive. I hope there's some legend or historical figure or time in their past where they worked with another alien race for a good outcome. My first priority is staying alive so I can help as long as possible."

"Fascinating." He leans forward and scrolls to the areas I direct him. "I mean, this is terrible. This is a disaster. I'm horrified. And at the same time, this is incredible. How did you know Allie?"

"She's one of the other passengers who shares my illness."

"Mm, that explains some things. We're not friends, so to hear her name from your father's mouth gave me a start, but she did pass through my life during a very tumultuous time, and I almost think... You know." He presses his fingers together. "If she could meet an Arrisan. One of importance. If she could get exposed to that lusteal and meet your captain, I think she could change any fate. Yours, certainly. Perhaps even more people's."

It's unfortunate then that she's millions of actungs behind me now. "I'll do my best."

"Of course. Okay, I'm contacting better scholars than I of Arrisan mythological history." He peruses the completely downloaded archive. The university servers must be straining. "Did you know this archive contains the actual schematics of the dreadnought?"

"Does it help us at all?"

"It's information. Can I call you back?"

"Honestly? I don't know."

He changes position, typing. "I've placed an emergency

call to the university chancellor. He knows our representative in the Humana Commission, and it would be good to know if or when our local overlords were going to tell us about the orbital move. Ah, and one of my friends is an earlier riser than I. The Arrisan home planet myths may, in fact, have what you're looking for. They're not part of any Arrisan training program so far as he knows, but that doesn't mean the myths haven't seeped into their consciousness in other ways. Maybe some imagery or iconography can help your case."

It's a place to start. "If I don't hear back, I'll contact you in a few clegs."

"Before you go, remember the keys to dealing with an Arrisan: never bargain." Dr. Ghaberi sits back in his seat and meets my gaze with sober warning. "Never beg. They don't respect either. I've studied the economic treaties of a hundred vassal planets, and all of them, including what happened on Earth—then, we called it Earth—turned disastrous. Bargaining and begging shows weakness. Compromise is an invitation for them to flatten you."

"Okay." We learned a little about the Arrisan brutality code in school, but not from studying hundreds of vassal planets. "The problem is remembering that when they hold a saw blade to your scalp."

"Stare down death, and they may actually let you live."

Yes, okay. Deep breath, let it out. "No matter how dire, I won't beg."

"Very good. And Catarine? Good luck."

Yeah, I'll need it.

I close the contact and settle in to read about their home planet.

Maybe this will do nothing. We are a lesser species to

the Arrisans, and knowing how many guns could force our planet out of orbit doesn't really help us at all.

But maybe we can do something. People who are smarter and better experts than me are looking into it.

And I really hope that someone can rescue my shipmates. Not someone from Humana—that would be too far away—but closer. Time is ticking down until they run out of atmosphere.

My shipmates are dying. Humana is at risk. I never would have believed it, but right now, I'm the one who's in the safest place of all.

And my fate all depends on what's happening in Sithe's conference.

TWELVE

SITHE

The captain's private conference chamber lies behind the bridge.

I am forced to wait for some time outside the room in view of other Arrisans. With my hood up, though, I make them nervous. The security guards swallow and clench their guns more tightly. Their weapons are designed to stop at the walls. Mine? Not so much.

Eventually, the door opens and the captain summons me. He and Ukuri have taken seats against the walls. My chair—in the Humana sense of the word—is a cage in the center with my back oriented to the door.

Ukuri grins with extreme satisfaction. His eyes are obscured behind dark lenses that reflect the room back at me, distorted.

The captain—Falkion—looks too young in person. His hair is deeper black with youth, and his broad, square features are accented by dark, slashing brows. He may have parlayed his fierce looks into his current position, but of course, a handsome appearance goes only so far. He is also here because he can rule.

And I am undermining him.

I stop beside the chair.

"Sit down," the captain orders.

I remain standing. "I thought a new dreadnought would have a more majestic interrogation chamber."

He studies me. Wise. He may rule this ship, but he does not rule me. "Since you cannot appreciate what you see, sit in an ordinary bench."

The chair folds into a stool, and I sit.

Precedent established.

"Now, explain to me why you have stolen a specimen and damaged a science office exam room."

"Because she is mine."

"Where are your orders explaining that?"

I cock my head at him. I have no requirement to show him or anyone else outside the Arsenal my orders. And he knows it.

He also knows I have not received any contact from my superior, Zai. The communication logs would show as much.

Can you just say no?

Catarine's question returns with greater force.

How agreeable I usually am. Executing my assignments, sharing unclassified information with anyone who asks, resting in my assigned tube, flying off again. Others irritate me. I need no one's good opinion. Usually, that attitude is directed inward, and it gets me across galaxies faster.

Do not waste time arguing with morons.

Right now, I have nothing but time.

"I can always demand your orders from Zai." The captain presses his palms together and rests his chin against his fingertips. "You really will not tell me?"

He can figure it out himself.

The silence lengthens.

Now, he should call my bluff and contact Zai.

Embarrass me in front of my supervisor. Show that the military will not be ordered around by one rogue blade.

But he does not.

Interesting.

Instead, the captain leans over to the science officer. "Can you not simply go out and collect another specimen to study?"

Ukuri still smiles with perverse satisfaction. It would make me nervous except for the fact that Catarine is now wearing my tracker. "The other lessers haven't been exposed to lusteal."

"So? Collect another escape pod and expose that one."

"It's impossible," Ukuri insists. "We've tried."

"Already?"

"No, other scientists have exposed Humana lessers to every known substance, including lusteal, and recorded their results. A small dusting of lusteal did not fuse to the test subjects. Sithe's lesser is a unique specimen."

Collect another escape pod? Wait. "We haven't left the site?"

The two fix on me, weighing how to respond, but this is an easy question I could answer myself as soon as the conference is over. I simply didn't think to ask it until now.

The captain comes to the same conclusion and leans back in his bench. "Yes, we have not yet left."

How interesting. "Waiting for someone?"

"As we are a new dreadnought, the engines need to be thoroughly inspected after our first jumps." He sounds skeptical.

So am I.

Something is amiss, and he doesn't know what.

Engineers are recalcitrant. The head engineer, as a blade, must be impossible. What are they scheming while we linger around a lesser accident site?

"I must have the specimen Sithe stole." Ukuri's eyes, shadowed by the lenses, seem to sink deeper into his sockets. "Don't make me file a formal requisition. It would allow me to enter any room and take whatever I desire in the name of science. Perhaps I will desire to study the blade who's so affected by a lesser."

I eject my blade a finger's length to scratch my chin.

They watch me with glittering anticipation.

Can you just say no?

We haven't left the area. The engines are stalled. Do I have more options right now than I think I do?

I retract my blade, rest my ankle on my knee, and hold it in place with both wrists down. The picture of relaxation. "No."

They both stare.

Ukuri stills.

The captain takes in a deep breath and releases it. "For what reason?"

"No."

"Do not repeat yourself, blade. I asked for the basis of your refusal."

But this path I've embarked on doesn't require it. It's terrifying and yet strangely freeing. As if I have a choice. "No."

They're both stunned. Absolutely.

"But this is my ship," the captain says, and both he and Ukuri uncoil into a ready position to challenge me. "You can't refuse me."

My blood begins pumping, hot and fast. I remain

perfectly balanced but am aware of all the different ways I can dodge and pivot their potential attacks. "Can't I?"

"Of course you can't. There is no higher position on this ship."

"Isn't there?"

His nostrils flare.

Captain is *not* the highest rank onboard a new dreadnought. There are special rooms reserved for a maiden voyage. Noncombatants with other types of positions that, when necessary, will be slotted into their place. Because there will always be order in the Arrisan empire.

And I have a *very nice* room.

Ukuri chews on his thumb. "You want to check the all-rankings list? Why not?" His grin deepens. "You might be surprised what you find out about living quarters on this ship."

"No." The captain holds up his palm.

The jagged lines of a blade greet me.

Falkion's a blade? My heart thuds once, hard. I slowly lower my ankle to the floor. Two against one isn't an even fight. And he's the captain.

"That's not necessary." The captain presses his palms together. He is more wary about checking the all-rankings list than I.

Does he think I'll try to take over this ship if I discover I have a higher ranking?

Could I have a higher ranking?

If we consider his blade rank before his captain's rank, I could easily outrank him.

And blades can refuse orders at all levels in order to execute their assignments.

It's tricky, the list. The logic. The order.

He knows it as well. "Will you not release your lesser?"

"No."

Ukuri shakes his head. "Then I have no choice but to submit the formal requisition."

"Denied," the captain returns. "Take another lesser or don't. Leave Sithe's alone."

Ukuri's lips tighten. "I can't simply infect another lesser."

"Why not? We have the recovered lusteal."

"It doesn't work that way. We've tried. His is a unique specimen."

"It's only a lesser."

"You must appreciate the significance."

The captain doesn't.

I stand. "It's been enlightening."

The captain's eyes narrow.

Reflections glare from Ukuri's lenses. But he still looks undeterred. "Now I'm even more determined to unlock her secrets, blade. You only incriminate yourself with your unguarded affection. I will appeal to the science center on Arris Central and see if you aren't both assigned to my examination room before this delay is over."

"Come and get me." I turn my shoulder on them both.

The walk back is strange. Euphoric. My head is not securely attached to my body, and the hall floors angle away from my feet.

I pass the bridge crew's quarters and continue to my own more prestigious door. The light is green. Locked. I swipe my hand over the panel and it slides open.

Catarine unfolds from her curious balled-up seat and rests a data tablet on her lap. Her long hair curtains half her face like a shroud, and she tucks it back behind one ear. Her eyes are bright with hope. "You're back."

Does all Humana verbalize what is obvious, or is it her own quirk? I had meant to study it. "Yes."

The door closes behind me.

"What happened?"

I report the highlights—that we have not moved, and that Ukuri is filing a formal requisition with the science center on Arris Central to have both of us reassigned to his science office.

Her chin lowers. "Can he do that?"

I slide into the seat beside her. "Not as long as I outrank him."

"What if one of them orders the captain to do it?"

"Same answer."

"You outrank the captain?" Her eyes widen. "Really? Is that normal?"

"No. He's another blade, so it depends on how the ranks are calculated but..." I stretch out beside her on the wide bench and tease the soft gauze of her dress between my fingers. "This is a nicer room than his."

"But is there someone else on this ship who outranks you?"

I shrug. If so, the captain doesn't want to involve them in this dispute.

"Then can you order the captain or the crew around?" she asks.

It's a natural question, but it will be tricky. "It depends."

She hops to her feet, holding the data tablet. "Can you collect the rest of my shipmates? Their escape pods?"

"The captain directed the science officer to do so, so yes."

She freezes. "Oh no. I don't want anyone to get vivisected. Can you stop that?"

"Stop Ukuri from collecting the pods until after your shipmates are dead?"

"Right. Leaving everyone where they are is bad and bringing them inside is worse. Let's..." She whirls, her gaze on the floor, fingers pressed together and tapping each other with the data tablet between them. "Can you have our cruiser repaired?"

The engineers didn't seem especially helpful. "It's possible."

"Have them bring it in, repair the damages so it's functional again, and then we can take it out and pick up the escape pods. They can't stop us, can they? If you're with me."

My euphoria leaks away as she describes the plan.

Leaving on a lesser ship is not good. In addition to the vulnerabilities and security flaws and the difficulty of keeping her safe, how can I serve the Arrisan empire and execute orders? Everything about this is bad.

But she carries on, getting more and more excited all on her own. "We could leave here together, find out who's in charge of food targets on Humana, and change it so that we're no longer in danger of having our orbit adjusted. And with you on our side, I'm sure the commission would tell us more of what was planned. You could even advocate for us. Allies get representation in the empire. Vassals should too."

Allies were represented because they had valuable things to trade with the empire and weren't just another repository of food.

I catch her wrist when she passes too close, dress swishing, and tug her onto the bench seat so I can curve my body around hers. It's better when she's touching me. The dangerous buzzing goes away.

She rests for a moment, then wriggles. "On the cruise

ship are my medical files. If you give that to the science officer, maybe he'll leave me alone."

"He will never touch you again."

"Ah, I'm not trying to bargain. But maybe if he knew there were records, he would be interested in getting those. The repaired cruiser could be a good way to get rid of us, and that could incentivize the captain to get it done."

She is clever.

Catarine pats my arms where they're looped around her waist. "How about it?"

I can see wanting to protect a planet. "Your shipmates are not your family."

"No, but they have their own families, and on our voyage, we shared a lot. They became like my family."

Having such compassion increases responsibilities and splits focus. That is why Arrisans are better; we serve only the empire. Allies becoming family? The network of rules Catarine must live by, with so many alliances changing at all times, must be exhausting. "It must be very difficult to live on a planet of lessers."

She smiles down and then pinches my cheek in a teasing way. "Will you make the requests?"

This sits like a weight in my belly.

Her reasoning is convoluted but consistent.

I roll upright, enter the communications console, and summon the captain before I change my mind. I don't give an order, but I do use Catarine's suggestions. "You should know that there are medical files on the cruiser. And a derelict harvester is of no use to anyone, but a well-repaired ship could be used to fly away any lessers who become a problem."

He stares at me with a long silence. His gaze shifts to behind me to where I know Catarine is visible.

I lean forward. "Questions?"

"When are you getting off my ship?"

"After I know Catarine will have a safe, secure voyage."

I can hear Falkion's words as if he were speaking them again. *It is only a lesser*.

She is only a lesser, but she is mine.

"Any other questions?"

His jaw muscles clench. "Next time, call me on my private line."

Maybe I will and maybe I won't. I close the connection and sit back.

Catarine throws her arms around me, the data tablet resting on my chest, and presses her lips to my cheek. "Thank you."

It almost touches the dread uncoiling in my belly.

This is another zig on a flight where I don't know the destination. Who am I becoming? What is going to happen?

I have never issued an order to another.

It's totally different from asserting that I can ignore others' orders. Now I am giving them. If they don't obey me, then what do I do? I can't actually injure another servant of the empire, only threaten, and to execute a threat, I have one weapon in my armory. The captain and Ukuri, even Atana, possess the same. Appealing to logic and shared goals circumvents that quandary, but is it enough?

All the blades I have encountered on this ship so far are men. That's unusual, although it is a small sample size. Are there others on this ship still hiding from me?

Catarine snuggles against me.

"Is this comfort?" I ask.

"It's whatever you want it to be."

Sexual release causes a particular absence of thinking, and right now, I very much feel a drive to solve my problems. Solve them before I face down blades, or before the buzzing comes back.

I pick her up, scooping her beneath the buttocks and carrying her up into a tall nook. She holds her breath and squeezes my neck, but after we land, she releases me carefully. Perhaps I have rested inadequately, or perhaps thinking so many new thoughts is too exhausting, but I don't have the will to return her comfort.

"Are you going to sleep?" she asks.

"I'm going to think."

She tucks her legs under her again and reviews the data tablet.

We rest here a long time.

Long enough for me to give up on thinking, give up on solving my problems, and revert to cycling my mantras. We rest in silence for some time, until her belly begins making the cavernous noises that she identifies as hunger, and I must feed her.

While I prepare nutrients, she touches the data tablet with total focus as though she's memorizing the statistics of the empire.

"What are you reading?"

"The origin myths of the Arrisan home world. They feature an early Arrisan named Grundi. Do you know them?"

I shake my head.

"I'm not surprised. This is how it starts: 'By the hundred years' flight of a kwil, beyond the fourth star, around the central planet, toward the hottest desert, across forty-four ice floes, beyond a mountain...' for sixteen marked passages of directions, it finally gets to 'Grundi washed his breakfast in the river.' Then there's another one, two, three...eight passages explaining how to identify this river from all the other major rivers on the Arris home world. And then it continues, 'But while he was washing, his friend Sirgoy beat him in the head and stole his breakfast. So he went back to the river, and his friend Sirgoy beat him in the head and stole his breakfast.' This goes on for a while, and I was thinking Sirgoy wasn't much of a friend, when..."

"Grundi destroyed Sirgoy and prevented anyone from touching anything of his ever again?"

"Not exactly, although I understand your reasoning." She flicks her fingers across the tablet. "Luckily, I got a message from someone on Humana who's studied the myths extensively. Some heroes of academia combed, condensed, and footnoted these stories, basically translating them into something I can understand. Sirgoy, it turns out, is a personification of the river, and when it says the river 'beat his head,' it means the river current was too strong and carried away whatever Grundi had planned to eat. This reading is supported because another early Arrisan named Amante washes her breakfast successfully on the other side of Sirgoy. Grundi watches Amante for a number of mornings and then finally asks her how she does it, and she shows him a...there's no translation for this. A 'pat-pat device.' Do you know what that is?"

Definitely I do not.

"We couldn't figure it out from context, but the next scene is that, inspired by her device, Grundi grows to ninety-six times his normal size and kicks Sirgoy so hard, he launches into the sky. The desert described in the earlier sixteen passages turns into an equally detailed description of a mist forest, and Sirgoy explodes into ninety-six children, or creeks, each one lovingly described. Then Grundi shows Amante how to grow ninety-six times her normal size, and they stomp mushrooms together."

I pour a hot gel pack into her nutrients. "Stomp mushrooms?"

"Yes, there was disagreement about it, but the myths loop, and one of the later loops is explicit that there's a kind of mushroom you stomp to spread its spores. Which fits the ground usually covered by origin myths: magical explanations for where everything comes from—food, water, us." She sets the data tablet on her lap and accepts the nutrient bowl without question. "Every culture has these, even alien cultures. It's fascinating. And you don't learn this in school?"

"If it's relevant, we learn the true origins, not mythical ones." I finish my meal with a few efficient crunches and gulps.

"I think we all do, but some aspects must have gone into your collective psyche and created foundational values about who you are." She swirls the bowl and then digs in her spoon. "At least, that's the theory of the scholars."

I don't particularly care about the lessers who've come up with theories, but learning about my homeland while eating around the brazier triggers some deep need in me. I put another bowl of gel on the sands—I do not need a stim pack, but hydration gel is only mildly wasteful since I do not strictly need it—and let the scent of the familiar liquid evoke the mist forests. "Is that all?"

"Huh? Oh no, that's just the first one." She crunches her food quickly, wincing. Lessers do not appreciate healthy food. "There are hundreds. Want me to keep going?"

I do.

She finishes her meal, tucks her feet under her, and unleashes more stories. Grundi creates time by eating up all the past and regretting it, Grundi destroys the mist forest to learn what is enough, Grundi scares off the Jut-Jut birds that steal unguarded toes. But many of them follow the same pattern: Grundi encounters some "friend" who turns out to be the personification of a planetary climate or geological feature, loses his breakfast to it, and then discovers that Amante has a clever trick that inspires him to grow ninety-six times his size to defeat it. Then he teaches her how to do the same thing, and they take over another territory.

Hearing these is like listening to a stranger tell a familiar story. Every time I begin to draw a conclusion, she mentions some detail or theory that yanks my thinking in a different direction. Not wrong, not right, just different.

When she starts yawning at the beginning of fourth shift, I order her to rest. She closes the data tablet and lingers by the bed. "What about you? Don't you need rest?"

But I have my mantras, so I shake my head.

Consequences are coming.

THIRTEEN

SITHE

Consequences come just after we finish our first meal.

Catarine's gaze edges toward me. She eats mouthfuls around reading aloud. The next story of Grundi looks like it will feature Amante, and it is interesting to settle into the rich landscape of this foreign planet, this world that I should have once called my own.

The communication panel chimes.

We both freeze.

My stomach traps the food, undigested, and acid burns the back of my throat.

She closes the data tablet and recedes above the resting nook to remain out of sight.

I rise soundlessly, float to the communication panel, and answer.

If everything is good, the captain will tell me the orders have been completed. There has been just enough time to accomplish them, I think. But if it's bad, they'll have only completed some of the orders, or none at all, and I'll have to figure out how to force them.

The captain regards me without emotion. "Come to the captain's conference chamber to receive a secure message."

"My assignment has arrived?"

He looks at me like I'm an idiot. If it's a secure message, he can't tell me the content on an unsecured line. I must be turning into one of the lessers, stating the obvious.

I confirm that I understand his summons and close the connection.

Catarine meets me at the door.

I tuck her hair behind her ear. Her dress is still stained. She looks so worried. "Is it your next assignment?"

"Yes."

"Will you be able to take me? Or will you come back?"

I don't know. "Visualize success, not failure."

A smile softens her mouth, but the wrinkles remain in her forehead. "Should I do anything?"

"Don't leave this room."

"Oh no. I'm going to try to contact Humana again, then keep reading."

She'll read more stories without me?

In spite of my other worries, I feel mild refusal. She shouldn't get ahead of me. I don't want to have to catch up.

I have never had difficulty focusing on my mission before.

And now these smaller impulses seem to take up so much of my own mind space.

She bites her lip. "Are you going to be okay?"

I take her hand, pressing the middle of her palm the way she often presses mine, and then pull her in for comfort. She lifts her chin. We kiss.

Her mouth is supple, intriguing. She leans into the contact, and wet need twists in my groin. I should have taken my release with her one more time, but I was too focused on the dangers, and it's too late now.

When she rests her weight on her heels again, her eyes look brighter, her lips darker. "Come back."

I don't state the obvious, but it's on my mind. *I'll try.*

I put up my hood, trigger the door, and step backward into the hall. My last sight is of her face. The door closes between us.

There were never any choices.

The floors are quiet even though we are midshift. We must still be stationary, and the crew is taking an opportunity for extra rests. Sometimes that leads to problems. Whenever Arrisans lose focus on the mission, some will self-destruct and others will follow. That is a problem for the captain, though.

This time when I arrive at the conference chamber, the guards let me in immediately. The door seals shut and block all internal signals.

Good thing I didn't delay.

The captain sits alone in the room. He gestures to the other wall seat. I sit.

He presses the transmission button, and the wall over the door resolves into my superior, the general master of the Arsenal.

"Who contacted you?" Zai's voice is deadly like velvet-coated steel, and his eyes are sharp like his blades. "Tell me their names and how they got to you. You won't be punished for this. I will annihilate them for treason."

My spine straightens. My legs urge me to stand, to be a less sluggish target, but obedience pins me to the wall. "No one contacted me."

"Don't protect them. Whatever lie they told to secure

your cooperation is nothing but that. A lie. I will enlighten you, Sithe. Tell me everything. Now."

I wish in the deepest fiber of my sinews that I could reveal these enemies to Zai.

He's not just my commander.

He rules the blades.

Defying him is worse than defying the emperor. The emperor has to manage the nobles. He's compromised the pride of Arrisans and the memory of our home planet for the wrong reasons before.

But Zai never has.

He's rarified honor, distilled protection, pure survival. He carries the core of the blades in his chest, and he never deviates from what is right.

There is no man I respect more in the empire.

That makes my current situation very uncomfortable. "I executed my assignment, and I'm awaiting the next one."

He steeples his fingers before his bloodless lips, and I can tell that he thinks he's going to have to do this the hard way. "You never pull rank. You never take a private room. And on the maiden voyage of the *Spiderwasp*, you do both of these things. A coincidence?"

I nod because it is. I would have done this on any ship. I think.

"How did you select your current room?"

"It was the farthest away from the science officer."

He lowers his hands. This does not fit whatever narrative he was building toward. "The science officer on the *Spiderwasp* is a blade."

Oh, I'm well aware of that.

"Did Ukuri tell you to take your current room?"

I shake my head.

Zai checks with Falkion. "Do either of them know who Sithe displaced?"

The captain shifts in his seat. "I don't believe so. They asked to check the all-rankings list, but I didn't want to reveal our guest without your permission."

Zai sizes me up, then orders the captain, "Show him."

The captain operates the controls, and the list displays on the closest viewscreen. My name is strangely at the top. Falkion's appears below mine. But between us is another I don't recognize: Arcturin din Orunfax.

Zai's watching me very closely. "You don't recognize it."

I shake my head again.

"You've never shown an interest in politics, so let me enlighten you. Arcturin is the eldest living son of High Commander Orunfax, genetic patriarch of House Orunfax, leader of the advisory board overseeing the Arsenal, and special liaison to the emperor. Does that bring up any memories?"

"No."

"Okay, let's try this another way. Why does Arris rule the empire?"

My shoulders pull back. "So we can protect the vassal planets and allies from the return of the Harsi."

"Yes. You might have heard that some believe the Harsi are gone forever."

I've heard that, but people think a lot of stupid things. "Are those lessers willing to bet their home planets?"

"Some who hold these beliefs are Arrisans."

My blades flex against my wrists. How can an Arrisan, any Arrisan, think so? After what we lost? How we barely survived?

"Well, I'm glad to see you share my disgruntlement." Zai's tone turns dry before returning to deadly serious.

"Here's the issue. Some Arrisans who hold these beliefs have infiltrated the High Command."

My stomach twists.

"The High Command controls the military," Zai continues. "The Arsenal only controls the blades. But if the blades hold the highest positions in every military vessel?"

"The Arsenal controls the military," I murmur.

"And we ensure the protection of the empire, precisely." Zai drums his fingers on his console. He's in his private office in the Arsenal, an area I've never seen except in the background of communications like this. The night shift lighting is tinted red and the room is austere. "We still need the support of the High Command to continue placing our blades, and antagonizing the son of the only high commander who's shown support is a sure way to end the program. That's why he will return to his private room and you will return to the tubes. Now."

Heat flushes my body, and my blades slide out to my fingertips. I pinch the metal to prevent them from extending any farther. My heart thumps in my belly. Blood roars in my ears. "I can't."

Zai's chin drops. He stares at me through his brows. His palms rise. "You can't?"

"My presence in the tubes will cause a disruption."

"What kind of disruption?"

"A...disruption."

Zai's eyes narrow. He uncoils his triple-blades, and the six weapons cross before his face in deadly warning. Each wrist has one long central pike flanked by two flat daggers that curl out and back at the ends. It was an earlier weapon class, a so-called failed blade type, but his skill has turned any doubters into mush.

"Explain."

There is no way to explain Catarine without losing her.

The silence presses my chest like pressure fracturing a hull. I can't take a full breath. My blades slide against my fingers. I must obey. But—

"Because of a lesser," Falkion says unexpectedly. His eyes are slits, and his hands clench his knees. He is as taut as I am. "Sithe picked up a lesser."

Zai's blades lower a fraction, and his tone flattens in disbelief. "A lesser?"

"From Humana."

"Where?"

"A small planet beyond Galacticus," Falkion says. "It doesn't matter. It got infected with lusteal."

Zai frowns as if Falkion is speaking a nonstandard language. "So?"

"Trapping it in a private room has avoided the behavioral problems caused by exposing nonblades to uncontained lusteal."

"Then why is it not contained?"

"It is now."

Zai eyes him hard. "Do you have this situation under control, Falkion?"

"Of course." Falkion places his ankle on his knee again. "Everything is proceeding according to plan. And at the first hint of any potential problem, I will contact you. Just as I have been doing."

Zai fixes on me again. "No more deviations, no more pulling rank, no more unusual actions. You stay in Arcturin's private room until your assignment is finalized, and then you leave. Do you understand?"

"Yes."

"Nothing jeopardizes this voyage. Not a blade who

should know better. And not a lesser from Humana." The viewscreen goes blank.

All my tension drains, leaving me shaky.

This is the best possible outcome.

I rise. "Call me when the cruiser is prepared."

"Why?" Falkion rises a beat behind me. His chin juts. "You're happy to risk the position of the blades, the safety of the empire, for a lesser? Lusteal wouldn't addle your brain when it isn't even here. Why do you care?"

This is a question I've been wrestling with for some time. "Blades protect lessers."

"From the Harsi."

"And others."

"Lessers have to contribute. When the time comes, we'll die to save their home planets. That's why it doesn't matter what happens now, here. If one or two lessers have to be sacrificed to give us an edge, they owe it to us to make that sacrifice uncomplaining."

I believe his words utterly. He's quoting from blade training. We are prepared to sacrifice ourselves, our lives, our resources to protect the empire and all within it from the Harsi. When the time comes, we will not hesitate.

But it's different.

With Catarine, it's different.

The longer I'm silent, the more his expression sets into something akin to disappointment. He turns on his heel and mutters, "I'll contact engineering."

Good.

I stalk back to our room. My muscles twitch from preparation. Our private quarters have everything but a good place to exercise, and I really need to do so.

But more than that, I need to return to Catarine.

She can't stay. I always knew it. Zai's orders confirm

what I already know. This time of hearing about origin myths and families on Humana and having choices must end. I will put them from my mind. There are mantras for shutting down urges, burying memories, cooling desires. I will recite them. My return to control, to serving the empire, begins tonight. By the time we each leave, I will not care that she is gone. I will not think of her at all.

The light at the door is red.

Unlocked?

I pass my hand over the unlocking panel, even though it opens from my presence.

The room is empty.

Catarine is gone.

FOURTEEN

SITHE

Catarine is gone.

My field of vision narrows. My skin grows cold.

There are signs of a struggle. The data tablet halfway across the room, screen cracked. Stim mug overturned, brazier lids ajar.

If she is dead...

I have a near-overwhelming urge to turn, exit, and carve the shape of Catarine's body out of the first person I see.

The screen in the communication panel is still on. Two lessers were talking quietly when the door opened; now they stare at me.

I lean in. "What happened?"

"He took her. An Arrisan." The angular one nervously folds his hands. He speaks with an accent. I suppose Catarine does too, but I never notice it. "He put her in a bag and carried her over his shoulder."

A bag? She's still alive. "How long ago?"

"Twenty...twenty-two clicks."

"Can you identify who took her?"

"A crew member."

"Uniform? Class?"

They both shake their heads.

I ask as a formality. I know where she's gone.

"Sithe." The younger, fatter one clears his throat. "Humana is scheduled for another movement that will cause catastrophic destruction. Will you help us?"

"No."

"But you have to—are you going to hurt Catarine?"

"No." My blades extend beyond my fingertips, and I tilt my chin so they can see my eyes while I let the blades flow. "I'm going to get her back."

The angular one shrinks in his seat.

The younger one blinks rapidly and then coughs. "Yes, but you see, destroying Humana will hurt Catarine because—"

I don't hear the rest. The door, sealing again after I exit into the hallway, cuts it off.

His words have no meaning. He is a lesser. I have a mission.

I pivot into more traveled halls. The Arrisans walking the opposite way see my blades and slam their backs against the walls, wrists down in surrender, as I jog past. Shoving my way through crowded junctures, I push first into the grav tube and float into the center to descend much faster than is recommended, free-falling across the levels of the dreadnought. My ears fill with a stuffy sensation as I approach the grav-induced pressurized atmosphere of the lower quarters.

The exit closest to the science office is still out of commission.

Not what I expected.

But I'll take the next one.

I slide into the normal region of the tube, skid past slower-moving Arrisans, and land on my designated floor much harder than I should. My skinsuit absorbs the shock, shuddering, and I take off running down the hall.

The escalator up to my destination is also blocked.

And so is the next best way, jammed with a shipment of cargo.

This is an interesting plot. Ukuri does have sway in the lower quadrant.

But I am a blade, and so I use brute force to tear the top crates down and squeeze through. It would be even faster to hook into the ceiling, but this would cause damage, and damage causes reports.

My heart beats fast. I am disobeying a direct order of my superior officer right now.

But so help me, I will destroy this entire dreadnought if Ukuri has damaged Catarine.

Come what may.

The hall around the science office is empty.

Ukuri thought to keep this area free of observers? He has done me a favor.

The door does not yield to my palm.

I have a duty to inform my victims of their choices.

I press the intercom. "Open the door."

There is an interminable pause before Ukuri replies. "You have no business here, blade."

"Open the door, or I will open it for you."

"It's reinforced bulkhead alloy. I'd like to see you try."

Thanks for the permission, Ukuri.

I step forward, jam my bent palms against the center of the door, and erupt my blades. They shoot into the metal.

It is thick, and much harder than anything I've ever

tested them against. I brace my feet and twist. They slowly slice through.

Every muscle in my body trembles. The blades warp and squeak.

It's not a matter of sharpness but density, and once I've started, I'm not sure I can pull them out. I should have cut into the wall, or better yet, the door activation machinery. If he activates the door before I sever the mechanism, it could yank me into the wall, and I'd be trapped; the blades could bend, and it could even crush me.

Sweat breaks out on my brow and upper lip as I force the cut. This choice was foolhardy, unwise, not well-considered, and yet I am committed now. The final motion twists into the activation machinery, and the door light goes out.

I can't yank my blades out.

Ill-conceived, like so many of my actions recently. Driven by rage rather than logic, by how I deserve to succeed rather than how I will. This is exactly why so many other blades fail their assignments. I've become ordinary because of a lesser from Humana.

My lesser from Humana.

I set my shoulder to the carved circle and push. My feet slide back. I anchor them and push, saw with my blades, squeaking them back and forth.

The circle moves.

I push harder, sawing and turning. This tactic would never work in an actual engagement. My enemy within would have too much time to mount a counterattack. I'll have to remember this the next time I'm forcing my way into a science office.

The large circle pushes through and falls inward, landing with a floor-shuddering clang.

A small creature faces me, palms down, wary.

I have startled a lesser.

But not *my* lesser.

I retract my blades into my throbbing, painful wrists and clamber through.

The exam room door hangs open. The circular saw blade is still embedded above the door, and the wall is still in need of repair. Ukuri kept the engineers so busy preventing me from reaching this office that he did not allow them to finish and make the room usable again.

Ukuri is nowhere to be seen.

"Where's Catarine?" I demand. "Who are you?"

The lesser lifts a black brow. She has a similar arrangement of features to Catarine, a deeper golden brown color to her skin, and shorn black hair not unlike an Arrisan. "I'm Captain Zeerah. Who are you?"

A captain? From Catarine's ship? "How did you get in here?"

"Your people brought in our pods. I came out to thank them, but they dumped me in here."

"Alone?"

"Until you showed up." She remains on guard.

Honestly? She doesn't look like the naïve, gushing, thankful type. She looks tough, like a survivor, and if she was clever enough to rig the pod magnets to evade the Eruvisans, she's probably also clever enough not to wait around inside a pod to be slapped into narco-stasis.

But she can't help me locate Catarine.

I slam the blank viewscreen to bring up the announcement system and flood the science office with my voice. "Ukuri. I'm warning you, I—"

"What?" He sounds irritated, as if I've interrupted his reading, and then the viewscreen resolves to show him in an entirely different room, not anywhere nearby. "You got inside? You... Oh." His face blanks.

"I accepted your invitation." I lift my wrists to show that my blades are still curved, although who knows if they're still sharp. "I hope you're pleased with the result."

He rubs his nose and lifts his chin so the reflection of the eye shields blocks his irises again, hiding him. "I'll submit the expense to Captain Falkion. The Arsenal is racking up quite the repair bill."

Funny. "Where are you holding Catarine?"

His brows lift and then his smile deepens. "Lost your lesser again, have you? Afraid I'm going to vivisect her?"

"Where?"

"I don't know, blade. Because of you, I had to go and get my own lesser like you see behind you. But guess what? It turns out Catarine might not be as unique as I thought."

"I don't believe you."

"Obviously." His smile flexes. "Why else would you carve through reinforced alloy? But it's quite true. It's been one thing after another in the lower quadrant, and I simply haven't had time to devise a plot to destroy you. I will, don't worry."

"I won't."

"But first I have to finish reading these medical files your lesser provided. They're unbelievably rustic—some of their practices for promoting good health are barbaric even by lesser standards—but they're simply fascinating. And they never performed any test for lusteal."

"Lusteal? Someone on Humana has our lusteal?"

"Mm, good point. They're barely able to exit their own solar system, so they probably don't *have* a test for lusteal on Humana. I'll have to run a full panel on my specimens. The gaps are really quite—"

"Specimens?" I growl. "Plural?"

"The unaffected lesser behind you to double-check baselines, and then one of the other lessers who's infected."

"Which is Catarine. You took her."

"I didn't, and if you're unable to process new information, it's a wonder you've gotten as far as you have, even for a simple blade."

I flex my weapons. "Come out and tell me that to my face."

"No, I don't think I will." He sighs. "But I suppose it is up to me to resolve your little mystery so you'll go away and leave me in peace." He taps his index finger against his chin, then grins. "Mm. You know, I wouldn't have the tools to enter your room in the highest quadrant anyway, would I?"

"You'd have found a way."

"I already have found a way simply by deducing the obvious. Let me be clear. I could not have taken your lesser. I wouldn't have the *tools* to enter your room. Do you get it now?"

I'm so certain he has Catarine.

Because he must be commanding the ones who do have the tools to enter my room.

But if he's not commanding them, then I must gain entrance to a region that I cannot use my blades to cut into. A region that does not obey Falkion nor any other authority. I must enter and take on perhaps a hundred Arrisans all armed with cutters that make my blades look like cosmetic picks.

"The engineers," I say.

FIFTEEN

CATARINE

Atana looks down on my prone form with a cruel gleam. "Hey, little human." He squats down to my level. "Remember me?"

I hold my breath.

"Oh, you do remember. Your blade insulted me in front of my crew. It's bad enough that he doesn't respect my territory but then he tries to get the captain to order me?"

Atana flips his wrist up. His blade extends.

The tip is on a diagonal, with the high side by his thumb and the low side by his pinky. The high side is thicker but still sharp; it tapers to the low side, which gleams with a woodgrain pattern.

"He might as well cut out a piece of my chest. So I'm going to cut out a piece of him. But he's not here. You are. And the way he's acting, hurting you is a good place to start." Atana waves the blade in front of my face. "Want to run?"

Crates line the engineering office's walls, forming a fortress, a maze.

If I run into the maze, he'll chase me.

And it's his maze.

So I won't win.

Stare death in the face. You'll gain their respect.

I've been terrified so long, I almost feel numb. My mind isn't quick. It's like the beginning of the fog rolling in again. My own stupidity will get me killed.

Don't cry.

But if I cannot cry, cannot run, and cannot see a way out of this trap, what can I do?

My silent terror seems to feed him.

He laughs, a great gusty sound from his belly as he stands and turns back to his panel.

Everything trembles. My neck aches from strain.

Oh.

I reach up and press Sithe's button.

Ding.

Atana glances up at a notification on the wall overhead, then smirks. "So, Sithe gave you the tracker from his skin-suit? Creative, and in the cargo bay it would work. But we have to test emergency equipment in this office, the kind that would cause a panic if it went off, and nothing penetrates these walls."

If he's lying, Sithe will come and get me, and if he's telling the truth, I'm at the same place I was before.

I rest my forehead on the hard floor.

This is how the rest of the empire sees Humana. Easily bruised, easily defeated, a means to an end for someone else. No one sees us as our own people. That's why Captain Zeerah made us get into the escape pods. How could we argue to the pirates that we were living, breathing, hoping, feeling creatures who deserved to live? They'd already cracked our hull. There was no way.

It's not only a problem for us in space, but also on

Humana. There will always be vulnerable people in the wrong place, crossing the wrong aggressor. No matter who you are, there's someone who wishes you harm or doesn't care. Old science fiction stories suggested that when something larger like deadly aliens attacked, fighting back would unite us against a common enemy and toward a common survival goal, but reality has shown the lie. We ought to unite against the Arrisans. The empire ought to unite against the aliens-who-must-not-be-named. But we don't, and they don't.

My mom sees this often in her war zones. Human nature, it seems, comes naturally to all races. There will always be people who have fallen into the muck, by accident or by design. Some will try to help and risk getting trapped too. Others will shove the victims in deeper.

I want to live.

And whatever that requires—*whatever it requires*—I will perform.

Because I'm the only one who can do anything.

I push myself up onto my sore knees. My pinky twinges. It's swollen out of proportion with my hand.

Deep breath. Let it out.

Here we go. "Do you have any healing ointment?"

"It won't make you faster." He frowns at his view out the office windows into the cargo bay.

"I'm not applying it to my feet. I think my finger's broken."

"I'm going to carve my name into your chest, and you want to heal a broken finger?"

"Yes."

He turns and eyes me. Calculating. "What'll you do for it?"

Never beg. Never bargain.

The point of this conversation isn't to heal my finger. It's to learn enough about him to convince him not to murder me. If I live, I win. "What do you think I should do for it?"

He launches himself at me.

There's no warning.

One moment he's across the office, the next he's a microtung from my face.

I freeze.

His breath is hot on mine, his blades so close, they're blurry. "I want you to run. Scream. Claw away from me, writhing with agony as I flay your skin from your bones and wear your face as a mask."

A long, wet thing lashes my cheek, and he stands again, looking down on me with disgust. "You taste like old grease."

He returns to the panel and chews on a long, thin cylinder with a red dot of superheated metal at the tip. A thread of smoke curls toward the ceiling.

The wet patch on my cheek evaporates.

My heart beat resumes and melts the ice holding my muscles taut.

Did he just lick me?

I fold my hands. This is one of those lucky times where my base reaction isn't to run away; highly useful in dealing with this sociopath, not so useful if, say, a dam was breaking. "Blame the bag your employee used to carry me."

He grunts.

"The bag also broke my finger."

"Lessers are weak. You break things all the time."

"My body didn't evolve for transport in a bag. Did yours?"

"No, but I'm not weak." He finally looks up from the

screen to sneer at me. "I could handle it." Then he looks back at the screen and explodes, the punk dropping out of his mouth, glancing off the panel, and hitting the floor. "No! I missed his face when he realized you were missing. Back it up, back it up. There. Aw. Disappointing." His shoulders slump.

A scent of burning reaches my nose.

He grips the panel, drumming his fingers on the metal, then drops down, wipes the punk off on his overalls, and leans against the panel, facing me.

I don't like the new danger in his eyes. "Sithe didn't give you a good expression?"

"His hood was on." Atana flicks his punk at the screen over his shoulder. "He thinks he's clever enough to order me? Go collect a junker, bring in debris. Repair the junker. Let's see how long it takes him to get through my maze."

Oh. "Did you? Do what he asks, I mean."

He extends his blade toward me. "I don't do anything because he orders me."

"You didn't bring in the cruiser or the escape pods?"

"Why should I? I don't exist to make him happy."

A new possibility opens. I don't know where it leads, but it's all I have.

"Those were my requests." I pull myself to my feet. "I was the one who asked him to do that. If you're going to be angry at someone for ordering you around, direct your anger at me."

Atana stills.

I brace.

Deep breath in, deep breath out. Deep breath in.

This threat is a bit of a cheat, really. I don't think he can be any angrier at me as this avatar of his nemesis. What's he going to do with this information? Since he's already planning to cut my face off and wear it as a mask.

Atana finally rests his elbow on one wrist and rests his chin on the other, totally unconcerned about having a deadly weapon braced against the underside of his jaw. "I don't understand."

"My friends are going to run out of atmosphere in the escape pods, and the cruiser magnet—"

"No, no." He waves his punk. "You *asked* him."

"Yes."

"Why?"

"Because the cruiser magnet was broken and—"

"No. *You asked him.* Why did you do that?"

"...Because I thought he would listen?"

Atana's brows draw together, and his lips poke to one side. "Why?"

"Because he listened to other things I said...?"

He drops his elbow and points his index finger. Now we're at the sticking point. "Why?"

"Um..." Honestly it's a good question, one that I haven't even bothered to ask up until now because my life was in such a precarious balance. I depend too much on Sithe to ask why he's helped me, why he's risked his life or at least his position. The truth is that I formed an unconscious opinion. One that was convenient to me. But I don't know if it's true. "Because we became friends."

"Allies?"

The Arrisan Standard word for friends has more connotations for allies than it does for any Humana equivalent. With allies, there's an implication of power equivalence, that neither partner has the possibility to gain control over the other. But from Atana's perspective, maybe even from

Sithe's perspective, he has much more control over me than I have over him.

With the Humana word, there's a sense of give and take. That if there was an opportunity to control the other, neither would take it because the goal of friendship is equivalence.

"Partners." I try on some more Arrisan Standard words. "Associates, confederates, accomplices..."

He looks increasingly confused.

Perhaps there is no word in Arrisan Standard. "There is an exchange. He makes me food, and I read him stories. He's doing so much more for me because this is his domain, but I did the same for him when we were on my cruiser. We both give and receive comfort."

"Comfort." Atana straightens so he's no longer leaning against the panel. He approaches, into my personal space, and his nostrils flare. I may taste like an old, greasy bag, but his pupils dilate as he scents the metal in my blood. "He breeds you like a female in the arena."

I force myself not to back away. "It's different."

He walks behind me. "Different how?"

"Have you ever been to the arena?"

He snorts, heat on the back of my neck. My skin prickles with bumps. His body is too close. "Engineers don't go to the arena. We're recognized for all the wrong reasons. I will never produce future Arrisans."

"You're also a blade."

Hot metal waves before my eyes. He's lifted his forearm even with my shoulder and holds the sharp edge at my neck. "Glad you noticed that."

Don't breathe. Don't speak. Don't swallow.

"But that means I simply have a second class to have no ranks in. A failure twice over as an Arrisan." His blade retracts. The heat recedes as he continues moving, my skin unmolested. "Why do I have no ranks? Because I have no assignments as a blade." He stops before me with poise. "And so I rot here, in engineering, the leader of the worst of the empire. Technically brilliant." His blades cross. "Genetically unsuitable. And here comes a blade who has all the rankings, who's been to the arena five times, and still he takes a lesser to fulfill his twisted, carnal urges to breed."

"It wasn't his idea." I won't be the victim to this madman, no matter what it costs. "I attacked him."

Atana tilts his head the opposite way. "He obliged you."

"Because of the lusteal. He didn't choose me to breed. I chose him."

"But he chooses you now." Atana flicks his punk over his shoulder at the obscured viewscreen. He slides toward me, and his eyes rove over my dirty, blood-stained dress down to my bare feet and up again. "And if I attack you, breed you, then I'll gain something over him."

He sets the punk down on a singed panel and reaches for my neck.

I set my feet. "It will not give you satisfaction."

He stops.

Honestly, the sex isn't my concern. If I actually thought it could buy me a way out of here, I'd get under this Arrisan in an instant. Or over him, or whatever he wanted. He'd be just another encounter in a dim back room, maybe a little sharper than the other memories because of my emotional state and raw awareness, but nothing to cry about.

"I might find satisfaction," he says.

"Not the kind you crave. You're angry at Sithe for what he is, for what he has, for what he's done. So you took something of his, and now you have me. Has that satisfied you? No. Will breeding with me do it? No. Will cutting off my face and wearing it like a mask give you the satisfaction you desire? No. You won't see him collapse, hear him cry, or become a higher rank. All you'll do is cause him a mild inconvenience. And that will give you no satisfaction at all."

His chin lifts. "You speak with such confidence for a lesser who won't have a face."

"I'll be dead, so I won't care. You'll go back to this engineering room, and he'll go on to his next assignment. You'll have accomplished nothing."

He lowers his hand. "Is this how you convinced him to help you?"

"No. Helping me wasn't in his best interest."

"He's an Arrisan. Breeding with you isn't in his best interests either. And yet..." Atana steps closer. From an ordinary distance, his silver irises look uniform like Sithe's, but they aren't. They're mixed shades of green-gray, blue-gray, and yellow-gray, all ringed with a micro line of black. "I saw what you did. Touching mouths. The door opened, and the sensor in the hall captured it. He enjoyed it."

"Because there's consent. I give him comfort freely, and he does the same. That's why, even if you and I breed, you will not achieve what he has. You can keep me here under force, trapped or enslaved, but you will never possess what he has because he and I work together by choice."

"You're his lesser."

This is where we're stuck. I have to change his thinking. "I'm his Amante."

Atana blinks. "His Amante?"

"From the origin myths. Amante helps Grundi and is also helped by him to discover the natural world and shape it."

He turns away. "Humana myths."

"No, actually, they're from your ancient home world. Arris."

He turns back. "Arris?"

"Sithe and I have been reading them together. I can show you."

He opens the archives, and I navigate through the system to what I received from the academics. The display fills with the stories, starting with where I left off on the data tablet. I make a copy so it will no longer be tied to my reading progress and scroll to the beginning. "This is where it starts. Not all of them are about Amante, but you'll get the idea."

"Read them."

Oh, boy.

I slide through the stories, reviewing footnotes. Which one might reach Atana? And not give him more ideas of how to torment me or Sithe?

There are no good answers.

I've been a student of Arrisan psyche for several intense shifts now, and I have yet to learn anything about de-escalating violence.

So I read a short one that seems fairly innocuous—nothing but a little eye trauma when Amante helpfully encourages Grundi to blind his opponent to get a tasty grain being hoarded—and another on how they crushed rowdy children for disrespecting the natural order.

He stands beside me listening, but as I finish the second story, I realize he's studying me from the corner of his eye.

I stop reading and swallow in a dry throat. "Another?"

He answers my question with his own. "Are all lessers from Humana like you?"

"Yes, depending on their education and opportunity. In

terms of shape, size, and mental capacity, I'm a typical example of my kind."

His gaze flicks over me again, and a frown pouts his mouth.

Is that good or bad?

I'm still alive, so I guess I'm winning.

A bowl of nutrient cubes rests on the panel. He grabs a handful, crunches them like potato chips, then offers them to me.

I take some—not too many, not too few—and crunch. These are different. Puffier, like they've been roasted and seasoned. "Did you want me to keep reading?"

"No." He finishes his handful and rubs his palms on his grease-streaked uniform. "You're right. Simply having you in my possession doesn't satisfy me. What will bring me satisfaction?"

"You said that you wanted to have a higher ranking and visit the arena to pass on your genes."

He waves his fingers. "A higher ranking is fine."

"How can you get a higher ranking?"

"It's impossible. I never completed the final trials, blade against blade, to set my starting level." He curves his hand into a claw and his blade extends to complete the cage. "I just want to see him on the ground, bleeding to death, as I stand over his cooling corpse and laugh."

My mouth goes dry.

He drops his hand and offers me the bowl.

I politely take some. I can't taste anything right now.

He refills the bowl with a canister overhead and rests it in its permanent spot, crunching. "Maybe I should lure him into a trap."

"Maybe"—I swallow roughly, hoping that this isn't

going to end terribly, especially not any more terribly than a trap—"you should challenge him to a fight."

His mouth drops as if he's literally never thought of this before. "A fight?"

"Atana." The voice of Ukuri plays from the distant viewscreen, his tone dry with tired amusement. "I'm in the middle of one of the greatest scientific discoveries of our lifetime, and your little prank has compromised the integrity of the science office. Send a team to repair it right away. Preferably before your target arrives."

"He's coming?" Atana lifts his wrists, blades partially extended, his silver eyes glistening like a child who's just won a prize. He grabs my arm—retracting his blade so he doesn't slice my limb off—and drags me out into the cargo bay toward a cleared section between parked ships.

Hey, isn't that ship in far corner our cruiser? But Atana said he didn't bring it in. Did he just lie? Why?

Sealed escape pods lie in a pile around it. They weren't supposed to bring anyone in, but it's good because now they're no longer at risk of floating off into space. It'll be bad if any Arrisan opens one, though. The women will pop out and try to embrace the Arrisans, and because they haven't been dusted by Eruvisan aliens with stolen lusteal, I don't think it will go too well.

I hope everyone's okay. They've been inside for some time.

He drags me out of the line of sight.

The engineers have constructed a gladiator arena and surrounded it with crates stacked to make tiers of seating. Atana plunks me in the very center of the seats. Engineers swarm him. He barks orders. They scramble, energetic and cheerful, to funnel Sithe into this pit.

But the ones he didn't assign a task draw near. They

look at me with dead expressions, nostrils flaring. Scenting me like a dog getting a whiff of prey.

Atana was terrifying in his office, but he wanted something. These engineers? There are too many for me to connect with, to reach. It's one thing to reason with a single person. It's an entirely different dynamic in a group.

Mobs obscure the choices of individuals.

Individuals commit violent acts.

Mobs tear their victims to pieces.

"This is great." Atana stands several tiers down. He casually extends his blade even with my throat. "Should I greet him like this?"

I hold very still.

Atana withdraws his blade from my throat and crosses it in front of his chest. "Or like this?"

I find my voice. "That one."

"Yeah, a classic challenge pose, okay. Want a stim pack or a canister of puff nutes?"

That must be the name of the seasoned nutrient cubes. "No, thanks."

Engineers take up positions along the walkways overhead. They point guns down at this pit Atana has constructed. He talked about mazes and traps. This is starting to look like both.

"Are you not going to challenge Sithe?"

"Oh yes. We'll try your fight." He grins at me as if I should share his excitement. "And if I don't feel satisfaction, my engineers will cut him to ribbons, and I'll wear *his* face while I kill you."

SIXTEEN

SITHE

I stride through the corridors to the cargo bay.

Yes, I know exactly where I'm going.

And I'm sore, and not thinking well. It's been too long since I've executed proper orders, and all the mantras in the Arsenal are not calming me right now. My blades are sore in my bones. They've been spooled out too far, and the skin is loose around them as if there isn't a way to get them seated again.

The corridors are oddly clear.

They know I'm coming.

I should do this differently, but I don't have time.

Catarine doesn't have time.

I already wasted too long in the science office.

Striding into the trap just to watch the barbed teeth snap shut is not an effective strategy.

And yet.

Here I am, moving purposefully to my destination.

The distant door opens, and the engineer I met on the first shift repairing the grav tubes exits. The door seals behind him as he wheels a bulkhead welder. Halfway to me, he puts on the brakes and leans against it with his hands buried in his overalls.

"Got that repair request." He leers. "Lots of repairs going on in the lower quadrant since you came on board."

I keep my hood on.

"Blades aren't supposed to lose their temper over every little thing." His eyes track my obscured face as I pass.

I walk straight past without giving him the satisfaction of acknowledging his words.

He rustles behind me. Something small whistles in the air.

I swing my left forearm up my back. My blade scythes the object. A dusty canister. It bumps my back and lands in two neat halves on the corridor.

He mutters something unintelligible. The squeak of the bulkhead welder recedes as he hustles down the hall away from me.

Good.

I retract my blade.

It slides into my skin unevenly, scraping against the inner sleeve.

My reactions are slow.

I need rest, a real rest, and treatment of my blade sleeves as well as sharpening and recalibrating.

Catarine has no time.

I stop at the door to the cargo bay.

Only a few shifts ago, I led Catarine away from here. How funny to retrace my steps, winding back into the past.

Shall I knock?

The door slides open.

Engineers form a bottleneck on either side of the doorway. They wear full welding suits and focus hull-cutter lasers on my chest.

I stop.

If one of them twitches, their laser blade will eject and slice me in half.

And it will slice into the wall behind me, and the wall behind it, and on and on until the laser hits space and dissipates as a rogue wave of energy into the blackness.

These hull-cutter lasers are as overpowered against my blades as the dreadnought is against my little sinusoid ship.

What I have is mobility and experience.

My blades might be ineffective against their reinforced welding suits, but they're not immune from each other. Assuming their first blasts missed, I could run down the center of their narrow column. It takes a special kind of training to follow a target *and stop shooting*.

But that assumes their first shots miss.

The engineer at the far end of the bottleneck lifts her eye protection to taunt me. "The boss's down below. Don't keep him waiting."

Drawing me into the trap, huh?

I enter the gauntlet.

The engineer hooks her thumbs in her tool belt bandolier and leans over to block me. "Your lesser is small and weak. But she smells like a puff nute. When I had her in my bag, I just wanted to open it up and crunch, crunch, crunch."

This is the person who took Catarine?

Who put her in a bag and *damaged* her?

I stop and look at the engineer.

My hood covers my face, so I don't know what she sees. But my stopping is enough to make her eyes dart over the blackness and avert, and for her to shuffle back, her sneer wavering.

I really shouldn't have destroyed the science office door.

And I really should not murder this woman.

I haven't lost all my loyalty to the empire, despite what I fear Zai will say when he finds out I've disobeyed his direct orders.

Beyond the engineers, my sinusoid floats at its dock attached with its magnet tether. For the first time ever, looking upon it I feel a hint of nostalgia. Nostalgia for a time when I could fly it to my next destination, my next assignment, and think of nothing else. That was a simple era. It's gone forever, I think.

The engineer gestures at a small grav tube used for conveying equipment to and from the pit below. "He's waiting."

I ignore the grav tube and hop over the railing, dropping to the lower bay. My skinsuit again absorbs the shock.

Debris clutters the wreckage of old parts and derelict vessels, the sort of detritus that gathers even in a new dreadnought's cargo bay. Some piles have been pushed into a circle to form a small maze. Tiers of crates are stacked around them.

Catarine sits in the center, hugging her elbows and knees, looking fragile and small. Engineers surround her. They sit far too close.

The head engineer balances dramatically atop the debris pile in the center. He opens his arms. "Welcome, blade."

Overhead, engineers shielded for welding clamber over struts and across the upper walkways, pointing their guns down on me.

This is a death trap, and I have walked straight into it.

Welcome indeed.

"You figured me out. It took you long enough." Atana

descends the debris pile, energetic. "This is what you get for trying to order around the engineering department."

Catarine does not seem hurt. No bruises or cuts that can't be healed by ointment, anyway.

But given the numbers, the arrangement, and the hull-cutters, I don't see how to get her out of here alive.

"I wanted to end you for your arrogance, but your lesser had a more intriguing idea." Atana lifts his wrists. "I have never been ranked as a blade. I missed that little part of our final trials. Wouldn't it be fun to test our metal? Find out how we both should really rank?"

There must be a trick. "You want me to attack you?"

He grins and ejects his blades, crossing them in invitation. "I want you to try."

How lucky that our desires should mirror each other's. I want nothing more than to slice him to pieces.

But if I defeat him, there will be no one to hold back his engineers.

I cannot scythe this whole department. One of them will get in a lucky shot. Or they'll let out all the atmosphere and Catarine, in her useless Humana fabric, will be sucked into space and die.

And even if that doesn't happen, Zai will hunt me down for treason. "I'm not allowed to kill anyone right now."

"Oh-ho." His exaggerated shock invigorates his crew, who clap and jeer. "You think you're just going to walk in here and kill me? I think you'll be surprised at what my men can cut down to size."

His employees shift overhead.

This engineer is insane. "If you willingly cause a hull breach, the next blade assigned to this ship will be charged with taking you in for judgment in the pits of Ranna."

"Why? I'm not the blade going rogue, who barged into

two departments where he doesn't belong. No one will look at me twice."

"If you're going to cut me down anyway, what's my incentive to fight?"

"You'll set my rank or watch me kill your lesser in the slowest, most agonizing way while you bleed out, helpless, in the lower bay."

Catarine watches me with hope.

Or fear.

I lower my hood and unseal my suit. "We fight to the mark." The suit peels off my shoulder, revealing the blade marks of those who bested me. "Anywhere outside the shoulder is a fail."

"For you." Atana kicks a crate over and hops atop it. "Noted."

I step out of my suit and enter the battle arena he's constructed nude. "Disrobe."

"Nah." He hooks a thumb in his slim tool belt bandolier. "You entered my domain. No one's given me any constraints about killing."

"You're not supposed to murder other Arrisans discharging their duties."

"Rules don't apply to me. I'm an engineer." He pats his chest. "And in my opinion, this ship would be better off if you weren't on it."

Under normal circumstances, practice fighting is useful exercise.

Atana's challenge to mark him beneath his skinsuit, which deflects shrapnel similar to blade strikes, is an interesting assignment.

And rank fights? The serious ones between blades are highly choreographed, a master lesson in self-possession and control. It's easy to kill someone and much harder to only leave a mark. Entire training methods are devoted to tricking your opponent into striking outside the shoulder.

But I am not in a place to give a master lesson.

My blades are dull. I've overextended myself.

Atana is fresh, rested, and has clearly been thinking about this for some time.

He's constructed this arena to suit his strengths.

Even if I succeed, Catarine can lose.

I do not like this.

No assignment happens when conditions are perfect.

But the consequences of failure on this are too high.

Catarine hugs her knees.

Fine. A test, then.

"You won't remove your bandolier tool belt?" I ask.

He scoffs at me. "Why should I?"

I erupt my blades at his face.

He jerks back and swings up his own to block.

I twist my left to engage his blades and hook my right edge under the bandoliers.

He drops his second blade to meet mine. Fast and effective, the sharps hiss like scissors.

I retract my blades.

He huffs a laugh and flashes his blades between us, one-two, the decorative metal gleaming. "You tried to surprise me and missed."

The bandolier separates and falls, hitting the floor with two thunks.

His smile flees.

"I'll remove it for you," I reply.

He shoulders out of his engineering overalls, kicking both out of the ring. "I didn't say to start. The next time you move before I order you, my men will cut you down."

Honestly, my test was to see if his crew would get overexcited and blindly attack.

But they did not. Good. So he must have assigned the guns to the employees he trusts, leaving Catarine under the guard of those who have less discipline.

He follows my gaze. "Don't worry. I'll execute her right behind you. I won't let you die alone."

His guards chuckle.

A sharp undercurrent snags their laughter.

The circle around Catarine tightens.

She squishes in, trying to maintain a safe distance.

There is no safe distance.

I extend my blade to my fingertips. "If anyone hurts her, this game ends and you die."

Her guards sneer at me.

Atana snorts. "No one's going to touch her."

I issued my warning.

But the only problem is that I don't know how I can possibly enforce it without dooming us all.

Catarine

Watching Sithe fight is horrifying.

He sets his feet. Atana does the same. Their blades extend just beyond the fingertips, and they begin some sort of strange dance.

Sithe holds his forearms down and walks swiftly counterclockwise, his gaze never leaving Atana.

Atana walks away at the same speed, his blades up by his head. He stomps forward, a threat.

Sithe veers back, maintaining an even distance, and

then ducks his chest and scoops his arm even with the floor. His blade scythes the ground.

Atana jumps over it, atop boxes, then casually down again.

They are testing each other's reactions.

It just increases the tension.

Sithe cut down the pirates without hesitation. Slash, slash, finished.

But he and Atana both move like loose electricity, jerky yet watchful. Once they commit and engage, the electricity will arch and someone—perhaps both—will be shocked, burnt up, maimed. The littlest nick in the wrong spot is all that's necessary to end a life.

Atana changes direction, pacing forward while Sithe backpedals, faster and faster.

Fear coils like a black snake in the pit of my stomach.

I want to do something. Fear for myself is terrible, but fear for Sithe is even more agonizing.

Atana's blade erupts.

It is long and straight, silver like a snake, with the tip cut into a diagonal.

Sithe slaps it away and leans into the strike, pinning Atana's blade to the floor.

Atana shoots out his other blade at Sithe's head.

Sithe turns his face.

Atana's woodgrain blade shoots past.

Sithe releases the pinned blade and strikes back.

Atana's blades clang against his. They push, and the blades hiss. Atana shoves off Sithe and presses forward. He slams his edges down.

Sithe stumbles.

Atana's blades snick toward his neck.

He rolls out of the way at the last moment and clambers back to his feet, unharmed.

They both retract their weapons and face each other, watchful, breathing heavily.

And then the deathly dance starts again.

Atana stalks him one way, then the opposite direction.

They clash a second time with a similar result—Sithe stumbling, Atana the aggressor—and a third.

Sithe's exhausted. He's slowing down. Atana's totally focused on him, and Sithe barely gets out of the way.

Sithe hasn't slept the entire time I've known him.

Atana speeds up.

Sithe darts behind a stack of crates.

Atana lunges and slices a crate at neck-level.

The boxes topple.

Sithe darts out the other side, shooting a blade at the level of his shoulder.

Atana dives and twists, swiping up and down to deflect a blade at his waist that I didn't even see Sithe eject.

Sithe advances, pushing down so his blades cross like long shears.

Atana slides onto a knee and pushes back.

The sound of their blades scraping against each other is like nails screeching against rock. My shoulders jump for my ears, and a shiver squirms up my spine.

Atana forces the blades apart and swipes at Sithe's ankles. Sithe balances on the uneven corner of a box. Atana leaps up and chases him, raining deadly blows, and Sithe runs backward.

But he's slow.

Much too slow.

This isn't good.

My guards know it.

The beginning of the fight diverted them, but now enough time has passed that Atana's victory is inevitable. And they know when Sithe is killed, I'll be next. Their time with me is limited. I'm a squishy new toy, and their owner has given them a deadline to chew on me.

They move. Subtle shifts. Knees bobbing, fingers drumming, they edge in. Priming themselves for action. One on the tier below me glances back. A creeping sense of awareness warns me they're moving behind me, too. Edging in closer.

I can't move.

But I can't stay.

I breathe shallowly

They can smell my fear. Not just the lusteal, although that's there too.

The one on my lower left grabs my hem.

I shrink in on myself.

But it's a mistake.

Everyone turns toward me.

Making myself smaller is the same as begging.

I can't distract Sithe.

Okay.

I force myself to sit up straight. I'm not begging.

I tug my hem.

The man's not expecting it, so I succeed in yanking it out of his hand.

He twists to grab it again.

I pull my dress tight around my legs and stuff the excess fabric under my seat. He can't have it.

I'm scared, but this is all I can do, so I do it.

He grabs my ankle.

Atana said they wouldn't touch me, but he was wrong.

I jerk back.

He holds on.

His eyes meet mine.

There's no flicker of interest. No hint of one intelligent creature greeting another. I am a thing, an object. Less than nothing. And for resisting him, I am the disobedient one. He can take my ankle and snap it if he wants to. I must accept being crippled because I'm not allowed my own will.

No.

I pull harder.

The pressure on my ankle increases.

He drags me down a step to—what is he even going to do? I don't know and I don't want to know. I try to yank free, contorting furiously.

Hands descend on me, manacling my arms, shoulders, thighs.

Ow. No! Ow-ow-ow—

They're yanking, smacking, tearing. Pain scores my collar. Someone claw-slaps my cheek. My vision blackens. Strange stars burst behind my eyes.

I try to curl in on myself.

They're shoving me, pummeling me. Feral growls fill my ears. Terrible squealing. Teeth snap near my ear.

Stop!

My fingers catch in something. A man snarls. Pain sears my hand.

Why?

Biting. So much biting. My chest, my side. Exposed skin, heat and blood, like they're tearing my flesh off.

This is...

Agony lances my ear.

I try to cover my head and survive.

Sithe

Atana is faster than I am.

He wasn't demoted for his lack of skill, something that I secretly believed despite Zai's explanation that this is part of a grander plan. Atana has the raw talent. He *is* a blade. He must have been placed on the dreadnought in engineering for another reason after all.

My experience has kept me alive.

Despite my exhaustion, despite my mistakes.

I still cannot see how to escape him and free Catarine.

A man who is embarrassed is more dangerous than a man who is defeated.

But the commotion of his guards forces my decision.

I don't see how the engagement starts, but I do see Catarine disappear into the crowd, and I dance back to the edge of Atana's makeshift arena, disengaging to give him a chance to deal with it, trying to figure out if I can use that distraction to do something useful.

But Atana isn't distracted. He breathes heavily. "You want to stop, blade?"

I jerk my chin. "Your guards—"

"Fight me, coward!" He rushes me.

Catarine screams.

Game ended.

I sidestep his lunge, dart forward, and slam the flat of my blade into his nose.

It makes a disgusting crunch.

He stumbles back, hands going to his face.

Everyone drops their guard the first time they get punched.

I grab him by the collar, pulse my blade into his shoulder, and throw him backward.

He ejects his blades at me as he falls.

Too fast.

It catches me by surprise. The tips score my temple, so fast and so sharp, it doesn't hurt, but I feel the skin separating.

I jerk back.

He swipes where I was an instant ago.

I pivot, scoop up my skinsuit, and leap into the crates stacked for seating.

The guards on the edges of the bloody frothing pile scramble back.

They will live today.

The ones attacking Catarine never look up.

I erupt my blades. Their hoods are back so they can attack, and my blades pierce skulls, curving. As my own skinsuit fastens around my body, I spit their heads like beads on a metal string. Their crazed snarls fall silent. They twitch and collapse.

Catarine lies in a bloody mess.

Her back curves to me, her face tucked under her elbow. They've torn off her dress. The shredded fabric across her broken skin makes her look even more fragile.

She doesn't move.

I will kill her attackers all over again.

The gunmen move overhead. If they cut me down now, they'll also desecrate their fallen friends. Half of them disappear, probably to get a better angle to shoot us.

We have to run.

I yank one of the twitching bodies off Catarine's legs, force her taut arm around my neck, and lift.

She hunches around me.

I stand and turn.

Engineers move out of the shadows with weapons

trained on me. Not hull-cutters, just ordinary solders, flares, metal shears, and makeshift pikes. They crowd between us and any exits.

I cannot run through them, not with Catarine vulnerable and naked.

I lower her to the crates again.

She sits and squints up like she doesn't know me.

In three swift motions, I slice off the overalls of the corpse closest to her size, peel apart the skinsuit, and roll the nude body off.

The suit flutters like a flag curling around itself, seeking skin to bond with and rejecting me because I'm already wearing one.

I flip it around her shoulders like a cape.

It suctions to her body, a little big on her, then smooths. The excess bunches in the back, forming a short train not unlike the Humana dress she has lost.

Now she has basic protection against ordinary weapons.

I haul her up again. She grips me tightly.

The missing gunmen crowd the escalator and block our exit.

We're trapped.

This was my nightmare.

I can probably trick the gunmen into firing indiscriminately. Probably.

But to do so while I escape with Catarine? In this state?

We will not make it.

Atana still sits in the center of the battle arena. He's jammed a white cleansing cloth up his nose and isn't smiling. "You executed my engineers."

"They hurt her."

His gaze flicks to Catarine. The long scratches beneath

her blackening eyes. Blood dripping from her nearly torn off ear.

She edges behind me.

Atana's eyes narrow, and he pushes his lips to one side, then pulls away the speckled cloth and spits a wad of blood on the floor. "You never finished our battle."

"Check your shoulder."

He looks down at his skinsuit. Then up through his brows at me.

I wait.

He flips open the shoulder.

One blood-crusted puncture, neat and precise, with a slight curve at the end.

He stares.

Any click now, he's going to feel it.

And while he's hesitating, mulling it over, I'm going to start putting distance between us. I hug Catarine to my side and stride purposefully between the engineers for the mini equipment grav tube nearest the exit.

One gunman drops from the grav tube, blocking our exit. She sets her feet and braces. "Freeze!"

The engineers behind us dive out of the way.

I stop.

Catarine trembles behind me.

This is it. The showdown. I'm out of options.

I'll try to keep her alive as long as possible. When the gunman cuts through the hull, and it sucks us out, I'll keep a tight hold on her because that's the best way to get her back inside.

The gunman flips the switch. Her hull-cutter sputters and then hums with a teeth-grinding whine. She centers the targeting beam on my chest.

Atana scoops up his tool bandolier. "Let them go."

"But he's insulted us." The gunman's lips curl back from her teeth. "He killed engineers in our own bay."

"He didn't kill them."

"I saw it with my own eyes!"

"You didn't see what you think." He fits the cut ends together, then lets them fall apart again.

The gunman splutters. "I saw him cut down the crew you rewarded with ringside seats by the lesser—"

"Rewarded?" Atana guffaws. He laughs so hard, his eyes water. With the blood spattered on his face, he appeals to the other engineers. "You think I rewarded that crew? You think it was a privilege?"

The bay echoes with his unsettling laughter.

"It wasn't a reward," he finally tells them, sobering. "It was a test. They failed. This is what happens when you don't listen *to me*."

"But...but..."

"It was all part of my plan. Have a little fun with one of my blade brethren. Weed out my followers who lack loyalty."

The other engineers straighten and flip up their eye shades.

The gunman does not. "We can do whatever we want to whoever we want in the engineering department."

"Because I let you. And what did I say?" Atana toes the nude corpse, rolls it over facedown. "I told you not to touch her."

"It's only a lesser!"

"You fool," Atana sneers at the engineer. "She's not just a lesser. She's his Amante."

The engineers look at each other. Confusion fills their faces.

"Oh, you don't know what that is?" Atana coughs and

dabs the blood-soaked cloth on his face. "Hmm. Even lessers know about *that* from our home world. And because she's his Amante, I knew he would do exactly what I wanted him to. But go ahead." He gestures at the gunman. "Question me again. This blade has finished serving his purpose for me this shift, so I'll have to think of a new test to ensure my remaining engineers are loyal."

The gunman lowers the muzzle of her hull-cutter. The whine fades as it powers down.

Atana's split lips do not make a full smile. He grins off-center at me. "See you later, Sithe."

His speech has nothing to do with me.

But I could not have fought my way out of here with Catarine, even if she is in a skinsuit, without a much higher body count.

Her gamble to tell Atana about the myths has brought us a respite.

Atana flicks his fingers for the remaining engineers to clean up the bodies. He turns and ambles toward the rear escalator to retreat to his office. He rubs his shoulder.

The mark, and when in our fight it appeared, is going to bother him for a long time.

But I'll take this dismissal.

I hurry Catarine to the mini grav tube and flip her hood, sealing her in for safety, then scoop her under the elbows and hold her against me. The dock zooms toward us. I hook the back of my blade around the railing and hop down, dragging her with me. Her feet tangle, and I don't let her slow. We have to get out of here before Atana changes his mind.

After all, he's going to have to explain this in a report.

And so will I.

SEVENTEEN

CATARINE

I put one foot in front of me after another.

My head pounds. Everything feels strange.

The suit Sithe put on me conforms to my body, and by the time we exit the cargo bay, the odd smell of the atmosphere inside it dissipates.

We travel through the ship. These walkways will never be familiar to me, but there's relative anonymity with the hood on. I can see out clearly, but no one can see me. No one looks over at us. Anyone who passes too close makes me startle and shrink away.

In the carless elevator, Sithe pulls me against his chest and looks down. Our hoods' tinting interferes in just the right way because I can see up into his eyes now. He's tired, concerned, but unstoppable. And no matter where I'm taken, he will find me.

This is deeply comforting.

We exit, and it's easier to move after him. A lot of small pains pop up as I walk, and my broken pinky throbs. We reach the room. He lets us in, seals the door behind us, and stops.

The silence stretches.

We're really here. We've made it back to this room. Alive.

He pulls back his hood, and it's not my imagination. He's as exhausted as I thought. He reaches for my hood. His fingers brush too close to my hot ear.

I twitch away from him.

He arrests his hand in the air. His frown deepens.

Oops.

I push back my hood, careful of my ear.

"Catarine!" The viewscreen is still connected to Humana, and Dr. Ghaberi is watching with deep hollows under his eyes. "You're back."

The man who works for a representative of the Humana Commission rouses from a couch in the background.

I don't feel well, but I lean into the communication panel to reply. "I'm sorry for frightening you."

"Oh, I'm fine. You look...are you all right?"

I'm honestly not sure. "My presence on the ship continues to cause problems."

"What happened?"

"I was kidnapped by the engineers so they could fight Sithe."

"It looks like they forced you into the ring too."

"I was supposed to be on the sidelines. Some of them got overexcited."

Dr. Ghaberi looks deeply concerned.

The commission assistant clears his throat and fiddles with his bow tie. "You need to convince your Arrisan to take Humana off the list for orbital changes."

"He doesn't have that power."

"Then he needs to find out who does."

"I don't know if we have time."

"Make time. Our world could end, Catarine."

"No, I mean, I don't know how much longer we have on this ship. Today I was kidnapped from a locked room while Sithe was being disciplined. Tomorrow...?" I turn to check with Sithe.

He's setting out the medical kit.

Again.

That's good, because my head is starting to swim. I must have lost a lot of muscle tone on the cruiser. I feel like I've been standing too long.

The assistant chokes. "Your ear..."

"Is it bad?" I'm afraid to touch it, and the look on Dr. Ghaberi's face suggests it's even worse than it feels. "I'm sorry. I still haven't found out what consequences Sithe will face for rescuing me from the science office, and this time, he had to carve his way into a crowd. I don't think those men will be all right. Once he leaves, there's no one else to ask for protection."

"Catarine." Dr. Ghaberi steps forward. "Are you going to be all right?"

It hurts to smile. "I'll do my best. But I think you should pin your hopes on another person."

"But you're the only one who's in any position to do something," the assistant insists.

This exhausts me. "I don't know what to say."

"Find some way to fight back. Make them listen. You did it once. Why can't you do it again?"

"I...really don't think..."

"End the call," Sithe orders.

I'm more than happy to bid them goodbye and retract the communication panel, then collapse on the bench.

He sits beside me and starts with my ear. The healing

substance stings, and the region grows even hotter.

Tears well in my eyes. I grit my teeth. "That's not ointment."

"It's glue." He lowers the tube—yes, it's blue and a different texture, more like putty than cream—and tilts my chin to study both sides of my head, pushing and poking the injured one until he's satisfied. He tosses the glue and grabs another thing I can't see, dabs it at the area.

I flinch away. "What's that?"

He shows me the tube. It's the ointment. The area around my ear cools.

Okay. I take a deep breath and let it out. I'm okay.

He smooths ointment onto my cheeks, nose, forehead, then on my neck. Then he stands in front of me and tugs my suit apart.

I jump and shy back.

He stops. His eyes flick to mine with a question.

"Sorry." But that's no answer, so I feel my way to an explanation. "I got so scared, I'm having trouble calming down."

He doesn't move for a long, long moment. The muscles in his jaw flex. He swipes his finger over the ointment and reaches for my collar.

I flinch.

He freezes.

"It's not you. My eyes know it, but the rest of me is... Just try a little slower, maybe."

He descends to one knee at half speed and applies the ointment in a now-familiar scene. Bites cover my arms, my hands. A vicious one mars my breast. That's just mean, really. Sithe works with infinite patience, in slow motion, and our breathing synchronizes, regular and soft. He tilts my body to balance on one cheek to administer to my back, then the other. From my crown to my toes, he touches me, heals me.

Again.

He studies my broken finger. The knuckle is swollen, nothing bends where it's supposed to, and my pinky tip is purple. This doesn't seem like the kind of injury that could be healed by ointment. He puts me into the gel bath, my skin enveloped by cleanser, and goes to the communication panel. The viewscreen is off, and he turns down the volume so much, I can't hear what's said.

I rest my palms on the side of the bath and my chin on my uninjured hand. "Can I put this cleanser on my face?"

He moves slowly, deliberately, to my side. "A cloth should provide adequate sanitation."

"He licked me." I point at my scratched cheek. "I want to peel my skin off."

Sithe's jaw muscles flex again.

Then he slowly kneels, scoops up the strangely textured ooze, and applies it where I direct him. Extra careful of my brows and eyes, skirting my lips and nostrils, he applies it only to peel it off again. It's a weird sensation, like being blotted with plastic fingers.

This man who knows nothing but death touches me with feather-soft kindness.

It is a view that only I see.

A gentleness he gives only to me.

And when I leave this room, I'll take this memory with me, wrapped in my heart. My view of a different life for him. A different way of being.

We were raised so differently, him to target and hunt and destroy, me to rebuild and protect and love.

In this ship, I wish I had more of his skills. I wish I could destroy his enemies or prevent myself from becoming their victim. I suppose right now, he wishes he had a different skill set, a different foreordained destiny too.

The door pings.

He stands—slowly—and eases to the intercom beside the door, murmurs an order to whoever is outside. "Leave it and go." After a moment, he unlocks the door, brings in a small box, and relocks the door.

Sithe pulls my injured hand out of the gel and carefully feeds it through a hole in the side of the box. The top lights up and shows my bones like an X-ray. Pins pierce my nerves, and then all sensation fades away. On the X-ray, long threads stick into my bones. My fingers twitch, but I don't actually feel it. The threads push the bones into place, including tiny chips and fractures, filling and fusing the cracks. The threads recede, the uncomfortable tingling sensation returns, and the light goes off.

He pulls my hand out.

My pinky is still red and puffy, but the fingertip is no longer purple, and the knuckles bend all the way to make a fist. It aches, but the pain is more like muscle soreness or strained tendons. He sprays my hand with the Arrisan equivalent of an ice-heat balm, a mist specifically for muscular and skeletal problems, and gives it a quick massage.

He's made me whole.

Again.

I could cry.

He rests my hand on top of the other and tends to himself, ejecting his blades so they curve around his body in a biology-defying display, and coats his blades with the ice-heat spray and retracts them. He applies ointment to a scratch on his jaw, the long wounds on his temples, and checks for other injuries in the data tablet, which he changes to a cracked mirror. Then he brings it to me to check for my own injuries.

My face spiderwebs in the reflection.

It's funny that the sawblade cut on my forehead, which went almost all the way to the skull, has healed so there's almost no blemish, whereas the scratch he got from something on the cruiser shifts ago is still a scab. These ointments are all optimized for Arrisans, but they work even better on me, it seems.

He takes the cracked tablet and bone-repairing box outside the door and murmurs into the communication panel for someone to collect them.

I drop my head to my elbow resting on the side of the tub and close my eyes. I'm one with the gel. "I should get out so you can have a turn."

His fingertips brush my shoulder. "Rest, Catarine."

He doesn't have to tell me twice.

But I've barely breathed out in a sigh when the sense of men attacking me, teeth and fists and rending, jerks me upright.

Sithe sits nude across from me, his back against the wall, eyes open and watchful.

My heart beats so fast. A sour taste fills my mouth. "S-sorry."

He checks the chronometer on the wall. It's been about half a cleg, just long enough for me to fall asleep. "You need more rest."

"I'm afraid I'm going to have nightmares." I try to lift myself out of the tub.

He silently glides to my side.

I hold up my hands, the gel peeling off, and he wraps my arms around his neck and pulls me free, then rests me on the lip.

I pull away so he can use the bath.

He holds me firmly. "I want to give you comfort."

I collapse against him. "Thank you."

He holds me for long, long minutes.

I can close my eyes and almost drift.

But my body twitches. The growling, the frenzied noises, the pain. It shakes me awake again.

He murmurs into my hair. "What can I do?"

"I don't know. I'm not used to this either." I nestle my cheek lower, off his shoulder, against his bare pectoral. His heart thuds in a comforting rhythm. "I was trying to cure my mental fog, but one benefit is that I never formed emotional memories of trauma. You killed those pirates practically on top of me, and I remember, but I have no feelings about it, positive or negative. And now I feel everything like a normal person would. It's horrible."

"Can you trigger the fog?"

I shudder in my soul and clench him tighter. "My deepest fear is that it will come back. We never figured out what caused it or why it's gone away. These terrors are bad, but I prefer them over dulling my brain."

He rubs his finger over one of the bites, although it already looks better from the ointment.

"I keep reliving the attack. It was so savage."

"Because of the lusteal."

"Oh?"

"Unlike lessers who grow up with procreation partners, Arrisans experience no feelings related to procreation at all. Lusteal causes a tickle in the mind, very uncomfortable, and those Arrisans had probably not been to the arena. They wouldn't know how to control their urges."

"Atana spent more time with me and didn't attack me like that."

"He's a blade. Engineer or not, his first training was in self-control."

I'm resting against Sithe's body, and he's being perfectly normal. "Do you feel it right now? An urge to procreate?"

"I have an awareness of it, yes. But more important is your comfort."

My heart thuds, just once. An echo of a thought I can't properly express.

There aren't enough words in Arrisan Standard for my feelings right now.

But Sithe is okay with silence.

This companionship is what I need. I just want to hear his voice, breathe in his scent, exist against him. "What happened at your conference with the captain?"

He tells me about the factions within the Arrisan empire, the reason for the engineer and science officer being blades, and that his superior will probably come now that he's drawn more attention to himself.

"Zai will have to punish me. It will be better if you're not nearby."

"How will he punish you? Will you be executed?"

"No..." But he doesn't sound as sure of it as he should be. "If he decides I am treasonous, he will execute me. If incompetent or disobedient, I will go before a tribunal and lose rank."

"Will he think it's treason?"

"I disobeyed a direct order that he threatened to call an act of treason. But he must know I will defend the empire against the Harsi."

I wake from my peaceful half doze with nervous laughter. "You can't just say their name."

"What name? The Harsi?"

My nervous laughter increases. He just casually throws

it around. "Stop."

"Why? The Harsi are my greatest enemy, the ones I train to face. How can I defend against an enemy I cannot name?"

"I don't know. You're not supposed to. It's like opening an umbrella inside or cutting your nails at night. You'll summon them."

"The Harsi will not appear because I say this name in my dreadnought. They will not hear it or respond." He traces the fold in my side to the hipbone and over the smooth curve, then cups me with gentle strength. "But someday, they will return. And on that day, all Arrisans will begin the final fight. All blades will assemble in our single-fighter sinusoids. All dreadnoughts will form the first, second, and final tiers of defense. We, along with the support of our allies, will make a net to catch them before they can tear apart the vassal planets. We will give our lives, our ships, everything to save their home worlds. We will fight off the Harsi even if we are pushed to the very last star."

"To the very last star…"

"And everything I do, everything the Arsenal prepares, everything the empire orders is organized around that goal. We are all preparing for the return of the Harsi." His chin rubs my crown. "Or, we're supposed to be."

"Against that canvas, one man's wish to keep company with a woman from Humana probably looks pretty small."

"Yes." He shifts, settling his other arm around me. "Although I do wonder. Why is this one thing not allowed? I'll still perform. I will assume my position for the final fight. The fate of the empire *is* the fate of Humana, whether it's first to fall or whether we save it, and I would fight equally for Vanadis or Eruvis. Who has looked at the grand order and decided that you cannot remain safely in my company for the rest of time?"

"Your superiors."

"Yes." His tone turns heavy, and he lets out a sigh. "Zai is a better blade than I."

The marks on his left shoulder reflect the light. They are precise as a tattoo, four perfect hash marks with slightly different edges. "Are those from training?"

"The final trials, yes. These were the rivals who defeated me. It is how we set our beginning rank when we graduate from training and are untested."

"Who marked you?"

"Zai." He touches the outermost mark. "The other three are dead."

"Why?"

"Mistake on an assignment." He taps the other marks in order. "Battle for the general master position. Bad luck."

"Bad luck?"

"His ship suffered a catastrophic engine failure on a routine flight between the Arsenal and Arris Central. It was pulverized by debris."

"That's bad luck." I rub the marks. "Some people must be covered in these."

"Zai. The general master has to fight every graduate. He does not deign to fight those beneath his abilities, and simply accepts their marks uncontested. It is a point of honor for him to deem you worthy to fight, and to bear his mark."

And that's the superior coming to discipline Sithe. The only man alive who's beaten him.

I have more scars than Sithe at the moment. I scratch at a strange tearing scar beside a scabbed, partial double-horse-shoe. "You wanted to bite me once."

He tilts his head, acknowledging that he'd asked.

"Where did you want to do it? On my throat? Or elsewhere?"

"No, although..." He shrugs. "You don't want to, so it doesn't matter."

And that, right there, is the difference. I scratch the scabs. "They bit me so much."

"It's a childhood behavior. When another tries to take your toy, you bite it to show it's yours. Is it not the same on Humana?"

"It's different. Sometimes people will lick food to stop someone else from eating it, but we only bite in anger."

He brushes my cheek. "Did you want me to lick you?"

"Hm?"

"So that you don't feel that Atana has claimed you?"

"Oh." That's kind of sweet. "I thought you did a good job when you peeled it off with the plasma."

He returns his hand to my shoulder.

Wait a minute. "Is that why you wanted to bite me?"

His breath slows. His muscles still.

"Want to bite me?" I amend, because he often ghosts his mouth over my body, despite the fact that he's respected my wishes every time.

His breathing returns to normal. "I don't know."

It's silent again, but strange. Not the companionable silence of before. A tension of words left unsaid.

Sithe shifts positions, his knee brushing mine. "Did you read the myths to Atana?"

"A couple, yes."

"He called you my Amante."

"I couldn't think of any other way to describe our friendship."

"Allies..." he muses, and the sense of something missing

from the Arrisan Standard word lingers in his tone too. "But Grundi and Amante do not have any control over the other."

"No."

"They don't always cross paths. Each lives their own lives, but when they come together, they grow ninety-six times their original size and accomplish great things."

"Like how your race came together and became rulers of the empire, I guess."

"I thought their relationship was more like your family."

My heart thuds again.

I pull back so I can look into his silver eyes. His strong jaw, his ordinary face. I cup his cheek. "My experience with you isn't the relationship of a parent and child."

"It is the relationship of your father and your mother." He has such calm, unbending certainty. "They brought a child into this universe, into a vassal planet with all its hardships, and relied on only each other to raise you. Their bond must be stronger than anything the empire understands."

How do you describe marriage, or lovers, to a race that doesn't have them? Sithe has found the words. "That's what I was trying to explain to Atana."

He rests his hand over mine. "Are you my Amante?"

I soak in his touch.

He leans toward me. His cock has grown, hardening into its arrow-straight precision.

"Am I?" I whisper.

Instead of answering, his mouth claims mine.

He kisses me slowly, sweetly, suctioning my skin in his mouth. His teeth slide across my tender flesh, but he still does not clamp down.

He has done so much for me. Continues to do so much

for me. And I want to give in, let him put his teeth where he wants them.

And yet my voice remains silent.

We haven't answered the most important questions. How can we escape, where can we go, how can we build a life together? He might be able to grow huge to save me, but I haven't figured out how to grow huge and save him.

I draw his hand to my breast, teach him how to cup me gently, lave my tender nipple with his tongue while I arch and moan for him. He asks how to comfort me? I show him exactly how I want to be comforted. Because I am allowed. I am allowed to experience comfort from him.

He cups my femininity, paints pleasure with his palm, his fingers, his tongue. And I can tell this is all strange to him. He doesn't understand my needs, but he fulfills them, everything I ask, as slow and as quick and as soft and as hard as I desire, and that is all that matters to me.

And this time when we couple, because his cock inside me is what I want, he slides into my wet interior and strokes me so infinitely slowly that it almost breaks my heart.

His forehead rests against mine, eyes locked, mouths open and kissing. It's almost too much, but it's just what I need right now.

And our bodies search together for a place where we can be happy. Where no one will try to take what we have or hurt either of us. Where there's a mist forest that goes for a hundred thousand actungs, and water sprouts from the cracked soil sweet enough that we can always drink it, and there is a land that has all the food that we ever want just growing outside, and no one else wants it. We can just have it.

We will find our own home world. A place no one can take away. A place where the two of us can finally belong.

EIGHTEEN

SITHE

"**M**aybe you have more choices than you think."

Catarine murmurs in my ear as her body rides mine, as we meet together and I lose myself in her again.

She shudders, another climax, and her neck is right beneath my teeth, her shoulder the perfect place for me to clamp down and have her...

But I do not.

My release comes, hard and perfect, and I hold myself taut, squeezing my teeth together as my liquid exits in a swift, final burst. I let out a pant, catching the breath that's gotten away from me. All the mantras in the world, all the exertions I've done, and nothing makes me sweat like Catarine. There is no other effort more important. No other woman more worthy of me than Catarine.

I disentangle us and put her in the bath again. While she soaks, I finally pop the tracker out of her skinsuit. No need for Atana to know where she is on the dreadnought should she ever leave here again. I help her into it. She nestles in, looking slightly too small for it, but perfectly adorable.

I should have found her a skinsuit immediately, before we left the cargo bay of the dreadnought that first time. Our lives would have been much easier if I could have slipped her through the ship.

She eats a meal with me, then tucks her legs under her and watches me sharpen my blades. They ache in my bones. It will take some time before I recover, but I must begin the long process of sharpening them now.

"If the worst happens, we could always make a run to your ship and escape," she says, continuing the conversation a cleg or two later. "Ideally we'd grab Captain Zeerah out of the science office before Ukuri can do anything to her, and everyone still in the escape pods in the cargo bay too. But if that's impossible, we could just run."

I am more than willing to go down this path. "And go where?"

"I don't know. Would they chase you?"

"Yes."

"How far? Would you become an assignment for someone else?"

I nod. It's most likely.

Zai, no longer able to predict my behavior, would have no choice. A blade who cannot keep his weapon sheathed is as deadly as one who does not draw them when needed.

She purses her lips, then chews on her thumb. Her eyes begin to close, and I pause to open the resting nook, tuck her in. She turns her large eyes on me. "I'm afraid I'll get nightmares."

I climb in beside her.

The pod stretches to fit the two of us. It's not designed for more than one, but I make it fit. If our room is breached right now, she'll survive. Sleep is somewhere I cannot chase her enemies, so I'll do all I can to protect her when she awakens.

She melts against my chest. Her breathing slows.

I'll do anything to protect her.

Anything.

But it's not enough that I want it. It also has to be what she wants.

Those engineers biting her, trying to make her theirs, didn't care that they were tearing her apart. They weren't trying to hurt her necessarily, although they clearly didn't care about her at all. They were only thinking about their wants.

I have never wanted anything for my own.

All that matters is the empire.

But now the empire matters even more because Catarine is in it.

There must be some way to join these two aims.

Right now, I can't see how.

A living thing always wants to live a little bit longer. No matter how doomed they are. No matter how small the hope. Just like Catarine's captain ejecting their pods into space, even though that choice doomed them.

What choices am I making to doom Catarine?

Catarine

I wake from a long, dreamless sleep.

Sithe is sleeping beside me. Long even breaths, on his back. I'm curled around his body like a kitten.

I feel a little cramped and a lot hungry. We must have

been here for a while. I don't remember what the chronometer said when I lay down, but I'm pretty sure I missed at least two meals.

Trying not to wake him, I ease up and inch my way out.

His eyes open and focus on me.

"I'm going to get up real fast," I murmur. "You can stay and sleep."

His eyes close. He turns over, his shoulder lifting off my trapped arm, and sighs back into sleep. He's really tired.

I clamber out, dragging my skinsuit with me. It feels weird. Not scratchy, not cottony like underwear, but some hybrid leather that's actually comfortable. It does feel a little bit like skin, which is disconcerting, but the longer I wear it, the less I notice, so it must be one of those things that you get used to. And it's quasimagnetic so you can pull it apart anywhere—cuff, hem, collar—with just the right tug.

That seems unsafe. If I caught it on a door handle, could I accidentally tear it off? In public?

Sithe has worn it in fights, though. It deflects gunfire, but at the same time, it doesn't feel heavy enough. Or secure enough.

I've watched him use the brazier a bunch. It takes me a while and I clank dishes, but I end up with a heated bowl of stims and nutrient cubes. I wonder where the engineers got their puff balls. They tasted pretty okay, but the walls of this room are only filled with normal food.

Should I make a bowl for Sithe?

He rolls over to face the wall.

No, then.

I put everything away and call Humana.

It's the middle of the night there. Dr. Ghaberi startles out of his chair and fumbles his glasses. "Catarine, I'm so glad to see you. You're looking better."

"A long rest and a hot meal will do that."

More people move in the background, and a distinguished woman appears flanked by bodyguards.

"Representative Khan, ambassador to the Humana Commission, is here to speak to you." Dr. Ghaberi moves aside.

"Hello, Catarine." She smiles warmly. Her competent manner is immediately soothing, and she looks a little like pictures of my dad's mother. We are—were—once a British colony, and also an intersection point for Tamil, islanders, indigenous Malay, and Chinese. "I understand you're on a new dreadnought, the *Spiderwasp*, and that your movement and time on the ship is limited."

"That's correct."

"We sincerely appreciate the archive you've sent us. It's helped to answer a few questions, specifically about how a planet of the empire goes from being a vassal planet to becoming an ally. When we've asked directly, the answers were not forthcoming, but the archive describes the path several planets have taken. I believe you can help us."

I'm holding my breath. I let it out in a rush. No one would ever change the orbit willy-nilly of an ally planet. "That's even an option?"

"It's one we've been pursuing very hard since the beginning for obvious reasons." She folds her hands in front of her chest. "The ally planets have reached their status at a median of ten generations." She bows her head once as though in prayer. "It is my personal goal to elevate Humana in five."

That would mean my grandchildren could be born into a world where they had some rights in the empire. I would be okay with that. "What about the legislation to move us from orbit?"

"If you happen to pass by a resource allocation council on Arris Central, please make our case."

"Oh." Yeah, that's not likely.

"One method to reach ally status is to hold a treasured resource that no other planet has, and we unfortunately do not. A second is to perfect a unique research area or skill. We are so behind the empire that it will take generations to reach a high enough level to qualify.

"A third option is to become allies with the other ally planets and force Arris Central to recognize our status. There, I think, we have some opportunity to shortcut the process. We currently have agents working on several ally planets, but we don't have anyone working on Vanadis."

"That's where I was going!"

"Precisely. I understand you're suffering from an illness. The research specialty on Vanadis is xeno-medicine, and so you may gain some celebrity that you can use to our advantage. Whenever possible, please promote Humana as a place of learning that would be an ideal partner."

"I will." I sink back into my seat. The magnitude of representing Humana, all of Humana, to another planet pushes down on my shoulders. "I'll do whatever I can."

"I've assembled some talking points." She tilts her head toward me as though peering into my soul. "Please don't feel like you need to personally gain the approval of the Premier Council of Vanadis. You're one person carrying a torch into the darkness, and you're not alone. There are many more. You may not see them, and you may not see the results of the work that you do, but it is important, and you should feel proud that you're doing it."

My chest lifts.

"Now." Representative Khan pulls out a digital planner.

"We've sent the talking points to your data tablet, but I want to go over these with you."

"Good, because the data tablet was broken in a scuffle."

"Ah, I see." She's businesslike about my situation. Like my mother, she accepts what is and uses the tools she has instead of wasting time lamenting what's gone, and I find it invigorating. "The first point when making a public appearance in front of the Vanadisans is to—"

The screen goes blank.

Oh no.

I press the communication button, calling back out of instinct. I may never get to Vanadis—I may never make it off this dreadnought—but I have to carry my torch. Someone's grandchildren depend on it.

The viewscreen displays the brutal face of Captain Falkion.

My stomach drops.

He blinks, as surprised to see me as I am to see him. "What are you doing on my comm? Where's Sithe?"

Never bargain, never beg.

I take a long, slow breath to compose my thoughts. "Captain Falkion."

"I asked you a question."

Another long, slow breath.

Sithe thought the captain couldn't come in. The engineers can, but Sithe still outranks the captain.

Probably.

I'm not sure if this is the right move. I have no idea what the right move is right now. "I heard it."

"Well?"

"I don't feel an obligation to answer."

He blinks again. "But you're a lesser."

"And you're a captain, yes."

His jaw juts forward and his brows pile up on his forehead. He looks flummoxed, but doesn't break into a rage, so that's good. "Get Sithe here. Now."

"No."

"What?"

"I'm sorry, but I won't. If you have a message for Sithe, you can give it to me."

"You can't tell me no. You're a lesser."

"It is a strange and painful thing to feel as though you ought to have more control over a situation than you do," I sympathize, and hover my index finger over the button to terminate the call. "As a lesser, I experience this quite often. I'll let Sithe know you called."

"Wait."

I pause.

"The general master of the Arsenal is flying here now. You know who that is?"

I nod.

"You understand how important it is?"

"Yes."

"Great. Get Sithe."

"I'll let him know." I rest my hand in my lap so he can't see my fingers tremble. "Anything else?"

He juts his jaw forward again. "Do you have any idea the chaos you've caused on this ship? The damage to a *new* dreadnought? Deaths during a so-called 'friendly training exercise' in engineering, as if they really thought I would believe that. All because of you?"

"Mm." This man is one indignant Arrisan. "And yet I didn't ask to be brought aboard. You brought me here."

His nose wrinkles and quickly smooths again, an aborted snarl. "And now I'd do anything to get you off here."

"Our wishes are the same, Captain."

I really wish I could have run this scenario past Representative Khan. She must have so much more experience reframing bargaining into mutually acceptable demands. I don't have that experience, so I'm left with telling the captain flat out what I want.

"I want a way off this ship for me and my crewmates without anyone else getting hurt. A way off that includes safe passage on a functional, well-repaired cruiser, preferably all the way to Vanadis."

He stares at something off-screen, then whips back to me. Something clicks for him. "You made Sithe order the repair of the cruiser."

It seems Atana didn't share much about our conversations in his training accident report.

"I didn't *make* Sithe do anything." Let's be clear on that. "But you're right that I requested it."

"Your cruiser was too damaged to be repaired. The engineers dismantled it for parts."

H. Double-H.

"That's disappointing," I say with a bit of an edge.

"But a Vanadisan expeditioner recently hailed us requesting permission to scour the accident site."

What? Really?

"I assumed they were scrapping. The Eruvisans have a long history of buying tech from Vanadis." He drums his fingers on the panel. "If I force them to take you, will you peacefully remove yourself from this dreadnought? Without causing any more damage? Alone?"

This is destiny. "As long as my shipmates are on the Vanadis expeditioner as well."

"I'll ensure that personally."

"Perfect."

He frowns, eyes narrowing. "You'll leave Sithe, and everything will return to normal?"

Leaving Sithe behind hurts.

It bores a hole inside my heart that no amount of blood will fill.

There's nowhere for us to go. Not without a crazy huge sacrifice on his part. And I understand that.

I asked him over and over last night, *Is there a place we can go where there wouldn't be any fighting? Where you wouldn't be hunted for leaving this place behind?* And his answer was often *maybe.* Sometimes, *I don't know.*

I'm just trying to stay alive. If I can help my shipmates and Humana, then that's a bonus.

But in order to go with me, Sithe has to give up his entire world.

And it's already been made clear what that entails. I've already seen the cost of it. He has to fight his own people. Kill his own people. That's so much bigger than anything I have to do.

I will leave, and everything will return to normal.

Right?

"I don't see why not," I say.

"Meet me at the cargo bay in two clegs," he says.

Oh, the cargo bay. "The engineers..."

"Will not be a problem." He lifts his wrists and displays a hooked blade. "You will exit the dreadnought with your shipmates, and no Arrisan will prevent your peaceful departure. I guarantee it."

NINETEEN

SITHE

I do not feel well.

Catarine ends the call with the captain and sits in silence.

Do her insides clench? Does her stomach churn like she's digesting fire? Does she not feel the need to peel off her skin, burst forth blades, cut through swaths of enemies and demand we remain together?

She eventually stands and exits the communication panel. Her beautiful brown irises meet mine. I'm sitting upright now, silent and blades neatly contained, atop the resting nook.

She pauses and links her fingers. "You heard."

I came out of a sound sleep at her change in tone. From the moment she greeted the captain, I listened.

"Your supervisor's coming, and the Vanadisans will be here in two clegs." She leans a hip against the cool tile of the closed brazier. "Vanadis is where I was headed anyway. I couldn't think of any other choice. This is..." She lets out a long sigh. "For the best."

These words tear strips out of my center.

She turns away and picks up her small bag.

I rise and follow as she gathers her things. She turns and bumps into me, then looks up and smiles. It pierces my chest in a hundred places.

She loops the bag onto her shoulder. "How long does it take to get to the cargo bay?"

"A few clicks."

She glances at the chronometer.

I want to hold her in my arms and never let her go. She's standing in front of me, but it feels like she's already gone.

"It's probably for the best," she says again and scrapes an invisible line on the floor with her skinsuit boot. "Is there any other option? Can you see one? Because this universe is big and dangerous. When I leave here, we'll no longer affect each other's lives, and this time together has been intense and precious to me."

She snatches my feelings out of the air and puts them into words. Yes, this time has been intense and precious to me too.

And while I've never feared for my life, being with her has torn off my skin and exposed hollow caverns beneath my bones where I thought I was whole. The longer we're together, the more I learn of what I lack.

My future, my past, everything has been altered by our meeting and interactions.

And yet, for all the ways I've changed, some things have stayed the same. "I can't think of anything."

"Well, I can, but..." She chuckles low and moves one arm expansively while hugging the other to her belly. "You could come with me. Just blow off everything and come. We'll go to Vanadis, and I'll get the lusteal taken out, or treated, or whatever they can do to make sure my fog's gone for good. No one would bother us if you were on our ship, and you'd make sure we got there safely and our needs were met. And then you'd help us get home again and—you know, it could actually work. We could stall the captain until your supervisor arrived. You could ask him if it was possible. Or maybe you could get stationed by Humana, and we...I could be an ambassador, and you could help us, maybe, try to get our vassal planet status upgraded, and we could become an ally."

She is all enthusiasm and smiles, starlight and hope. Envisioning it is as uplifting as the sensation of floating in orbit with the gravs off.

But then there's the plummet.

"Blades are never stationed anywhere except on Arris Central," I point out, telling myself as much as I explain it to her. "And I can't demand an assignment. If I actively move against Zai, he'll have me killed. 'A weapon in the wrong hands is worse than a broken blade.' I must pledge my loyalty and obey."

Her face falls.

But she's not surprised.

She wriggles her fingers into my clenched fist, and I open it to interlace my fingers with her small, fragile digits. "I know. And I can't stay on this ship because someone's always going to be against us. Last time was Atana, but next time, it'll be the science officer again, and then it'll be someone new that we're not expecting. You'll eventually get an assignment that you have to go to, and I won't be able to go with you, and so this will happen anyway."

She's right.

The chaos in my head calms.

She understands everything so clearly, explains it so thoughtfully. It makes sense. I feel like she's given me an order, even though she's said nothing but what is now obvious. It's obvious because she makes it so.

Catarine sniffs and presses a hand to her mouth, then smiles up at me again through watery eyes. Rains in the desert, sere brown turned to a dark sea. She presses her lips to mine and murmurs, "Can we? One more time?"

I hook a finger in my skinsuit and tear it off in one fluid motion. She drops her bag and falls into me, meshing our mouths, her suit parting to meld our chests. My desperation is equivalent. I must feel her, squeeze her, know every part of her is still here, still with me, still mine. Her breasts swell in my hands and her socket slips beneath my fingers. Her arms wind around my neck. I lift her onto my already hard jack, and she wraps her legs around my waist, hooking ankles. My jack eases home, and she moans.

Then she grips my hair in her hands and forces her fierce gaze into mine. "Why do we fit together so perfectly in every position?"

You were made for me, I want to say, *and I was made by you*.

But it isn't enough.

It isn't nearly enough.

"You can be rougher." She bites my mouth, making me shudder. "I want to feel you everywhere."

I thrust into her, walking her back across the room to fall—controlled, always controlled—onto the cool tile of the closed brazier, my forearms landing first. I cup her fragile skull, and then I pulse into her socket, twisting in the ways I know she likes, hearing her moans turn into gasping cries and then back-arching shivers.

She will never forget me because we will never part. This moment will never end. I will own her and she will own me, for all of space, for all of time.

She arches so hard, I continue the roll, pushing her over onto her stomach, and I drag her hips back to meet my full thrusts. She goes boneless beneath me, quivering, just like the first time I took her on her cruiser, when it was my choice and we were both learning who the other was. Now I know her more intimately than I know myself. And still I am discovering more. The dimples on her lower back just above her perfect buttocks. Did I notice those before? The muss when her hair spills wildly across the tile, the hypnotizing way her breasts swing when I pull her to meet me, the scent of her musk coating my body in lust and utter contentment. I was born to be here, right now, buried balls-deep in this woman from Humana, making her moan my name over and over. I have no other purpose but this.

She turns her head to look back at me, exposing her shoulder. The smooth, warm beige skin whispers to me. I should put my head down, do it now. She will not stop me. It will be done.

I clench my jaw so hard, my teeth ache.

"Sithe." She gasps, sobs. "Sithe."

The release whips through me. I arch over her body. My lips graze her shoulder, the back of her neck, all the golden beige skin I could so easily taste, embed, make mine, and I stop with a kiss because that is what she has allowed me. A gentle kiss. Because I love every part of her, marked or unmarked, even her boundaries.

The room feels very still. We lie, me on my elbows over her, her hunched beneath me.

I will protect you. I promise her silently. *No matter what. Forever.*

She takes a deep, shuddering breath.

I start to rise.

"Sithe." She arrests me with a hand on my hip. "I was

going to say you can do it. I couldn't get the words out because everything was so...intense. But I was trying to say it's okay. You can do the bite. I consent."

Hot blood shoots into me again.

"Ah, you're growing." She wiggles her hips as I'm still buried in her.

I pull out.

She protests with a moan.

I pick her up and sit on the inert brazier cover, now warmed to her body temperature, and set her knees to straddle my hips. My jack pierces her wet folds, and she shudders. "Oh, we should have done this for clegs. Every moment alone. We wasted so much time."

I move, a slow and gentle rhythm in comparison to what we just shared, and her tremors start deep. She gels onto my body like the viscoplastic, hugs my torso, and rests her cheek on my shoulder.

This is where we fit.

Everything is perfect here.

"Bite me," I order.

"I thought...you were going to...mmm...bite me?" Her words are dreamy, interspersed with guttural moans of satisfaction.

"I will. You do it too."

"At the same time?"

"Yeah."

"Okay." She turns her head and opens her mouth, gnawing gently. "Mm."

"Harder."

"Nn?"

"I want to feel you all the way into my bones."

She clamps down.

An urgent sensation tickles the base of my skull. "Harder."

She clenches, and the sensation turns to a sizzling need. Her grip loosens.

"Keep going."

Her words slur against my shoulder. "I taste blood."

"Drink it." I rock her more intensely against my jack, building the sensations in tandem, my need to release and my need for her teeth. "Tear my shoulder off."

She shrugs, gives an adorable growl, and bites me so hard, I can't breathe.

White heat sears me.

I drop my mouth to her skin, sink in, and ravage her pure shoulder, my jack pounding into her socket as I lose control of every nerve bundle. My whole body convulses, and she matches me, shudder for shudder, as my liquid pulses into her channel, unloading my deepest essence.

And then it is done.

I release her shoulder.

I bit her much harder than I meant to, and yet it still feels right. There's no blood, just white indentations.

My shoulder pounds, hot and painful.

She sucks in a deep breath and chuckles. "Oh, H, I bit you so hard. Look at these teeth."

But I don't want to look at them.

I don't want this to end.

We hold each other for long clicks, just resting against each other, soaking in this last feeling of warmth and touching, this last sensation of our weight in each other's arms, our bodies connected.

And then she lifts her head, and liquid drips down my legs. Life moves on, time continues, this moment ends, and we have to disentangle.

"Ugh." She slides to a wobbly stand and tightens her thighs. "I have to get the gel bath again, but there's no time."

The Vanadis ship will be docking now.

I pick up her skinsuit. "Your suit should compensate."

Her brows draw together. "Um, it's a lot of...I don't think it will."

I seal it up to her collar, leaving the bite—my bite —exposed.

She dances as if something is dripping down her legs and she's trying to avoid getting it on the suit. "I told you it... Oh." She stills, then her mouth makes a confused O that's caught between acceptance and displeasure. "Oh, it actually does. That's convenient. Sort of a strange sensation."

I scoop up her bag. "You'll get used to it."

She shoulders the strap, then gasps and pokes at the indentations on her skin where the strap rests. "What did you do to me?"

"I bit you."

"That's what I thought, but with what? A drill press?" She pushes her pinky into one indentation. "Look at this. I can get it up to the cuticle. That's insane." She drops her bag on the brazier cover and rummages in it, muttering about machining tools.

"It's not a tool. It's my recessed teeth."

She stops and looks up. "Recessed teeth?"

I open my mouth and move my tongue out of the way. She peers in. The moment she sees my two recessed teeth lying flat against the floor of my mouth, she recoils. "You have secret snake fangs? And nobody ever told me? Oh, H." She claps her hand on her back, identifying the indentations from my top recessed teeth. "Today I learned the Arrisans have demon teeth. Because you're not terrifying enough with blades that fly out of your wrists."

She hands me the ointment and turns, pulling her hair out of the way.

"The blades are constructed." I pull down her skinsuit again and dot the ointment over the scratches and blemishes her skin seems to attract, especially when I'm less careful, such as just now. The clicks are passing. I finish and offer her the ointment.

"I'm glad I didn't know you had those, because I would have said no." She gestures at the bite. "You forgot these marks."

I didn't forget them. "Does it hurt?"

"No. It's weird and scary, but not painful. At least, I don't think it hurt when you did it, but I was kind of distracted."

I hold the tube, but I can't force myself to smear the ointment. I just can't.

She cocks her head. "Did you want it to hurt?"

No, of course not.

I smear the ointment into the depressions, recap the tube, and hand it to her.

She pulls my skinsuit down to expose my blistering, swollen shoulder. Her teeth made bloody crescents. She shudders and squeezes out ointment. "Let me get some of this on you."

"No." I grab her hand. "Don't waste it."

"It has to hurt."

"This isn't an injury."

"I bit you hard. I bet I bit you harder than you bit me in spite of everything. You don't want to have a scar." She pushes against my hands.

I fold hers over the tube, gentle but unyielding. "It doesn't hurt, and I don't care if it scars. I want a mark. It would be an..." No, that's too heavy to say aloud.

Her smile melts away. "It would be an honor?"

Of course she hears my unspoken words. The thoughts I don't even realize I have.

I nod.

She strokes my cheek gently, then caps the ointment after all. "You had a thought to put a mark on me that couldn't be erased with ointment."

I hadn't thought to do so, I'd just...craved to. Needed to. All this time, without even realizing it, that's what I'd wanted.

"You've already put a mark on me inside." Her voice roughens, and her eyes fill with moisture again. "You saved me so many times. I'll never forget you gave back my clarity."

That is a good feeling.

She finishes repacking.

The captain summons us on the communication panel. "Where are you?"

She looks at me. Small, strong, ready.

I flip her hood, sealing in her secrets, and flip mine as well, then take her hand.

She squeezes my fingers, nervous and excited.

I answer the captain. "On our way."

TWENTY

SITHE

I guide Catarine to the cargo bay. The journey through the ship is uneventful.

That in itself is strange.

The captain has stationed crew members at intersections to safeguard our passage, but the other Arrisans ignore us. Catarine's hood seals in the atmosphere, her scent, and conceals her image. The only one who knows she's beneath the hood is me.

Our return journey passes too quickly. We are directed through the main cargo entrance rather than the narrow personnel hall, and at least as many upper-quadrant officers stand respectfully at attention outside the cargo bay as engineers move inside it.

The Vanadis ship, a cargo-class expedition vessel, slides through the atmosphere veil. Engineers pilot it to the dock.

Captain Falkion himself stands at the end of the dock. His feet are set, shoulders back, and his hands rest in front of him, one clasping the other, wrists pointed inward to his body in confident relaxation. His hood is down. He stares at us with piercing eyes.

Catarine stops beside me.

An engineer pilots the escape pods up from the lower floor and drags them onto the dock behind us. The pods have been dumped into racks, topsy-turvy, and the magnetic dolly beeps a warning as it approaches our section of elevated dock.

We step to the side.

Each pod has been retrofitted with gas intake tubes. The readouts blink, showing that they've been flooded with narco-stasis gas, which means the occupants won't be awake to experience the bouncing that must have occurred when they were jumbled into the racks.

Catarine's index finger lifts, and her lips move soundlessly.

The expeditioner airlock hisses at the slight pressure differential, and their bay doors slide open. A willowy Vanadisan stands inside, wearing their version of a skin-suit; the hood is fixed with bolts, and they sacrifice mobility for greater blunt-force protection. He struts forward.

The engineer guns the dolly, and the pods rattle. The Vanadisan jumps out of the way with a squawk. He recovers and marches to Captain Falkion, protesting with the accent that makes all Vanadisans sound irritated. This time, it's accurate. "What is this? We have no room for this. You said we will take the lessers, not these metal roller balls."

"The lessers are inside."

"Then get them out."

"After you've cleared our nearspace, do what you want."

He mutters, "You said lessers who are humans. These are metal eggs. They are sleeping."

"One is awake." The captain lifts a hand to indicate us. "That one."

"Huh? Where?" He looks past Catarine at me. "Ay... that is...an Arrisan?"

"No, the lesser. In front of him."

Catarine lowers her hood, exposing herself.

"Ah." The Vanadisan straightens and waves his large, flat hand. "Come, come. Onto the ship, lesser. We go now."

She turns to me and clasps my hands in front of her chest. "Thank you for everything."

"Now, lesser." The Vanadisan shows off his wrists imperiously.

I tilt my head to expose my face so he can see my glare.

He drops his hand and stumbles back. "In a moment, sure."

The dolly beeps as it exits the Vanadisan expeditioner, racks empty. The engineer's gaze sears us. Everyone, it seems, is looking.

Because of the hood.

I remove one of my hands from her grip and cup her upper arm, drawing her nearer, then stroke her long hair. It is a show of possession, but I also have a need to feel the fine brown threads, soft and fluffy, one more time.

She swallows. The rims of her eyes redden, and moisture gathers at the corners. "I'll never forget this."

Neither will I. "If you need anything, contact me."

"Oh, yeah." She reaches up and touches the back of her neck. "I still have the tracker. Not that it helped in the engineering office."

"Shielding."

"Right. Did you need it back?"

"No, keep it."

"I guess it's only going to work in nearspace anyway."

She lowers her hand to mine again. Her lips wobble between a smile and sadness. "If we're ever in the same nearspace, look for me."

"I will."

She nods and worries her lower lip between her teeth. "Um, I guess I should go." She takes a deep breath and pats my hand. "Goodbye, Sithe."

"Goodbye."

Her fingers loosen around mine as she turns away.

No.

This is wrong, this is—

She turns back and lifts my own hand to push back my hood, her lips aimed to press against my cheek. But I follow her movement and capture her mouth with mine.

Catarine melts to me, opening to my comfort, her tongue catching my thrusts and plunging into my mouth in turbulent desperation. This is what is right. Her body meshed to mine, her gasp my pant, our limbs entwined, an endless spiral of us combined.

And then she draws back and rests on her heels.

Her lips are damp with my liquid, her eyes bright and active from my stroking, her golden-beige cheeks flushed with readiness.

And I am ready for her too.

She flips on her hood.

Because mine has fallen back, I can no longer see into hers. For the first time, her face is fully shadowed from mine.

She squeezes my hands and whispers, "Thank you."

My throat closes. I cannot respond.

She turns away.

I take a step to follow, then rock back on my heel.

She stops before the captain. "Thank you for arranging this transport."

"Get on it," he says stiffly.

"Was that really every pod?"

His chin dips. "Wasn't it?"

"I think...I could be wrong, but I think some pods are missing."

He catches the attention of the rack pilot idling his dolly by the mini grav tube. "I ordered you to get all the pods off my ship."

The engineer gestures at his machinery. "You see any in my racks? You think I'm hiding one in my overalls?" He grips his overalls at the lower abdomen and pulls them away from his body. "My package isn't that big."

Catarine looks down, then faces the captain once more. "Promise me that nothing bad will happen to Sithe."

He squints at her. Since his hood is also off, he can't see her any better than I can, and that must be disconcerting for a man of his stature. "What?"

"Don't punish him."

"Punish? I have no control over... That's the role of the general master." His frown deepens. "Why do you care?"

She hikes the loop of her pack higher up her fully covered shoulder. "I could explain, but it would take too much time."

He looks at me as if I have the answer.

But I feel empty. Like this is happening to someone else. The man in my skinsuit is reporting my sensations back to me in another room. I am unmoored.

"You're a strange lesser," the captain says to Catarine.

"No." The tone of her smile becomes richer. "I am typical of Humana, actually."

The Vanadisan calls, "Come, lesser. Do not irritate the Arrisans. We leave."

She crosses the dock and steps onto the Vanadisan ship.

The Vanadisan moves his leg to kick at her to hurry up.

I step forward.

The captain steps in front of me.

Catarine disappears inside.

The Vanadisan turns the switch on his airlock. He sees us standing nearer and jumps in surprise. The airlock closes, sealing him in.

I dislike how he treats Catarine.

I dislike it very much.

"Zai is on his way." The captain gestures behind me. "Go to your assigned tube and await his summons."

I barely hear him.

Loaders tow the Vanadisan ship to the atmosphere veil. It disappears through and is gone.

My pulse increases.

I become aware of all the crew in this area. The engineers idling the dolly, pooling around this dock, forming a barrier to reach my sinusoid.

There's no reason to cross all these observers and go after her.

She's on her way to her original destination with her shipmates.

And I'm on my way to my tube to await the summons of Zai.

This is how things must be.

If I repeat it enough, I'll begin to believe it.

I slide back a pace.

And from this distance I realize the captain has turned his wrist, the curved edge his blade out, ready to gut me unawares.

I lift my chin so he can meet my eyes.

He doesn't avert his. "Are you going to your tube?"

I give the barest nod.

He retracts his blade and covers that hand with the other. "Good."

Well. That's interesting.

I turn, fully taking in just how many different ways the captain has me under observation. Two engineers pretending to work on another ship with their hull-cutters suddenly busy themselves in their tool chests. The first-quadrant officers stand at attention just outside. All our escorts to ensure we reached the cargo bay. So many officers, and all loyal to Falkion.

I have had a bad practice of running into situations beyond my estimates lately. This would have been another one.

If I were going to steal my ship, then I should do so intelligently. Think over the problem. Review everything about the cargo bay and who's assigned here until the answer moves into focus.

Like any assignment.

But Catarine is not my assignment.

I walk around the cargo bay, choosing to leave from the smaller personnel hall. It's a more direct route to the crew quarters where I'm assigned. It also gives me a chance to study the environment.

I shouldn't.

Although I am here and my body is here, a small part of my mind is on the expeditioner with Catarine, voyaging out onto an alternate path.

Which is closed to me.

I stand before the personnel exit and look back at the captain, the observers, my ship one last time.

The emptiness inside unsettles me.

But it will go.

Yes.

Honestly? In a short time, I'll forget all of this. I'll forget the feeling of Catarine nestled against my body. I'll forget the feeling of choices that I have. I'll forget the questions that were raised about who I can be or what I can have. I'll go back to being the weapon arm of the empire, the unsheathed blade that executes all who would stand against us.

Atana swaggers up to me, scabs on his broken nose, a smoking igniter punk clamped between his teeth. A small device is tucked under his arm. "So, she wasn't your Amante after all."

I would still like to kill him for his role in hurting Catarine. My blades jump under my skin. They are sore but functional. Hopefully, Zai won't ask me to demonstrate my readiness, but I'd be willing to do it again if I could have a fair chance at Atana. "What?"

"You let her go."

"And?"

"It's in the story."

"What about the story?"

He grins, and the igniter punk lifts. "You didn't read to the end?"

The...end?

Atana hands me my data tablet. The crack is barely visible. The repair has made a small scar that will smooth away in time. He positively beams, thrilled to know something I don't. "Pleasant reading, Sithe."

He ambles away, his breath making a musical tone against the igniter.

I will punch him harder in the face next time.

The captain is still watching us. Watching me.

For nothing.

I pivot on my heel and stride out of the cargo bay.

The implant tells me the most direct route to my tube, but I remember the way from before, and this time, the grav tube to the crew quarters is in perfect running order. The dreadnought is ready to move on. It will surely go as soon as we receive Zai.

I reach the dorm and cycle through my pre-resting routine with sharp efficiency, then slide into my assigned tube.

I should recite mantras until Zai summons me or I fall asleep.

Instead, I pull out the data tablet. It opens to the last story Catarine was reading to me before her kidnapping. I flip to the end.

Grundi picked up her jawbone and added it to the pile in his bag. His journey had just begun.

Huh?

I flip back to the start of this story. Amante finds a hole in the mist forest. Grundi is too busy sleeping after his great feast to explore it with her.

A small number floats above the text.

I press it.

Gray words appears over the top of the story. *This is one of the very few times Grundi denies Amante aid.*

Okay. These must be the scholarly notes Catarine read to help us understand what was happening. I click the number again, and the gray text fades. The story continues.

After a while, Grundi comes out of his food coma and realizes he hasn't seen Amante in some time. A small animal —another gray note identifies it as a grain-eating louse—tells Grundi that the river god, angry that Amante taught

Grundi how to outsmart him, tripped Amante and then dropped her into the hole, where she was torn apart and devoured by demons. Grundi goes on a great rampage that devastates the mist forest. The river god, now properly frightened, tells him that if he brings Amante's body back, the river god will restore her life with his water. Grundi descends into the hole and punches the first demon, who regurgitates Amante's jawbone.

I read the final line again.

Grundi picked up her jawbone and added it to the pile in his bag. His journey had just begun.

What kind of an ending is this?

All the other stories ended with Grundi and Amante growing ninety-six times their previous size and destroying whoever stood in their way. This is unfinished. One punch of one demon? There should be at least ninety-six punches of ninety-six demons.

Another small number floats behind the last letter. I tap it with irritation.

The next hundred tales describe Grundi's journey through the underworld. We are in the process of translating and annotating them. Sincerely, the Second Harvard Restored School of Arrisan Mythology.

Atana told me to read this story to irritate me.

I rest the data tablet on my chest, stretch, and recite my starting mantras for calm, for control, for discipline.

The tube quietly beeps. The captain's voice emerges from the private intercom. "You are summoned to the conference room immediately."

I am not calm.

This is not good.

I slide out of the tube, grab the overhead bar to pivot upright, and lightly drop twenty boot-lengths to the ground.

The data tablet isn't mine. It was assigned to the room I appropriated. All that's assigned to my person is my skinsuit.

I leave the data tablet on a common table for someone else to return and head to the captain's private conference room.

TWENTY-ONE

CATARINE

My shoulder twinges.

I scratch Sithe's bite mark, digging my finger under the skinsuit.

The puncture is now raised and red.

Strange.

Usually, the ointment works so well. Is this an allergic reaction? I have a hard time believing I'm allergic to Sithe after all the saliva we shared.

Was there something inside those crazy weird snake teeth that he was so casual about? Like, he knew about them all along, but they sure never showed up in any schoolwork or training materials.

Maybe they were in the archive I downloaded to the university. The empire has never denied us information, assuming we could do nothing useful with it, but they haven't bothered to give us deep or relevant details either. Like the entry on Humana, lots of their technology skips from the stone age to the intergalactic age and assumes we have the processing power to create resources not locally available.

But if we become an ally, that will change.

I sit quietly on a large tool chest off to the side of the cargo bay where my new hosts left me.

The Vanadisans are still arguing over what to do about the pods.

I know a little bit about their planet from reading early in the voyage when I could still put together thoughts. They are a birdlike people, lighter than they look, with graceful swooping movements. I think there's diversity on Vanadis just like there is on Humana. Different colorations and patterns. It's amazing how similar we all are, honestly.

"Heavy-footed Arrisans," the smaller, more wiry one mutters as he pushes one pod to the top of his pyramid with three gravity-assist handles. He wears something that looks like a trench coat with more volume. "They think we're the lessers. They push us around."

The Vanadisan who ushered me onto the ship is taller, and I consider him the commander. "What are they still waiting for? This suit is heavy." He taps the external viewscreen. The personal evac-jet he dragged out rests against the wall by his knees. "Go. You are done here. Be gone."

"You could take the short-hop orbiter outside," the handler says, waving at the two-man ship parked in the middle of the cargo bay. When their fingers are all pressed together, the seams fade, and their hands look like paddles. "No suit required."

"Eh, we got trapped inside for a few shifts when the expeditioner broke down. It still smells."

An intercom crackles, and a third voice trills out something in their language.

The commander stabs the communication button and whistles right back, then switches to Arrisan Standard. "You want to tell Fuzig we didn't search the wreckage? Or you want to go out and search it with the gunship watching your every move?"

The intercom trills some more.

"That's what I thought." The commander lets out a breath, and a hollow reed noise echoes in the cargo bay. He sticks out a long finger at the handler. "We should crack those pods. Take out the patients and dump the containers. Then I have an excuse to go out."

"If we crack them, they wake up. We have to feed them, clean their messes."

The commander grunts. "We have to crack one. Fuzig needs to begin. How can we identify his first patient? We must crack them."

I stand. "I can identify patients for you."

They both look at me as though they've forgotten I'm here.

"Identify them?" the commander repeats. "Inside the closed pods?"

"Yes, I can look through the window and see who they are."

The pyramid has been arranged so some windows face into the ground or the walls.

The handler rolls his head around on his neck like he has no bones. "Why did you not say this earlier?"

"I did."

They ignore my answer, jostling me out of the way while they rearrange the pyramid again.

I really wish I could have received the talking points from Representative Khan. I'm sure she would have told me how to deal with the Vanadisans. It was ultimately helpful in speaking with the Arrisans to know not to bargain or beg. Would the Vanadisans react better to bargains? The same work can be accomplished. It's all a matter of phrasing.

The commander ushers me to the first pod. "Okay, lesser, identify it."

"I'm Catarine."

"Not you." Then he marks something off on his folding data tablet. "Yes, okay. Catarine... Ah. Mental stupid. I understand." He looks at me pityingly and slows his speech. "You, lesser. Identify. Who inside Pod 2851?"

I fold my hands in front of me. "I do suffer from mind fog when I'm afflicted by my illness, but I'm not suffering those effects right now. You can speak to me like another Vanadisan. I'll understand."

The commander whistles through his nose. "Mental stupid."

The handler echoes the sound, resting an elongated elbow on the overturned pod. "Yep, mental stupid."

Perhaps this is not the way to communicate with them.

I really wish Sithe were here.

Even on Humana, there are people who won't listen unless you make them.

But Sithe isn't here. I'll just have to do my best.

I peer through the window. Dark ebony lids regally closed, springy finger coils that take so much time and patience, hands resting in her lap as though she were already sitting in her destined throne. I can almost hear her voice. *Assert yourself, Cat. You've got the smarts. Quit waiting for your opportunity. Get into the ring and knock it out.* The kingmaker.

"Allie," I tell the Vanadisan.

He marks it down. "Next."

I peer inside and tell him, moving through the pods one by one. "Nisha. Maeve. Graciela. Fahari. Lilja."

A small pinch of tension releases from my shoulders as I identify them.

These women are in a comatose sleep, but I have saved them. We're saved.

Most are secured with the hazard straps, so it's easy to look through the tiny portal and see them passed out. One or two weren't strapped in, and they're splayed in wonky directions. I worry about them, and at the end of the tally, my worst fears are realized.

I draw out the last name. "Salome."

The commander looks up. "Sure?"

"Yes."

"You sound unsure. Too long hesitation."

"Because we're missing four people."

"Who?"

"Captain Zeerah, for one."

He waves his fingers. "That is no importance. She is no patient."

"Right, but she had a contract." Captain Zeerah must still be on the *Spiderwasp*. And after I asked Captain Falkion whether he'd gotten everyone on board. He'd said yes, but he'd lied.

"We're also missing..." I tap my fingers together, shuffling through the faces that were around me for so many weeks.

If they can't cure me, I'll take this dagger and cut out my heart. "Noemi."

He huffs as he notes it. "Patient eighty-one. Too bad."

Oh, Catarine, your cat ears made a funny indent in your bangs. Did you know that kale has every essential vitamin a growing girl needs? Come here, your tag is showing. "Lia."

"Patient sixty-five."

And I didn't see a tell-tale helmet. *You know, if we*

crash-landed on a hostile alien planet, you'd actually want me around to hold off predators. You don't have to be faster than them, just faster than me, and since I pass out every time I sneeze, I'm like the perfect life preserver. "Esme."

"Aye. Patient twenty-three?"

"She's probably just outside near the wreckage. They probably all are."

He raises his voice, ignoring me. "Chuk. We don't have Patient twenty-three, sixty-five, or eighty-one."

"Twenty-three?" The handler drops the pod he was angling back into place with a loud clack, and they share a furious conversation in their language.

I don't know what's so special about the ingénue over the housewife or the ace, but they seem to be focused on Esme due to how often her number is repeated amid the flurry of other noise-words.

Vanadisan is a nasal-tonal language that vibrates parts inside the nose that I don't think should vibrate. Most people from Humana don't have much of a problem with Arrisan Standard. I know people who study other languages, such as Irubarys, which requires fixing an air bladder under your tongue because otherwise, it's impossible to make the sounds. Vanadis has a breathy whistle, and it's possible for us to speak it, but our anatomy is just different enough to make it difficult.

Humans are completely incompatible with great swaths of the universe, which makes it even more amazing that I was so compatible with Sithe.

A sick ache fills my chest.

I think I'm going to cry really hard as soon as we get underway. Right now, the dreadnought's still so close and I'm still so uncertain about the Vanadisans, but once I can get back to a bunk, hug my knees, and close my eyes, they'll produce the Second Flood down my cheeks, guaranteed.

I don't know how my mom ever stopped crying over the tragedies, but she's seen so much. I have a lot of respect for her fortitude.

The Vanadisans fall silent and hover over a communication device.

Oh. Hey, we're in nearspace with the dreadnought, which has intergalactic comms. "Is it possible to contact Humana?"

The commander glances at me, then turns away without answering.

I really, really wish that I would have heard those talking points.

A burst of crunchy whistles emerges from the comm. They respond stiffly, then the viewscreen darkens and they squawk at each other. The handler secures the pods with cheerful energy. The commander throws off his space suit, revealing a puffy trench coat, and stows the evac-jet.

The commander strides farther out of the cargo bay into his ship. "Come, lesser."

Wait. "You're not going to rescue the patients outside?"

"I said come."

I set my feet. "But what about the patients who are missing?"

"Fuzig recalls us," he calls from down the hall. "Now I have an excuse not to go outside."

"But the others..."

"They will die, or they are already dead." He returns shaking a small canister and shrugs. "Who cares?"

"I do."

"You're mental stupid, lesser."

"No." I represented my shipmates to the Arrisans.

Somehow, I got us all here. Now I will represent them to the Vanadisans, who are supposed to be our saviors, and I'll do my best even without knowing the talking points. "You want the missing people."

"I want nothing."

"Ah." I lift my finger. "You want me to go to our lab. I want you to rescue my friends. We can work together and accomplish both things."

He squints at me. "What, you think you are Arrisan now? You're going to kick me around?" He and the handler both make strange hoots. He clacks his lips at me. "You are a lesser."

"Well, I want to be an ally."

"Oh-ho, an ally? Humana?" The two Vanadisans whistle louder. Laughter.

"Humana ally," the handler chortles.

"You want to call my cousin?" the commander hoots. "On the Premier Council?"

"Call Fuzig, call the Premier," the handler parrots.

They shake and hoot.

I guess it's good that Representative Khan didn't expect me to change their opinion of Humana in a single interaction.

"Enough. We begin." The commander lifts the cylinder to show it to me.

I step closer to parse the small glyphs. I know a little Vanadisan. Their written script is easier. *Hazard*.

He depresses the top button.

Liquid sprays me in the face.

I jerk up my hands and stumble back. "What?"

The liquid burns my throat. I cough and rapidly draw in a big mouthful. My eyes water, my nose drips, and I feel like I've just gone over the edge of a cliff. My heart races, pumping the burning sensation through my body, down to my toenails and up into my brain.

Pepper spray?

But then it all goes numb.

The world recedes.

And this is infinitely worse.

I know this numb sensation.

I remember the burning deep inside, a fire licking at my veins with urgent need while my mind tumbled across soft, foamy clouds.

My stomach roils, dread bashing against panic.

I scrub my face hard enough to rip off skin.

"No scratching." The commander prods me in the lower back. "Go to the lab now."

I resist. "What did you do?"

"We sprayed you for the examination."

"Why?"

"The Arrisan seed, it called the small amount of lusteal in your body to a controlled place." He gestures at my midsection. "I sprayed you with a three hundred times concentration so the urge of the metal spills out and travels all over, especially up to your brain, and controls you again."

The wave of lust rolls up my body. Sweat drips down the back of my knees. It lubricates between my thighs. And whatever is in the...skinsuit...yes, that's what it's called...is utterly unable to handle my sudden furnace.

But...

Sithe is not in the lab.

Nothing I need is in the lab.

The lab is bad. Bad for me, bad for Sithe.

No matter what, I must resist going to the lab.

"Why does nothing go today?" The commander shakes the spray. "You don't go, the Arrisans don't go, my pilot doesn't go. Should I spray you again? The metal is precious."

"Fuzig has more," the handler says.

"He says not to waste it. We have no luck stealing it, yes? And Fuzig's supplier has too many demands for this little metal, but any more and the controllers become suspicious."

"Maybe the spray takes time to activate," the handler says.

"The others obeyed right away."

"She neutralized her metal with Arrisan seed. Maybe a lot of seed still inside."

"Hmm. Oh, Humana patients follow male genitalia." The commander prods the handler. "Show her."

The handler opens his trench coat to expose his skin. "Follow?"

Vanadisans are biologically incompatible with humans. The ingénue told me about it. They have a...a....what was I saying? Pouch babies. Marsupial stage.

The handler's genitals are fuzzy, pliable, and the end is forked like a bundle of pipe cleaners.

The poor other Humana patients.

I know their cravings. I've impaled myself on bed posts. Closet door handles. Anything and everything remotely possible to give me relief. Nothing satisfied.

Nothing was Sithe.

And right now, thank everything, he is all I desire.

I have never been less attracted to a phallic object in my life.

The handler waves his pipe cleaners. "Lesser, come to the lab. Should we try?"

"Disgusting," the commander twitters.

"Eh, why not? The metal makes her crazed. Here, lesser." He grabs my hand.

I pull back. "I have bloodworms."

The handler freezes.

"You...what?" The commander gapes at me. "Bloodworms?"

"Everywhere." I hold up my hands, wrist-first, in a threatening gesture. "I'm infested."

The handler quickly fastens his trench coat, and they both give me a wide berth.

"Come," the commander tries again. "I give you a vaccine in the lab."

"No. There's something else you need to do. Something about my shipmates..."

They watch the fog roll over me.

My thoughts disintegrate.

When I first battled the mental fog, I recited numbers over and over, things I should know but suddenly couldn't place. I sought out long passages with complicated concepts and panicked because I could no longer hold all the ideas, then not even two ideas. Then, not even one.

"You infected me," I repeat, trying to wind back my thoughts the same old way.

"To study the metal in your blood. We can't study if you're cured." He prods me with a distant kicking motion. "Come. We cure you. I get the vaccine."

Okay, so they're still going to cure me. They had to spray me so they could give me the cure.

Does that make sense?

I can't tell anymore.

The commander leads me down a short, dim hallway to a large room with a metal slab. "Get on."

"Skinsuit," the handler says.

"Yes, need that off."

The two Vanadisans yank on my suit.

I want it off. I want my skin sliding against another male. I want him taking me, reckless, furious. I want...

Not these two.

I do not want these males. "Stop."

"Need off," the commander insists. "For the cure."

Oh.

I drop the skinsuit from my right shoulder. The left still itches. The commander touches a skinny cylinder to my biceps. *Hiss.* "You should have been vaccinated before you left orbit."

"Humana," the handler reminds him. "A food production planet."

"Yes. Okay." The commander pulls on my skinsuit, trying to pull it lower. "Take off. All the way. It will interfere with the saw."

"Saw?" Overhead hangs a rotating saw just like in the science office. "I don't want the saw."

"We cut you open just a little, watch how the metal moves through your blood, attaches to your nerve endings, penetrates the brain."

"But you cured me."

"Of bloodworms. Now we can touch your lusteal blood, drain it, apply bleach."

"Bleach will kill me." I'm fairly certain of that.

"And then the examination is complete." He tugs my arm. "Off. It does not come. Chuk, the seam. Find it."

They work together on the suit.

I must be missing something. "You're not supposed to kill me. You're supposed to help me."

"Help you? No. You help us."

"I do?"

"Arrisans don't share the metal. But you, somehow, you

have the metal inside. A small amount. Somehow." The commander stands back frowning at the skinsuit. "The metal in you makes the Arrisans crazy. We study the metal in you, we develop a weapon, we destroy Arris." He flips on a light. "Vanadis rules the empire."

The overhead light is blinding.

I shield my eyes. "What about the others?"

"When your body gives out, we start again with...Allie."

I haven't saved anyone. I've delivered them into the hands of our new science officers.

My skinsuit separates and pools at my feet.

"Ay, what's this?" The commander prods my inflamed shoulder. "No medical record."

Red streaks away from Sithe's bite. Four raised puncture marks. The red lines form a spiral blade pattern that's almost a...art. Image. Thing. Ah! Tribal tattoo.

Sithe's bite is on fire.

Yes, Sithe is what I need right now.

I crave a male, one male. The one who fixed me before. Cleared my head.

Mine.

He marked me. Made me his.

I want no other male. No other Arrisan. No other will ever satisfy me.

Never again.

He is my weapon. My shield.

My warrior.

See? I can be clearheaded when I'm getting my fix.

And now?

My fix is Sithe.

I reach up to the hairline above the back of my neck and press his button. I press it so hard.

Ding.

The intercom makes a noise.

"Ay?" The handler brings up a viewscreen. "Skinsuit?"

The viewscreen displays our nearspace. There's the dreadnought.

Then, it's gone.

Sithe left.

"Hmph. Strange." The handler closes the screen again.

"We're on our way." The commander pats his chest proudly. "Back to Vanadis. We will rule the empire. I will be the hero."

Oh, Sithe didn't leave. We did.

"Fuzig will have the recognition," the handler says. "Unless the experiment fails because the patient has a shoulder poison. And bloodworms."

"No bloodworms now. And yes, the red marks. I will identify them, then perform the experiments." The commander pushes me into a small containment room.

My head nearly brushes the ceiling. I can take five small steps in each direction.

Through the glass, the handler arranges a box of laser saw attachments next to their operating slab.

Both Vanadisans hum cheerfully as they prepare to cut me open.

Did the tracking button work? Were we still close enough?

And if he got my plea, is Sithe coming?

TWENTY-TWO

SITHE

The discipline conference with Zai is worse than any nightmare.

I sit on an open-backed bench.

Zai stands across from me, his triple-blades crossed, his fury so cold, it freezes me in place. "Which is it? You and Atana are collaborating to weaken the blades and collapse the empire for your own reasons? Or you decided to execute the traitors who approached you on your own, before I could interrogate them and find out how deep your treason runs?"

Every muscle tenses.

Sweat pours down my back.

Zai extends his central pike. The deadly piercing tip waves in front of my throat. "Which is it?"

"Neither." My voice cracks.

His lids lower to half. "Come on, Sithe. You really expect me to believe you executed those engineers in a training accident?"

Zai looks worse than he did on our last visual contact. His cheeks are sunken, his skin grayer than usual with exhaustion, and his lips more bloodless. Even the whites of his eyes have yellowed, as though his body is falling apart beneath him, despite his will to continue.

He could still fillet me before I could blink.

And I need him to think well of me.

He's the only one I know in this universe who always does the right thing.

But everything I can think to say makes me look stupid and weak.

I have to stick to the truth.

It's hard to swallow. "Atana challenged me to a ranked fight."

"And how did he do that if you were in Arcturin's room? Where I ordered you to remain?"

Everything about this is bad. "His engineers entered my room."

"Then why didn't you execute them in your room?"

"They came while I was meeting with you and Falkion." I have no choice but to be honest. It's not smart, and it's not going to make anything better, but I am no Catarine. She knows how to explain things so they make sense. I don't. "They stole from me."

"Stole?" He squints at me. "From you?"

"And I had to get what they stole back."

Zai abruptly seats himself on the bench opposite me. He is tall, angular, bony. And he has always been so wise. But right now, he's looking at me like I'm the mystery. "Why didn't you contact me to explain?"

"There wasn't time."

"How is that possible?"

"Because Atana was going to damage her. Did damage her."

"Her?"

"My...Catarine."

"Your Catarine?"

"From Humana."

"The lesser?" Zai tilts his head one way, then the other. "Of all the lies, this is the strangest one."

"Captain Falkion told you about her."

"Yes, and I asked him if he was compromised too."

I take a deep breath and let it out. "It's the truth."

Zai tips his head back against the wall and stares up at the ceiling. "I've always liked you, Sithe. I can tell you that now since it isn't going to matter very soon."

A cold, hard ball rolls in my guts. "I didn't commit treason."

"You're not a complex thinker, but whoever recruited you to betray me could have come up with a better lie."

Zai casually extends his pike to a high ceiling panel and tucks in a dangling wire with precise control. As his central blade extends longer than his forearm, the flat side-blades emerge. At the tips, they curve back toward his body like deadly ribbons, and he flexes each one individually in his sheaths like terrifying fingers. He can stab with his central blades, but he can carve and flay with his side blades. Where is the weakness? It's hard to understand why we ever changed away from his class's blade style.

"I'll interrogate Atana next," he muses. "I thought he was too perverse to get taken in by conspirators, but even I can be wrong."

"I'm not lying."

"You want to know how I know you are?"

I nod.

He retracts his triple- blades with a *shink* and tosses over a data tablet. It's open to a child psychological profile.

"I always study the profiles of my blades, the behaviors,

especially in childhood. That is who you are, at your base, before the training. You want to know yours?"

Oh, this is mine?

"You never took any toys. That's why I assigned you the richest, rarest stolen goods to retrieve. You never took any for yourself. You were never even tempted. Assigning you the right missions led you to your current ranking."

I read the highlighted portion of the profile.

When an older or larger child takes Sithe's toys, he sits with his back to the wall and watches until the others lose interest. He never retaliates, never protests. He waits to play with it again after the others have left.

I don't remember that time well.

But I do remember the feeling of absolute giddiness when I got blades. I endlessly flexed them in my forearms. They were a part of me that no one else could take. They're fused into my bones. I will slice anyone who tries.

And Zai is right.

The assignments I excel at are always getting something back. The monetary value isn't important. It belongs to the empire, and is therefore, mine.

Mine.

The Vanadis ship is still outside. It's visible on one of the many screens Zai has used to create a small command center to try to catch me in my supposed lie.

Catarine's still nearby.

The urge wells up in me.

Distract Zai. Slip out of this room. Jog down the hall to the grav tube; make it look like you're on a mission. Pick up overalls from the welder's bin outside the cargo bay and carry a hull-slicer to the sinusoid. If anyone notices, cut them down and slice through the outer hull. In the chaos, escape.

I force it back down.

Catarine chose to go. She asked to go. Her will is important. It matters more than my desire.

"My assignment strategy led to your current ranking," Zai continues, "and your current vulnerability as a target. So tell me." He leans forward and extends his central blade at the viewscreen displaying the images of the high commanders. "Which one of these men turned you? Will you tell me, or shall I explain how each of them is unworthy of your protection?"

I steel myself.

Zai begins to talk. "These men do not deserve your loyalty. Listen."

The things he tells me are horrifying.

The men of the High Command are honored military generals who've surpassed every ordinary ranking. They craft the assignments I execute. Zai sends us out at his discretion, but always to fulfill the will of the emperor—who is guided by these men.

And yet, they do not possess great and noble desires.

I wish to serve the empire. The origin of my orders has never mattered to me, only executing them.

But now I find out—in gross detail—that I am wielded by a weak, floppy arm filled with conflict, directionless posturing, and petty revenge. These rulers have small and selfish hungers, appetites like a...well, like a lesser.

This is the worst realization of all.

"Yes, they behave just like lessers, all of them." Zai studies me carefully as I gape over this conclusion. "You understand well. Does this kind of truth interest you? Perhaps investigating the High Command and uncovering their worst activities is your future."

Is it?

It isn't how I imagined my future.

Sometimes, I do something new, and everything makes sense, like sheathing my blades the first time. The weight in my forearms felt right. Enforcing the will of the empire with them was what I was meant to do. These blades were missing pieces of myself that I hadn't known that I needed.

After I got the sheaths and I walked through the halls, no one bothered me. They kept their distance, and that was how I liked it.

I rub my thumbs over the skin flaps.

"You could retire your blades," Zai says, reading my thoughts. "The high commanders battle each other with clever words. You must outthink them."

This is ideal work for Catarine. She's influenced every Arrisan she's encountered, and she has done so with only words. She understands and observes more than I do. More than I want to.

You could come with me. Just blow off everything and come.

She made that offer.

I should have considered it more seriously.

"You still won't reveal the traitors? Even after knowing the truth?" Zai sighs, then straightens abruptly and barks, "Do you pledge yourself to the empire?"

I jolt. "Yes."

"Do you pledge to obey the grand master of the Arsenal instantly and without question?"

It's the same question they ask us when we join the blades. My shoulders pull back. "I so pledge."

"Then reveal the reason you executed those engineers."

"They attacked Catarine."

He blinks. Then he nods slowly and taps his fingertips together. "Okay. That's your final answer?"

It's the truth, so it is.

"Very well. I have your next assignment." He takes back the data tablet and scrolls.

Next...assignment?

I'm not going to be tried for treason, summarily judged, or executed right in this room?

Truly?

"Your assignment is to infiltrate House Orunfax and confirm his loyalty." Zai hands me back the data tablet with the assignment outlined. "You'll be placed in his personal guard on Arris Central. The last three blades assigned to this position were killed, and I have yet to find out whether they were victims of rival commanders or of Orunfax himself."

Oh.

This is not good.

Zai goes over the details.

I listen respectfully.

But my feeling is bitter.

When I last took the pledge, the only enemies I ever considered were the Harsi.

Now I must prepare to fight Arrisans.

If I must fight them anyway, why did I not escape with Catarine?

My implant tingles.

My skinsuit is in nearspace, moving away.

I still.

Normally, this message is supposed to ding on the nearest comm screen, but the screens all remain silent.

Have I imagined this message because I've wanted it so badly?

"Sithe." Zai looks deeply into my eyes. He must know I haven't been listening. "Your place is here. Accept my final assignment. Obey me."

I nod to show my understanding.

He returns to his complicated terms, tapping the data tablet.

My heart thumps hard.

This is my place.

I am a blade.

There is nowhere I can go with Catarine and keep her safe. We will always be hunted. Even worse now that Zai has told me his secrets.

The Vanadisan ship fires up and disappears from the viewscreen.

She's gone.

My knees rattle. My blades nudge my wrists.

She's gone, and this is my place.

This is...

The story.

Amante and Grundi.

She calls me because she needs me. If I don't go to her right now, she'll be torn to pieces, and I won't be there. And I can't find her later. I don't know any river god to put her back together again or bring her back to life with his waters.

Zai stops his speaking and looks at me again. "Are you paying attention?"

"I have a question." I point to the viewscreen farthest away. "If you doubt High Commander Orunfax's loyalty, why don't you tell the emperor?"

"Because if I do and the emperor decides not to act, Orunfax will have me removed from the Arsenal."

"He can't do that."

"There are ways." Zai stands and walks to the far viewscreen that shows the chart about who rules the Arsenal if the grand master is suddenly incapacitated. "More ways than you'd think."

"The blades would rebel."

"Not necessarily." His back is to me. "I've considered it from every angle."

"Only blades can replace a general master. And choosing a new one requires ranking fights, trials. Tests."

"There are ways to circumvent the usual methods. Let me explain."

I actually want to sit and hear this. I want to argue with him. The High Command can't just replace the general master. Not even the emperor can do it on a whim. Not without a huge uproar.

But my genuine incredulity fuels the deception.

"In every successorship system, there are failsafes." Zai twists the viewscreen frame one way, then the other, as though trying to force the pieces into place.

I silently rise and back toward the exit. The door whooshes open. I freeze.

"The most obvious exception is what to do when we're attacked by the Harsi and, say, I'm killed in the first wave."

I turn and walk through the door.

"But equally plausible is if..."

The door closes.

No guards stand here. The captain has kept our meeting quiet.

Still pretending that this is a normal maiden voyage on a very abnormal dreadnought.

I flip my hood and stride into the occupied hall. Purposeful but not too fast.

This is what I've trained for.

Every time I rush headlong after Catarine, I make mistakes.

Because every time I rush after Catarine, I attempt something I have never tried before.

But even though I made mistakes, I accomplished my goal.

Every time.

She is mine.

This is what I'm good at.

Taking back what is mine.

And I will use my skill to serve the empire.

Except the empire is not my number one priority any longer.

She is.

TWENTY-THREE

ZAI

"So you see, Sithe, there are almost as many ways to remove me from the Arsenal as there are ways to remove you." I turn to gauge my new protégé's reaction. "Sithe?"

The conference bench is empty.

He's gone.

How long?

The pounding of my headache, barely contained for the last few clegs, presses on my skull. My vision blurs. I rest my weight on my palms.

It's devastating that my enemies have gotten to Sithe.

He's the one blade who never worried me.

If they can get to him, they can get to anyone.

They can get to me.

And I want to be wrong about him so badly. I've taken risks, stupid risks, hoping against hope he'll prove his loyalty.

I, who once heard the whisper of a blade ejecting from a sheath at fifty paces in a busy spaceport, did not hear him leave. In my weakened state, Sithe could have walked up and slit my throat.

I close all viewscreens and tidy the data tablet. This action is supposed to give me time to think. But I am so, so tired.

Captain Falkion enters, waits until the door closes for privacy, and announces, "Arcturin din Orunfax wishes to speak to you."

Of course he does.

I'd hoped to avoid this, but knew it was inevitable. He's the kind of man who'll check the all-ranking list every other cleg just to make sure he's still on top, so he would have seen when my name showed up on the local listing.

But the matter of treason comes first. "Where's Sithe?"

"I'll summon him." The captain taps his forehead to access his shipwide implant, then lowers his hand, clearly remembering that this private room blocks all ordinary comm signals. The only kind of wave that might get through is something totally useless like a skinsuit tracker. "Where did you assign him?"

"We were not quite finished setting the assignment."

The captain pauses to process this. "He left without being dismissed?"

"Find him, Falkion. Quietly."

Falkion dips his head in assent and exits smartly. The door closes.

I'm alone.

I allow myself to slump against the wall bench and rest my head against the unforgiving steel.

There's a reason Falkion has become a captain at his age. I wish I had his energy. This job has crushed it out of me, squeezing and twisting and wringing me out until now

I'm a papery husk of my former self. I'm not much older than him. I too was considered something of a prodigy and I too was given a huge command earlier than most said I should have it. I fought my way to the place of respect I hold now, and yet, the fight is never-ending. I must always prove myself. Before, I was too young, and now I'm too used up.

The pounding headache gouges electric fingers into my temples.

I drop forward, resting my elbows on my knees, and rub the useless flesh.

It's bad today. Worse than usual.

In the stillness, my heartbeat races and slows, races and slows. My hands tremble.

I want to slide forward and sleep for a hundred clegs, but every moment I sleep, my enemies turn my blades against me.

The door whooshes open. Captain Falkion leads in Arcturin din Orunfax.

I rise and scrape up energy I don't feel. "Welcome."

The captain steps out again, and the door closes.

Arcturin din Orunfax lowers his hood. He has the pure silver hair and bland features of a male who was created by a house breeding program in a genetic combinator rather than the aggressive selection process in the arena. In fact, his hair shines. He probably colors it.

His lips curl. "Why are you here?"

"The same reason you are."

"Your father ordered you to make sure these new blade officers give house leaders their proper respect?"

When I trained so hard as a young blade, I always imagined it was so that I could have the last slash. Take down my enemy with my dying breath so we expired together.

I did not imagine I would use it to appease a man too

influential to be given the response he deserves. "How are your observations?"

"I was displaced from my room by a rogue."

"A test of the new ranking system your father implemented." I force a pleased smile. "It's operating exactly as we expected."

"You didn't tell me."

"That was to make the test more accurate."

"Hm." He nudges my blank data tablet and sighs. "Then it was effective, I guess. I'm back in my room now."

"Very good."

He walks around the room, plucking at the sleeves of his skinsuit. His wrists are bare, unmarked. A regular Arrisan.

Once, the Arsenal was more than a training ground, more than a dispatch center hustling to fulfill the whims of the High Command.

Now?

The high commanders use us to jockey for control of the empire. Rare luxuries matter more than planets. Pride matters more than security.

But that is going to change.

Soon.

"Do you think the ship will ever move?" Arcturin asks.

"As the newest dreadnought in the fleet, I certainly hope so."

"I suppose." He finally yawns with boredom, flips his hood, and departs.

Captain Falkion nods to him respectfully outside, then enters and waits for the door to seal. "Sithe is no longer on the *Spiderwasp*."

I stagger.

His eyes widen.

I turn it into a hard lean against the wall. He escaped right after I told him how to displace me? "I see."

"But we think we know where he's gone."

I lock eyes with the captain. "We?"

"I." Captain Falkion clears his throat. "I think that he's gone after the Vanadisans."

But the Vanadisans have nothing to do with my plans. "Why?"

"He's gone to get his lesser."

That makes no sense. Is the captain pandering to me? He can't know my full plans either, but he is bright. Perhaps he worked some of them out for himself. "Are you sure?"

He nods, grim, as though Sithe following a lesser is the worst outcome he can think of.

Trust me, there are many worse. "I can't understand anything about this."

"There's something you should see." Captain Falkion leads me through the dreadnought and down to, of all places, the science office.

A massive hole has been carved in the reinforced door, and an engineer has her tools set out, welder in hand, snapping at her assistant about the mess and the stupidity of higher-ups who...

"Captain." The engineer grins, straightening, and powers down the welder. "General Master. Here to check out my work? I haven't done much of this inside with people on board—don't get much call for it now that the Harsi aren't peeling all the skin off our ships and scooping us out like honey ants, you see—but don't worry, we'll get it done."

The captain nods at her confidence and gestures at the hole. "Sithe did this."

The hole is carved all the way through the reinforced metal, almost as thick as my torso.

Again, the significance escapes me. "He stole a hull-cutter from engineering?"

"This was done with his own blades."

Impossible.

But the engineers are grinning. "He's a mini Harsi, he is. My boss almost took him down. Had him on the run and everything."

"He crushed the other engineers, cut 'em to pieces," the assistant chimes in.

The captain juts his chin. "Your boss submitted their deaths as a training accident."

"It was." The lead engineer stretches her lips wider. "He and the boss were training, you see. The dead ones got in the way of his blades."

The captain's eyes narrow, but he turns away.

Behind him, the lead engineer stops smiling and shoves the assistant, and the assistant shoves back, then notices me watching and quickly straightens his overalls.

They honestly believe Sithe did this. "You're certain it was done with blades?"

"The boss was expecting it. He put up a recorder," the engineer says agreeably.

"Show me."

She drags out a greasy data tablet with three cracks on the screen—typical that an engineer would carry around a cracked data tablet instead of taking the short time to apply her own gel to repair it—and scrolls through some videos of lessers doing questionable things to a low-resolution feed. The camera was positioned in a corner of the corridor that would show this whole area.

Sithe storms up to the door, speaks into the intercom—

there is no sound, only images—and then sets his feet *and carves a man-sized hole through reinforced steel.*

It's a bad placement, honestly. If he was going to cut into the office, he should have gone through the wall. The sliding door could have severed his wrists or snapped off his blades.

That aside, *who is this man?* The look on his face is different from any I've ever seen. Focused, driven. Obsessed. This is the energy I wanted to harness. A man like this *will* stop our enemies. He'll restore the blades and secure the empire from invasion. He'll never let Arris fall again.

Sithe pushes through the hole and enters.

"Why did he do this?" I ask.

The engineer grins. "He thought his woman was inside."

"His what?"

"His lesser," the captain clarifies.

He has this great rage within him and it is in service to *a lesser?*

Yes, Sithe and Falkion and now these engineers have all told me the exact same story, and yes, I am still incredulous.

It's a lesser. *A lesser.* Who cares that much about a lesser?

Sithe does.

Somehow.

I need to have him examined. This is more than lust. He's had the metal before. I've had it too. The lusteal compels us to breed. It doesn't do this.

This is something else. "How did she command him to destroy the door?"

"She wasn't even in there," the engineer confides. "But

she didn't command him. He has a natural alliance with her."

"What's a natural alliance?"

The assistant pipes up, "She's his Amante."

"His what?" the captain says.

"From the origin myths," the lead engineer says. "On the Arris home world."

"Oh?" the captain says.

"Yeah, you know. Her and Grundi?"

The captain sets his feet. "Refresh my memory."

"They do everything together. She comes up with the clever engineering solutions. She's got a real head on her shoulders. She'd be great in a cargo bay. And that old Grundi, he just keeps going back to her. He'd be a good engineer too, if he wasn't so busy eating and sleeping."

The captain catches my eye.

I shake my head. I've never heard of this either.

He interrogates the engineer. "Where did you read about this?"

"Oh, everybody knows," the engineer boasts. "Right?"

Her assistant nods eagerly. "Amante, Grundi, Sirgoy—he's the river god. They're from the home world, you know."

"Uh-huh..." the captain says.

"It's all over the quadrants. Anybody who's got a data tablet's reading it."

This is something interesting. A new training for the military? From the High Command? I didn't teach it to my blades. It's very strange.

During this conversation, the engineer's video is still playing in her hands. A flicker of movement on the screen catches my eye.

A lesser squeezes through the hole, looks both ways down the corridor, and scurries off the screen.

The captain freezes. He noticed it too. "What was that? What just crawled out of the office?"

"I don't know," the engineer says, and her assistant shakes his head. "We never watched it this far."

The captain backs up the video. We watch the lesser escape again.

Falkion takes a deep breath and strides into the science office. "Ukuri?"

"He's not here," the engineer calls. "He's in his private office."

"I don't recall issuing him private office."

"Uh...never mind, forget I said anything." The engineer busies herself. She and her assistant quickly exit.

Hmm.

There are so many oddities on this ship, I would get a headache if I didn't already have one. I press the hollows beneath my jaw. The muscle feels loose.

I have too much to do to die.

Falkion hits the viewscreen. "Ukuri, report."

It crackles to display the science officer in some sort of private quarters, all right. A repurposed storage bay. "Captain Falkion. To what do I owe the pleasure of your visit to my science office?"

"Were you ever going to tell me that I have a lesser creeping around on my ship?"

"Of course not, Captain." His clever smile deepens, and the reflective lenses hide his eyes. Being a science officer suits him, as I knew it would. "Don't worry. She's neatly contained right here. Noemi? Greet the captain."

A lesser leans into the camera and waves her fingers. "Hi."

"That is a different lesser," the captain grinds out.

Ukuri keeps his grin in place. "Why, Captain, how can you tell? Don't they all look the same?"

"She has different hair length, coloration, and body proportions."

Falkion's observational skills are impressive. I can train myself to find a lesser target when needed, but he recalled the details immediately.

Ukuri's smile remains fixed. "We'll find her, Captain. I've got people looking all over the ship."

"You didn't tag her?"

"I didn't expect her to be mobile long enough to need a tag. And I didn't expect Sithe to cut a great hole in my door. Atana's pranks go too far."

The captain growled. "I want no more lusteal-related chaos on this ship."

"Good news, Captain. The escaped lesser was the only one definitely *not* infected with lusteal."

He pauses, then considers. "So no one will notice her. If she's resourceful, she could hide in corridors for kortans."

"Oh, it won't be that long, Captain. She's only a lesser."

He shakes his head and mutters, "There's something about these lessers. They are too Arrisan." He raises his voice to a normal level. "Don't expose any more of them to my crew."

"But just think of how intriguing the experiments could be. If a lesser can drive a blade like Sithe to destroy a science office, what would happen if we exposed a whole army to one? What could she drive that army to do?"

Is that intriguing?

Or terrifying?

"How many of these lessers did you give to the Vanadisans?" I ask the captain.

"Twenty. Maybe twenty-five."

"Hail their ship. Order them to bring the infected lessers back."

The captain grimaces. "Bring them back?"

"Immediately."

He taps his forehead and murmurs for the bridge communications officer.

Ukuri watches pleasantly.

I step into view. "Ukuri."

The smile drops off his face. He removes his eye shields and straightens. "General Master."

"Don't kill your lesser."

She sits in the background, more of a silhouette, and doesn't react to my order at all.

Ukuri's gaze meets mine unwaveringly. "No, I didn't intend to."

"Keep the other Arrisans away from her and don't report any results of your current experiments, preliminary or otherwise, to Arris Central until I give the command."

He rubs his jaw. That movement is the signature of the scientists. His core orders are butting against each other.

It was my greatest objection to this plan. Arris is already divided. No good can come of dividing the loyalties of our blades. But I was overruled.

Now we will see which core will prevail.

"You know that when you were removed from the Arsenal, my predecessor took you aside and explained you were chosen. Remember that? You were sent away because he believed that you could endure the training of the other center, but never forget that you are, first and always, a blade."

He sits very still.

"Remember?" I push. "You were stationed here for a

reason. And if you ever doubted or questioned our purpose, that reason is about to become clear."

The captain lifts a finger. "The Vanadisans are ignoring our hails."

"Of course they are." I focus on Ukuri. "Do you understand?"

Ukuri releases his breath. "I will not report my results until your command."

"Protect the empire," I tell him, and close the connection.

"What do you want to do about the Vanadisans?" the captain asks, following me from the science office and into the grav tube for the bridge.

"Chase them down."

"Firing on them would be awkward. They're allies."

"When we match velocities, if they still haven't accepted our call, I'll go speak with them personally."

He studies me from the side. We exit the grav tube together, and my hand slips on the guide rail. My grip is weak. He averts his eyes.

I have been so focused on Arris Central and the High Command that this incident with lessers and lusteal has blindsided me.

Thieves sometimes attack our depots, steal our superior weapons, rip off our technology. Lusteal has gone missing in accidents or explosions. Our enemies have stolen it at the same time as more valuable minerals, and I always assumed it was taken by mistake.

But now I have to revisit that assumption.

These lessers who are infected, are they part of a plot?

Or some completely new threat from an unexpected adversary?

I am grasping for the shards of a broken shuttle and trying to flail toward other survivors.

Our race has always been doing this. Since the Harsi destroyed our home world, hunted us to the ends of our galaxy, feasted on the meager survivors, we have done whatever we needed to live. To defend ourselves. To prepare for their inevitable return.

Our own rulers forget.

The Arsenal never sleeps.

It's why I've had this headache for two standard years.

Maybe Sithe has not committed treason after all.

He is too fine of a weapon to be broken and reforged.

But who will wield him?

TWENTY-FOUR

CATARINE

I pace the confines of the glass box.

My world has closed in.

I can't think.

The itch scratches at my brain.

Get out of here. Capture a man. Seek relief.

Only one man will give me relief.

Sithe is coming.

He must be coming.

I'm antsy and hot. Burning hot, my skin is crawling off my bones, and I need someone to fix it into place.

I need Sithe.

The Vanadisan commander sets aside his data tablet with a stretch and taps the glass with his knuckle. "You, mental stupid. How did you get that red mark?"

He has to let me out. "It's an Arrisan bite."

"Bite?" the commander repeats. "No Arrisan bites like this."

"They have recessed teeth."

"But do not use them."

"I saw him. He bit me. It made this mark."

The commander looks at the handler.

The handler shrugs. "Mental stupid."

"Mm, mental stupid." He opens the door—freedom!— and sprays me in the face.

Again!

I scrub at the burning spray while he and the handler force me onto the operating slab. The light brightens. The laser saw turns on.

I thrash. "Don't cut me!"

"Stay still." He tightens restraint loops around my torso. "It will be over for you soon."

I have no weapons to fight back. I've only ever had my words. And my mind is gone.

Once, I had Sithe.

But I made him stay away.

No, he's a weapon I still have.

Be clever, me.

"He's coming for me."

"Mm?" The commander prods my bitten shoulder with a silver awl-type implement.

I barely feel the jab. "I summoned him. He's coming."

"Mm-hm. Who?"

"When he gets here, he's going to eject his blades and cut you open. For every cut you make on me, he's going to do it back to you times...times ninety-six."

"Sure, sure."

"He's going to kill you without a thought."

The handler murmurs something in their language.

The commander waggles the silver awl at him, then switches to Arrisan Standard. "No one is coming. You are a lesser. A nothing. No one cares about you, and no one's coming for you."

"He is."

"Then we are very surprised. Okay? Don't move."

The saw descends.

The intercom crackles.

They both jump.

The handler shuts off the saw.

The commander frowns and berates him in their language, but the intercom emits frantic trills and squeals, and the commander freezes.

The squeals continue.

Both Vanadisans look at me. The commander drops his awl. It clatters to the ground. Both take a step back from me on the slab.

This is how someone should react when they know a blade is about to board.

I don't understand their language, but I understand this. I arch my back against the restraints. "Sithe!"

The intercom cuts out.

I writhe on the slab. "He's coming."

They hurry to the intercom and jab it, talking furiously.

There's no answer.

The commander looks lost. The handler bounces worriedly.

"Let me go," I coo, so helpful now. "Do as I say. I'll ask him not to kill you. Not right away, anyway."

The commander sneers, "You don't ask a blade anything."

"You're right. I won't ask." Power surges through my veins. I twist the opposite way. These bands are too tight, but I don't mind. Everything amuses me, and I widen my eyes to relish their growing terror. "I'll demand it."

The commander is unnerved by my confidence.

Then he picks up his awl with renewed determination.

The handler squeaks and pulls at his arm.

He snaps, "We finish fast and dump the body. If a blade is coming, he never knows."

"Oh, he'll know." I let a deep breath fill my lungs, relishing Sithe's arrival. "As soon as he carves up your ship, he'll sense me. He'll feel the metal in his brain, taste my blood on the air."

The handler backs away.

"You won't be here," the commander insists.

"So? If I'm outside, dead, then he'll have no reason to hold back."

Something thumps the ceiling.

They both look up.

"He's cutting his way in." I stretch, hot and ready for him. "He carves open ships. Cuts down his enemies from outside the hull."

The handler babbles incoherently.

The commander lifts his hand for silence.

I jerk once in each direction, like a fish. "Let. Me. Go."

The commander shakes, indecisive, then presses a button. The restraints unfasten and retract into the slab.

I sit up and turn to the doorway.

Sithe enters like a silver ghost. His head is down, his shoulders are up, and his pose makes him look wider than he is tall. His long blades extend like spider's fangs. His hood shadows his face, but I know it's him.

I open my arms.

He hesitates.

The Vanadisans shriek and stampede into the corner.

I slide off the slab and run to my Arrisan.

He retracts his blades and straightens, ready for me.

I leap into his arms, and my enthusiasm staggers him. He stumbles back into a stack of crates and ends up sitting on one. I straddle him and press kisses to the impenetrable air shield.

He pulls back his hood, revealing his familiar face, tender, and then he meets me with heat and hunger. Our kisses are rough, hard, the opposite of comforting, and I just want to eat him, consume him, become him from the inside out.

And then I issue my command. I will *not* be denied. "Take me right now. Fill me to the brim. Possess me, make me yours. Now."

His lips curve into a smile.

I claw at his skinsuit. He hooks a finger in the collar, parting it, and I tear it off to bare his erect cock. His brows lift at my animalistic frenzy, but his hands guide my waist as I spear myself on him, taking him in all the way to the hilt. *Yes.* This is what I need. This is the itch that I must have scratched.

Others made me sick, but he is the one I choose for my cure.

I buck and slide, dragging my wet channel up and down his throbbing shaft. Pleasure torments his expression. I drive him wilder with everything I've learned from our couplings.

Release. Release already. I need to think.

Sweat beads above his lip, above his brows. His fingers score deep imprints on my hips as he struggles to hold on.

"Give it to me," I demand. "It's mine."

His lips part, suffocating to a pant.

I will steal his air, his essence, his everything.

He is mine.

Look. There's my mark on him. My double-horseshoe bite. He wanted it deeper? I will not deny him.

I chomp his shoulder.

He jerks and clenches, releasing his heat into me with an intense roar.

It crashes inside, cosmic and eternal.

And my insides tingle.

He's curing me, but I got sprayed so much. I release his shoulder and bob against his still-hard shaft. He sucks in a breath through his clenched teeth and meets my gaze, then kisses me softly, filling his hands with my breasts, kneading my soft cheeks, and he moves with me. I ride him, longer and sweeter, until the orgasms build with every thrust, until I can feel everything. Until all of me comes back to myself. Until I'm the one who's kissing him. His mouth, his face, his nose. Every part.

I pull back and meet his eyes, telling him now that I'm me again. "You're mine."

"I'm yours," he says.

And I get it.

When we were parting on the dreadnought, I daydreamed about Sithe staying with me. I asked in a passive way, painted a "wouldn't it be nice?" kind of picture. He understands orders, not wishes, and my mistake almost cost us everything. His skill is weapons and mine is words. I must take greater care in how I use them.

I represent all of Humana to any aliens who've never met one of us before.

I must not hesitate to use my resources—all my resources—again.

Something falls over behind me.

The Vanadisans, probably.

Sithe has had a good field of view this whole time, and I'm pretty sure he would have cut down any threats even in the middle of his release, so they still need to be dealt with.

I clamber off, muscles twinging and liquids dripping as usual. I'm sore, but in a good way.

Sithe lies back, arms loose and hands lax in his lap, perhaps savoring the feeling of having reached me in time, yet again.

Let him enjoy it.

I feel a little antsy still, like the first wave of my cravings has passed, but that I'll need him to neutralize the rest of it. I'm going to need him a lot in a short time I think.

But first, I grab my skinsuit still pooled on the floor by the operating slab and whirl it around my neck. It flows like a cape and suctions to me, sealing down to my wrists and ankles and bunching up behind me. I'm an expert even though I've only put it on three times.

Sithe rocks forward and methodically seals himself up again so that he too can experience the nice drying factor of the suit. It evaporates liquid like a warm breeze does after one emerges from the sea.

The Vanadisans huddle in the corner.

We block the only exit.

Sithe stands beside me and stretches. His blades extend to the ceiling and curve behind him like a deadly frame.

The Vanadisans quiver.

"You got here just in time." I pick up the commander's data tablet.

It displays images of Arrisans and humans, including many more of Humana than were in the archives I passed on to Second Harvard. Oh, this is interesting.

I address the commander. "There's a lot more pictures than what I found in the dreadnought archives."

The commander rises and coughs. "Yes, the scientific archives are separate and locked."

"Why?"

"Data collection."

"What does that mean?"

He shifts his weight. "Vassals become allies. Allies don't like how the data was collected when they were lessers. So, locked."

No surprise.

But that reminds me. "You were doing these experiments on behalf of someone named Fuzig. Who is he, and what does he want with us?"

"We won't tell you."

I turn to Sithe conversationally. "They sprayed me with a lusteal solution three hundred percent stronger than what was in my blood before, and were planning to experiment on me to the death."

He turns on them. "*You* infected her with lusteal?"

The handler shrinks.

The commander clutches his throat in distress. "No! We infect nothing. She had it already. We just add more, make its effect strong."

"Where did you get more?"

"Fuzig. Fuzig!"

"And what about this Fuzig?" I press, riding on Sithe's deadly focus. "And his tests?"

"We don't know."

Sithe points his blades at the Vanadisans.

They shriek.

"No! Please. We don't. Only that here is these patients and here is these tests we must do. In the data tablet. All there."

"I think a great scientist would know more about the experiments he's doing," I say.

He blubbers. "I am not a great scientist. I just do what

Fuzig tells me, and I only have this position because of my cousin."

"It's true," the handler squeaks from his huddle on the floor. "He is terrible at science, but his cousin is a great man."

"Assistant to a Premier Councilor."

"High," the handler says. "High man."

Hmm. Interesting. "Okay, then I have a few questions for your cousin."

"My cousin? He does not know Fuzig."

"That's okay. I want to talk to someone in your government too."

"But, he...is very busy..."

I turn to Sithe. "Do you think if you cut them up a bit, his cousin will free up his schedule?"

Sithe scrapes his blades against each other, the *sching* sound causing the Vanadisans to shudder.

"Ah, I call, I..." The commander operates the communication panel.

Sithe steps to the side, out of the view of the camera.

That's fine. I won't use him unless I have to.

But if I have to, I *will* use him.

A Vanadisan appears on the viewscreen. He wears long colorful strips of fabric. The commander speaks to him urgently in their language. After some back and forth, the view changes to another Vanadisan in a different outfit and background, and another tense conversation occurs. The view changes to a third Vanadisan. The commander gestures at me while talking. His paddle-shaped hands tremble.

And to think, not ten clicks ago, these were the same hands that were going to hurry up and cut me open to quickly get rid of my body.

This third Vanadisan snaps.

The commander shuts up and hunches his shoulders.

The Vanadisan—his cousin?—focuses on me. His accent is flawless. "You are a lesser? And you assaulted and rendered a blade helpless, tore off his clothes, and forced him to breed with you?"

I laugh. Is that what they saw?

The cousin looks unamused.

I don't owe him any explanation. I compose myself. "I'm from Humana. We seek to become allies with Vanadis, and you—"

He laughs in my face, openly displaying scorn and a slight whistle. Unlike when I had to guess at the commander's laughter before, there is no mistaking his. "You will not become an ally for a thousand generations! I know Humana. Smoking earth and too much water."

"You're in a position to speak to the Premier Council," I continue, undaunted. "Please consider us a future partner."

"Partner, pah. You mean 'friend.' Yes, I have heard of this Humana term." He lifts a long finger. "I will not speak one word of Humana to the Premier Council until you have a spaceport. Understand?"

"We have a—"

"You have a dirt field. Without a proper spaceport, Vanadis does not even consider Humana a vassal planet. You are an asteroid. A comet rotting with semi-sentient mold. You see?"

"But—"

"After you have a spaceport, an interstellar shipyard, a catalog of your valuable metals and biologics, and the most basic extragalactic communications network, then maybe I will mention you in passing. One time."

"We're working on it. All of it."

"You cannot reach the edges of your own solar system. How can you offer anything of value to Vanadis? You cannot even speak so we can hear."

Although I doubt any of this is new information, I will report it to Representative Khan. "Okay. I'll call you back when we have an extragalactic communications network."

"Ah, wait." He holds up his hand—a human gesture, nice—and points at the side where Sithe is lurking. "Is that...?"

Hah. I kiss Sithe just off screen and terminate the connection. Let him wonder.

Sithe absorbs my kiss, sucking and teasing my lips, and the need streaks between my thighs again.

Soon.

He nuzzles me. "Can Humana make an extragalactic communications network?"

"I don't know. I'll pass the information, along with the scientific archives on this ship, to my people and find out."

My ears pop.

Sithe glances behind him with a frown. The cargo bay is that way, and this science lab is now empty.

"Where did the Vanadisans go?"

"I guess the short-hop orbiter." Sithe pads down the hall, then pauses and kisses me.

Mm, this is good.

He pulls back and flips both of our hoods, then peers into the cargo bay. The pods are secure, but there's a big empty space where the orbiter was.

"Can they fly back to Vanadis in that?" I ask.

"Yes, but it's a long trip with no grav. They won't be happy."

"Can we fly back to Humana in this?"

"Yes. Is that your destination?"

"I think so."

The Vanadisans were plotting something. Whoever this Fuzig person is, the researchers at Second Harvard can review his tests and maybe reverse engineer what he was trying to do.

"Maybe, now that we know lusteal causes our illness, the Second Harvard researchers can figure out what cures us. Other than you," I tell Sithe. "Or any Arrisan, I guess. But ever since you cleared my mind, I've only been attracted to you."

He presses my hand briefly, then looks disturbed. "But who's supplying the Vanadisans? We account for every barrel. It's tightly controlled."

"That's what it sounded like. They said Fuzig had had no luck stealing it."

"So how did they infect you on Humana?"

"I don't think they did."

He frowns. "You weren't infected?"

"I was, and I'm developing a theory. You told me once that your sinusoid has all the material in it to restart the Arrisan race. That includes lusteal?"

He nods.

"I spent a lot of my childhood at excavations near Arrisan crash sites. Humana didn't bring down many Arrisan vessels, but I would have visited most of them. And Esme's mother was exposed to a ship crash where it rained glitter for days."

He makes the connection that glitter could equal lusteal. "Then why isn't every human affected?"

"Maybe it takes multiple types of exposures. Maybe a genetic factor activates it, or maybe we share a mutation that causes us to accumulate it. Now that they know what to look for, the Second Harvard team will try to answer these questions."

"Then let's get you to them." He pivots away.

I give one last glance to the pods full of my sleeping shipmates.

How funny that we've gone on this massive journey across galaxies only to turn around and head right back home for the cure.

But the journey was necessary.

Knowing what we're actually fighting makes all the difference.

And while I don't think the Vanadisans personally infected us, they must have noticed our sensitivity to the ointment and other Arrisan medicines. They've definitely got some of us imprisoned. We're their guinea pigs, their laboratory mice, their hapless victims, important to them only because of how our physiognomy mirrors their true target, the Arrisans.

We are important in ourselves.

And someday, we will prove it.

I follow Sithe through the Vanadis vessel.

This ship is smaller than our old cruiser, and the corridors are filled with crates. On top of one stack rests a cat carrier, of all things, and inside purrs an orange-marmalade tom. He sniffs my finger through the bent wire and then rubs his chin on me. His coat is glossy, and he seems well fed.

Huh. That purring cat just mesmerizes me. "Do the Vanadisans normally fly around with pets?"

"No. But they're science officers, so..."

Sithe stops in a doorway. The room beyond hums with whirring machines. He arrests me and turns my chin to prevent me from looking inside the room.

I obediently look away. "What's going on?"

"They're almost done cleaning."

"Cleaning? What?"

"The pilot." Sithe eyes me, measuring my reaction. "I ordered him to freeze. He didn't."

Oh. Lucky freezing is my default action.

"You were sad after the attack in engineering. After your mind was cleared."

He's right. I have no need to see bloodshed. "That's very thoughtful, thank you."

The small cleaner robots clatter through the hall. The caged cat meows at them like they're familiar friends.

Sithe and I enter the bridge.

It's smaller than the cruiser's but there are similarities. The open area, lots of viewscreens. Sithe goes to a central panel and tenses.

My stomach drops, reacting on instinct. "What?"

He points at blinking scripts. "Missing hails. They've come after us."

"Who has?"

He levels his gaze on mine. "The dreadnought."

TWENTY-FIVE

SITHE

I watch the dreadnought grow larger on the expeditioner's navigation screen.

We have nowhere to go.

I have come this far, and there is no escape. No way to evade. I can slice down any lesser, any ally, any Arrisan who gets in my way. On a great day, I could possibly slow down Zai. I would at least try.

But I cannot take down a dreadnought.

And yet I must.

The comm button blinks.

"They're hailing us again," I tell Catarine.

She touches her dusky lips, thinking. "Is it wise to run?"

"We can't run."

"Not even in your smaller ship?"

I shake my head. "I'm sorry."

"I understand. I just wanted to know my options." She drops her hand and treats me to a confident, no, radiant smile that warms the inside of my soul. "I'm willing to advocate for us if you're willing to follow me. Can you? As far as we can go, no matter what I have to say?"

Because it's her? "I will. Even if we're pushed to the very last star."

Her smile deepens. "To the very last star. Okay. Sit out of view of the camera. Where's the center?"

I direct her and then move back as she asks, stationing myself beyond where I expect the lens to capture. Although I'm tense, I feel a little better. As when she wanted information from the Vanadisan science officers, I will be ready in an instant when she needs me, but fighting a battle without weapons is her domain.

It's all up to her now.

She straightens, smooths her dark hair and her gray skinsuit, and answers the hail.

"*Spiderwasp* in." Captain Falkion hails us in a nearly empty communications room, with Zai silhouetted in the background. "Ignoring our hail strains our alliance and will result in our... Oh. It's you."

"Hello, Captain Falkion." Catarine smiles quietly, holding her secrets to her chest. "I'm sorry the pilot didn't answer. He was unfortunately dead."

"Where's Sithe?"

"Nearby."

"Show him to me."

"No, I don't think I will."

The captain's eyes widen. It's the same conversation that she had with him when I was resting, and I can only imagine how he's enjoying the experience for a second time. "I want to speak with him."

"That's very nice, but you're going to have to speak with me."

"The punishment for treason is execution, and he's in dereliction of his duty, rejecting orders, abandoning his station, and endangering the empire."

My blades jump in my sleeves.

He's right. Every count is true.

And yet...

"I disagree," Catarine says.

The captain blinks.

Zai's profile turns to look at her.

Even I am surprised.

"Sithe is not in dereliction of duty. He uncovered a clandestine operation perpetuated by an ally to cripple the Arrisans and take over the empire, and he acted immediately to stop that ally."

The captain's lips droop and his brows rise. "By Humana?"

"Thank you so much, Captain, for confusing Humana with one of your allies. It is my deeply held wish that we'll soon be elevated, and I'll rely on your support at such a time as that if it should become necessary."

While she's talking and the captain is trying very hard to control the jut of his chin and the flaring of his nostrils in embarrassment, Zai ambles up behind him and leans over the screen. "Vanadis."

"Yes, correct. Who are you?"

He edges the captain out of the way. "General master of the Arsenal, Sithe's highest superior."

"Hello, Zai. I'm Catarine."

He doesn't react to his name. "What is this plot?"

"As we've recently discovered, lusteal mixed in human blood creates a more potent tincture than the metal alone. A Vanadisan research program headed by a scientist named Fuzig is studying how to refine the substance to produce a weapon, destroy Arris, and assume control of the empire."

Zai gets it instantly. "They hired the Eruvisans to steal our lusteal."

"Yes, and I think the Eruvisans were also supposed to escort us to Vanadis. They made a mistake attaching to our cruiser, though. Cracking our hull spooked Captain Zeerah."

"Their environmental system was overextended, so they had to connect, and they wouldn't have expected your captain to attempt suicide by forcing you into pods." He taps his fingertips together. "I wonder how many of their thefts have been successful."

"None, according to the Vanadisans who used it on me. Fuzig received his supply from someone else."

"Who?"

"Someone who has access to a controlled supply."

His eyes take on a deadly intensity. "Which noble house?"

Oh. Yes. House breeding programs will, of course, receive a small amount of lusteal.

"The Vanadisans didn't share names," Catarine tells him, "but this ship contains the experiments they intended to perform, and probably much more. Our medical doctors will review the findings and, with our greater knowledge of our own biology, confirm the results."

"No." Zai straightens. "You tell no one. Return to the dreadnought. Now."

She purses her lips. "That's one option."

"The other option is I destroy your vessel and you on it."

"Then you'll get nothing." She rotates her finger to indicate the expeditioner. "The tests, the records. Your lusteal."

"Neither does anyone else."

"We're the only ones who need it. The Vanadisans are running a whole program with captive Humana patients elsewhere. This little operation of theirs was just one part, and they must be getting close to a big result, or else why risk associating us with the Eruvisans? There are some very odd things on this ship, Zai. We're not interrupting the beginning stage of some plot. We're stumbling in at the end."

Zai takes a long breath and lets it out.

Blades give orders, and Catarine sidesteps his by weaving a noose of words that make so much sense. She calms me. But based on his expression, I do not think she calms him.

But he is not the general master of the Arsenal because of inflexibility or false pride.

He addresses her like a blade. "You can't fly a Vanadis expeditioner back to Humana without resistance. If you're right and this *is* part of a larger conspiracy, one that includes houses on Arris Central, the conspirators will do everything in their power to take it back or destroy it. And you."

"Sithe's ship will give any non-Arrisan raiders pause. And if someone attacks anyway, that might be quite interesting information for you, don't you think?"

His chin drops. "You want me to assign Sithe to your vessel?"

"I want you to assign Sithe to me."

Zai's eyes narrow.

But he's actually considering it.

This is more than I ever thought possible.

"If I and my other shipmates were taken by conspirators, I would hate for Sithe to miss out on learning who they are because of a misguided requirement to stay with the ship," she says logically. "His mere presence should deter all but the guiltiest parties. And it would be terrible if, upon returning to Humana, our researchers discovered something of vital importance to the Arrisan empire but failed to report it because we had no Arrisan present to understand its significance."

"It would be terrible," Zai echoes dryly. "But you cannot take everything with you. Send us the data, the lusteal solution, and half your shipmates. The rest of you can go."

Catarine rubs her fingertips across her skinsuit. "I will share the data. It makes perfect sense to have a backup, or several. The data should contain the formula so you can create your own lusteal solution."

She rubs her fingertips across her suited thigh again. Agitation. She doesn't want him to access our ship because she doesn't want to give up her shipmates.

I don't need to know her reason why. My blades extend just beyond the line of my wrists, ready to enforce her will however it needs to be.

But Catarine takes the extra moments to consider Zai's perspective. "What do you want with half my shipmates?"

"We're the experts in lusteal. Our science officers will catch up to the Vanadisans easily by using them to study."

"Using them..." She sucks in a deep breath and lets it out. "No."

"You don't tell me no. I am a blade. You are a—"

"First of all, you already have at least one of my shipmates."

"Two," Zai says testily.

"Three," I murmur.

Catarine turns to me. "Three?"

"I saw two empty and one full pod tucked away in the engineering offices of the cargo bay."

"In plain view?" she asks, irritated, like she can't believe she missed it.

I shake my head. I used a nontraditional entrance.

"They're not in a visible or accessible area."

Her gaze darts around the bridge as though she's searching her memory. She focuses on Zai. "Do you know which two people you have?"

"An escapee from the science office," the captain growls from the middle of the room. It must be her Captain Zeerah.

"The other was identified as Noemi," Zai supplies.

"The ace," Catarine murmurs, and consults me again. "Did you get a look at who was inside the occupied pod?"

In fact, while I contorted through the passageway that was not quite big enough for the both of us, I got a pretty detailed look. "Strange, puffy footwear." I motion at my boots. "Pink."

"Pink bunny slippers? That would be the housewife. Which leaves..." She leans on an elbow. "Zai, you have to go back to the accident site. One of us is still out there, floating in space. Your dreadnought can get there much faster than we can."

"Anyone who's been in an escape pod this long is already dead."

"Which, horrible as that would be, makes her a more palatable test subject. I'm hoping she's still alive, but if she has died, I want to be able to tell her parents something."

"Her parents should know that voyaging into space on a modified harvester is asking for death."

"I know. But I want to give them closure. Will you do this?"

"The dreadnought has other assignments; however, I'm leaving soon and I will consider flying that route back to the Arsenal." Zai focuses on the edge of the screen. "Sithe. Show yourself."

My guts clench.

Catarine looks at me with a question.

If I do not want to speak to Zai, she will refuse to cede. She will cut off this communication, redirect, do whatever she must. She silently tells me that with her, always, I have a choice.

I have a choice.

So I choose this.

A heavy weight presses on my shoulders, and it feels like I must lift the whole empire as I stand and nod. I will face my superior.

She steps back and gives me the central spot.

Zai studies me. A million small twitches show the emotions he's suppressing. Finally, he settles on his military snap. "You pledged to obey the grand master of the Arsenal instantly and without question. And then you refused your assignment and abandoned your duty. That's treason."

Catarine makes a small sound.

Zai ignores it. "We both know the truth. No fine words about your subsequent discoveries disguise it."

I nod heavily.

"No one approached you with a plot to betray me, and there are no known traitors on this dreadnought, are there?"

I shake my head.

"This, and all other treasonous actions, are the result of chasing after a lesser who has lusteal mixed into human blood. This substance rendered the Arrisan engineers into unthinking animals, and it's warped the loyalty of a blade who's studied nothing but control and obedience. Correct?"

The answer tears my throat. "Yes."

"Then there is clearly no greater present, active danger to the empire than this lusteal-Humana cocktail."

What?

"You will escort these infected lessers back to Humana,

establish a secret research program with the sole objective to eclipse the Vanadisans and reverse the effects of the substance, and report directly to me. Understand?"

Zai has just assigned me to Catarine.

I can barely speak. My voice is rough, and the syllables clog my throat. "Understood."

"Transfer the expeditioner's data to the dreadnought." He moves to terminate the communication. "This conference is—"

"Wait." Catarine pushes into the center again. I stand behind her, augmenting and guarding her, where I now officially belong. "Humana is scheduled to be moved in orbit. That will be catastrophic for our planet, and it will seriously impact our research."

"Move your researchers off-planet with the rest of your population until the surface has settled."

"We don't have the infrastructure to do that yet."

Zai lifts his chin, studying the ceiling. "Because you're not an ally. I forget you..." He glances back at the captain, who also forgot Humana wasn't an ally, then focuses again on Catarine. "I'll see that the orbital move is stopped."

She leans against me. "Thank you. Not having to worry about it will make us so much more productive. It's a real gift."

"It is not a gift. Humana is necessary to protect the empire, and therefore, its inhabitants are all under the protection of the Arsenal. For now." He closes the connection.

And it is done.

We transmit the expeditioner data to the dreadnought. I stand beside Catarine, helping her to figure out the controls. This ship was constructed by a vassal planet of our allies, but there are enough similarities.

The dreadnought receives our data and disappears from our screen. It's gone.

We change the destination from Vanadis to Humana. The ship begins the recalculation process to divert to the new coordinates.

We're done.

She lets out a great sigh and whirls in my arms. A smile teases her lips, and her eyes sparkle. "Except for that last part, I feel like I got gifted a whole star."

I know exactly what she means.

I want to jump out of my own body, bounce up the wall, blade-walk across the ceiling, drop down again, and run, run, run around.

Instead, I clamp her waist and swing her in a circle. She gasps and laughs.

I don't have to go with Zai and fight Arrisans for the rest of my life. I'm assigned to Catarine. Protecting her serves the empire. Our paths finally intertwine.

All because I made a choice.

Because she gave choices to me.

I slow my spin, feeling every bit of her soft body slide down mine. Now, I want to make another choice. And by the way she eagerly melts against me and pulls at my suit, she shares my desire.

I tug my suit open. While she fumbles with hers, I lower her onto one of the Vanadisan's open benches. She separates the material from torso to knee just in time for my hard jack to slide into her already liquid socket.

She closes her eyes in a moan, and then she teases her teeth over my chin, my jaw, my earlobe. Her little nips make me shudder.

Burying my jack deep in her, connecting and reconnecting over and over, feels so right, it makes me dizzy. I rest my elbow above her head, stroke her as I mold her pliable body, fit her endlessly to me.

This is where I belong.

My assignment is to comfort, defend, and treasure Catarine.

I have never had such full-bodied alignment.

She sobs gently, shuddering as she releases her pleasure with increasing urgency. She clings to me, ratcheting my pleasure higher, and then grabs my backside, and I surge. My release pours into her. She is my airlock, my breath of oxygen. She is the ship I return to, the dock in my long flight.

I let out all my agonies in one gust of air and drop my head to her shoulder.

She rests a hand on my head, rubbing the short threads of my dark hair.

"Oh, you know." She wiggles, so I rise up on my elbow. She worms her skinsuit down to her elbows. "I jumped you so aggressively before, you probably missed it, but there's something wrong with your bite."

Wrong?

"I think I'm having an allergic reaction. It's inflamed."

I help her upright, seating her on the bench with her legs pointing one way, and I sit on the same bench with my legs pointing the opposite direction so I can get a close look.

Flames are an accurate description.

The marks of my recessed teeth have pushed out like four coordinates. From them spiral long red streaks that interconnect like fiery vines. "Strange."

"You've never seen this before?" Her tone dips into worry. "Not even when you bit something else?"

"I rarely bite. Not since I was a child, and even then, never an animate object."

"What about other Arrisans? Like at the arena?"

"No one bites at the arena."

"You don't?"

"The arena is generative. Emotionless. There is no possession." But the weird thing is that I *have* seen this before. Not on skin. In her stories of the origin myths. "Ninety-six."

She cranes to see it better. "Where?"

"The marking." I trace the dominant red swirls, ignoring the web-like offshoots. "The original writing system. It's used for accounts, inventory, regiment numbers."

"Your bite got inflamed in the pattern of a number? That's a weird coincidence."

I wonder.

The old writing pattern came from natural features. Geographic. Physical.

"Ninety-six is an important number," I tell her. "A sacred number."

"I guess that's why Grundi's always growing to that size." She lowers her shoulder. "You know, the Vanadisans didn't believe you bit me. They said Arrisans didn't even use your recessed teeth, and they've been studying you much longer than Humana has. Kind of funny, huh?"

It is funny.

We have lost many things from our past. When our home world was destroyed, we did whatever we needed to survive. The few things we saved from the destruction were important. Precious. Like these origin myths that Catarine has given back to us.

We have changed so much since that early time. How we breed, how we live, how we survive. We've forgotten the reason we saved these precious things.

Now, perhaps, we will remember.

I could never have defied Zai before I met Catarine.

She made me grow ninety-six times my size.

And today, she defied both the Vanadisans and the Arrisans, stomping her opponents open like a mushroom spore and spreading truth with her bladelike words.

This is only the beginning for her. For us. For Humana, and, in turn, for Arris.

Today, she grew the same size.

"Hey." She closes her skinsuit and makes that funny shuffling motion where she's angling the evaporators within to do their work. It's just adorable how she moves. "Do you think this ship can contact Humana?"

"Not as the dreadnought did. We have to match velocities with a satellite, which we'll have to do when we give Zai any reports."

"Then, when we report to Zai, I also want to contact Humana." She hugs me. "I want to introduce you to my family."

My chest aches.

"I can think of no greater honor," I manage.

"When we get married, you'll be connected to them too."

My first connections. To her, to her parents. To a family.

This is a strange new journey we are embarking on together. But with Catarine by my side, we'll change the empire.

I'll be her blade. She'll be my tongue. And together we'll create a future where we can belong. Because our love will endure like our drive to defend it, we will fight.

To the very last star.

EPILOGUE

CATARINE

The last thing I hear at night is Sithe breathing.

He pulls me closer and kisses me. And no matter where we are, no matter what we're doing, we melt together.

His shoulders relax, his thumb strokes my cheek, he presses our bellies together with a hand against my lower back. We create each other's peace. And I am so glad the one I met, the one I crave, is Sithe.

Once, I wanted to be someone important like my mom. I wanted to build bridges like my dad. I wanted to change the world.

I had dreams.

Now I'm living them.

My illness is cured.

Humana is saved.

For now.

I'm guarding my shipmates, and soon I'll be home. My parents are so proud of me. They welcomed Sithe warmly, even though he sat stiff and silent with nerves. They have their own worries about us, I can tell. But I'm sure it helped that they saw how I nudged him, teased him, couldn't keep the grin from my face.

Things are changing. The conspiracies run deep.

My shipmates and I are the key.

And the ultimate question is, where will we end up? We who have been infected with lusteal and pulled into a war we were never meant to understand? What will happen to our small and helpless planet, Humana?

Representative Khan wants us to become allies in three more generations.

But you know what? I think we're going to do it in one.

The metal was my greatest weakness.

Then it became what saved me.

It's the same with Humana. I know it.

Sithe never leaves my side. He understands.

The empire is about to catch fire.

Today is only the beginning.

ZAI

After leaving the dreadnought, I return to the site of the attack.

Here, the Eruvisans pounced on the helpless harvester. Here, Sithe unveiled a new reason for me to stay up at night.

Here, it ends.

There's one pod left? I set the ship on deep scan and stand.

My head swims.

I lean against the panel.

Too many sleepless nights. Too many stim pack-filled days.

And a new nightmare to challenge my blades' loyalties.

As if they didn't already have enough.

Why was Sithe so compelled by his lesser?

Is the metal in their blood *that* addictive?

The watery sensation fades. I straighten and go to the food stores, break the seal on a self-heating stim pack, and shake it. The bag warms in my hands.

When did my fingers get so cold?

I tear open the pack, dump in a scoop of regen powder, and gulp the contents. My predecessor claimed the powder helped him live a hundred standard years. But I can tell it's not working like that for me. Based on my current health, I can only hope for another...what, five?

The deep scan beeps.

I secure my mess and pilot to the debris the scanner tagged as a potential escape pod, but it's a blown fragment of the Eruvisan hull. Someone took potshots at it, blew it into chunks.

It wasn't the Vanadisan expeditioner. The dreadnought would have noticed their arms.

Was another ship lurking, powered down, missed by both the dreadnought and the Vanadisans? Waiting for its chance to destroy evidence and taking it as soon as we were gone?

These are the reasons I don't sleep.

It's not hard to hide in space. Our external sensors are primed for intentional movement and only register drift when it threatens our hulls. An entire fleet could drift by the dreadnought, and so long as they calculated their vectors properly—and didn't get unlucky—they could pass undetected.

The deep scan identifies two more potentials—duds both—and my chronometer set to Arsenal time warns me that there are meetings to attend and high commanders to appease. Conspiracies to put down.

On cue, my viewscreen beeps, and I accept the call.

"General Master." My most bloodthirsty student grips the screen. "I've defeated the last trainer."

How did he get my private comm? I keep my tone and my expression emotionless. "Congratulations, Verit."

"All that's left is you." Verit is sweating, his muscles

taut, the trial ring lights behind him. He must have defeated the last trainer moments ago. "I'm ready. Let's finish this."

"Verit?" His class adviser shoves him away from the screen; he's also sweating, but because he's flustered. "General Master, my greatest apologies. I don't know how he got your private contact number."

"High Commander Orunfax gave it to me." Verit curls his lip in an imperious grin. "Just in case."

"In case of what? Huh? What?" The class adviser pushes Verit's shoulder, his tone high-pitched from embarrassment. "Come on. You can't call the general master for no reason."

"I called him to fight me."

"No one fights the general master until graduation." The class adviser forces Verit away from the terminal and tips his head to me in apology. "I've told him a hundred times lack of patience is lack of control. Now that he's out of fighting partners, he can meditate on his shortcomings and impress you with his new self-knowledge on graduation day."

"Three goras." Verit pulls back his lips in a feral grin. "We fight."

"Don't state the obvious like a lesser. Off."

A sliver of real irritation shows on Verit's sweating face.

The class adviser terminates the communication.

I close the viewscreen and rest my forehead in my hands.

In every class, there's one who trains extra hard to defeat me. Malicious, obsessed. Some are cold, some are easily enraged.

None have the backing of High Commander Orunfax.

Sithe would have destroyed Verit.

And in my current state...

I don't know how I will put Verit down, but I must.

I'm trying to take over the military with my blades. The High Command is trying to take over the Arsenal with their students. And from what I can tell, they're doing it better.

This strange lusteal-Humana weapon conspiracy... I have no strength to defeat another threat to Arris, but I must. If perfected, this weapon would take down the entire empire, military and noncombatant alike.

Ping.

The deep scan has found another object. It's in a rubbish cloud. No wonder the engineers didn't investigate.

I match velocities as closely as I dare.

Shards dent my hull. I can't fly close enough. Collecting the pod will require an evac.

The engineers wouldn't do this because of the difficulty. That's the difference with me.

No object is out of my reach.

I am relentless.

I collect my jet clamps and flip on my hood. The escape chute evacuates the atmosphere around the command center in my sinusoid. I crack my hatch.

Vacuum meets vacuum. Silent.

Floating weightless into space is such freedom. Out in the open, all you see are stars. The universe unfurls endlessly in every direction. This must be what it's like when you die. No one will ever find you. That must be very peaceful. There is no right, no wrong; there are no gray areas. It just is.

But death is not for me today.

I push off my ship and sail into the storm.

Dust scrapes my skinsuit, leaving a hundred tiny craters, each of which hastens the destruction as they abrade the fabric. Each miniscule impact pushes me slightly off trajectory, but not enough to matter.

As I near the pod, I stretch my left arm. My long central pike threads the pod's top ring. I swing around and rest my feet on the thin, heavily dented curved wall.

I stick the magnetized clamps on their three marks and activate the jets.

One doesn't activate.

Because that's my luck lately.

The two that do fire cause the pod to rotate in place instead of moving us back to my ship.

I thump the dead clamp.

The pod spins faster and faster. My feet fly off and my blade slips through the ring. I swiftly eject my two side blades. They fly out and then curve backward, hooking the ring. Stretching to the limit of my side blades, I shut off the working clamps with my suited fingertips.

The jets turn off.

We spin like a quasar, frictionless in the void.

My stomach roils.

I have not thrown up on an evac since before blade training.

I will not do so now.

I will grit my teeth. Get through this.

I unstick one working clamp and pulse it against the direction of the spin. When my eyeballs stop rolling around in my head and I can focus on objects again, I hold out the clamp and activate the jet to push us back to my sinusoid.

The jet fights me, whipping against my tendons. It's like holding on to a leviathan, and if I let go of the head, it will coil up and devour me.

We finally escape the debris field and reach my ship.

The pod is too big to go through my escape chute, so I

have to hover us next to the cargo airlock without actually scraping my hull. The blade-lined cargo portal unfurls, stretching wide like a toothed mouth. I hold us steady. Control. We enter the cargo bay. My whole body trembles.

The cargo bay seals. Gravity and atmosphere return, and we land with the smallest bump. I release the ring and slide down the outside of the pod, landing on my feet.

My knees fold.

I slam into the floor of the bay, retract my blades, rest my shaking palms on the floor, and breathe.

In and out.

Swallow down the sickness.

Breathe.

The shakes worsen.

I need more than a stim-pack in my belly.

I force myself to my feet.

The pod sits upright, a funny egg in my cargo bay.

What kind of creature will it hatch?

Or is the embryo already dead?

Its atmosphere content is low.

I crack its hatch.

The air hisses as it opens, sucking in atmosphere.

The lesser inside is slumped over. With the influx of air, she moans and twitches, but does not open her eyes.

So, she's still alive.

Probably because she's put herself into narco-stasis. Most lessers panic as the atmosphere drops, using it up even faster. This one is either lucky, clever, or very disciplined.

A monstrous hard shell with ventilated ridges covers her head. Perhaps to contain her brain? I do not know much about the lessers of Humana. The ones I've seen so far have piled mounds of shaggy hair on their heads, and perhaps it is for some type of armor. I will learn more shortly.

Sithe's lesser had warm beige skin and fluffy, dark hair.

This one has bronze skin and thick hair as black as space. Her cheeks are speckled with dark flecks like reverse stars.

And there is a scent.

Not what I expect from being stranded in a pod beyond its environmental capacity.

Something else.

Something...unnerving.

It slithers up my nose, into my skull, and quiets the headache. Just for a moment.

Beep.

Another call, another emergency.

I stagger away from the pod. My headache returns, hotter now, more agonizing. I make it to the communication panel. My hand trembles over the answer button.

No. I can't speak to anyone like this. I'll collapse. I have to eat something, regardless of how I feel.

I shake a few nutrient cubes into a bowl.

Pain lances my chest.

This is not normal.

I have twinges sometimes after overexerting. Just a few warnings here and there. But this... This is not a warning.

This I cannot ignore.

The weight of inevitability squeezes away my breath.

I can't draw it back in again.

Doom pounds in my temples.

I can't die now. I can't leave the blades to be overrun by students like Verit, and I can't leave the empire to be ruled by the High Command.

And the Vanadisans...and their weapon...and the Harsi...

Medical kit.

I drop to my knees, drag it out. The automatic scanner verifies that my heart is pumping erratically. Its green light emphasizes the urgency.

How funny that the lesser has survived certain death in space, and yet she may awaken to find herself the only one alive on my ship. Without my ability to drive it, it will be a slightly larger prison than her pod. At least she won't have to worry about food or atmosphere.

There's the medical hypo-syringe.

It's already loaded.

I just have to crack open my skinsuit, slump against the wall to expose my chest, and drive the needle...drive the...into my...

ABOUT THE AUTHOR

USA Today bestselling author Starla Night was born on a hot July at midnight. She hikes, scuba dives, and swims naked in the ocean. She writes about smokin' hot dragons and tattooed mermen at StarlaNight.com.

9 781943 110674